Buried In Between

A BELLETHORPE NOVEL

LEANNE LOVEGROVE

To Annie Seaton, thank you for your help, endless guidance and friendship.
You are the reason I'm still writing.

Prologue

MARCH *2017*

Claridge's Hotel was the home of timeless elegance. What girl didn't want to get married here? And now, she, Ava Montgomery, simple Australian girl, was fulfilling the dreams of women around the world.

Unlike the bedroom she'd dressed in that had been delicately decorated in powderpuff pink, the ballroom housing the wedding reception was a white extravaganza. Nothing overstated; everything was sophisticated and classy from the ornate crystal chandeliers suspended from the ceiling to the expensive silverware and crisp linen tablecloths. The only splash of colour was the greenery in amongst the large floral creations on each table.

Beauty and luxury was everywhere; in the high-couture gowns worn by the female guests; in the jewels sparkling at their necks and wrists and adorning their lobes. In the fine-cut linen suits dressing the men and their slick hair and European leather shoes. These guests were hand-picked, people with status like politicians and members of state from various countries, friends and allies. Then there were the gentlemen of tradition, elders who wore the turban-style headdress of white cotton matched with dark, trimmed beards lining their chins.

It was a wedding fit for the social pages. An event she was sure could have been replicated at the British Museum amongst the classical statutes of ancient Egypt. Who knew the museum held wedding celebrations? A fact unknown to Ava until she'd announced her engagement to her work colleagues as her head was buried in the catalogue of an ancient, recently discovered artefact. At the time she'd brushed it off as an interesting piece of information, but in amongst this pageantry she would have found strange comfort in the cool temperature of the gallery, and the calm and foreboding statutes of the ancient world. Ava thought of her favourite, the Mummy Mask, an Egyptian head dress covered in gold leaf dating back to 1500 BC. That cold-eyed stare had always captivated her. She'd see it again soon, for now, she searched the room for her parents and brother. Finding them, she smiled.

What must her family think of the acrobatic performers trawling the room, entertaining and indulging the guests; of the royal members they'd never heard of, the thirteen flower girls and boys who had traipsed down the aisle before her? And not to mention, the lobster and venison and top shelf champagne and liqueurs?

None of that mattered though. Claridge's had greater meaning than the luxurious and spacious rooms accommodating the hundreds of guests with the finest and most expensive food and wine.

Yes, it was owned by her husband's family, but it was also where they first met. The work function where she'd met Henry and fallen helplessly in love with his easy charm, intelligence and movie-star good looks. That was the night her life changed forever.

CHAPTER
One

JANUARY 2023

A sleek black crow squawked in the tops of the nearby trees and Ava flinched, rubbed her arms. It was just a bird and shielding her eyes with her hand, she watched it take flight, wings flapping until she couldn't see it any more in the haze of the horizon.

She'd forgotten about the endless open landscapes with their vast skies, the fresh country air, the unbearable dry heat and blinding glare of the outback Australian sun. It was both welcome and familiar and evoked feelings of home. Even though, these days Ava wasn't sure where home was.

She closed her eyes as childhood memories engulfed her. If she listened hard enough, she could almost hear the happy squeals as she and her brother raced through grassy pastures. Of those long, bright summer days where they'd swim in the creek and race under the sprinkler and devour icy cold drinks, letting the liquid run down their chins. The carefree abandon of country life.

Watching her son sprint after another mob of kangaroos brought her back to the present. He'd been chasing them all morning with no luck, unaware that the wild creatures surrounding the house didn't want to be caught. Here in the outcrop that was Bellethorpe, in remote

Queensland, it seemed they had their own animal sanctuary, much to her son's delight.

Ava placed her hand to her stomach and the nerves settled a little. She could relax now, they were finally here, were safe. Ismail raced away from the kangaroos and bounded up onto a large rectangular trampoline in the corner of the yard. His body flew into the air, legs dangling before bouncing again. Her tummy twisted as he fell. There was no safety netting around the edge but at five years of age and hardly the weight of a feather, she guessed he'd be unlikely to hurt himself. Plus, he was having so much fun. Her heart squeezed at his giggles of childhood delight.

Yes, she'd done the right thing. But still her hands trembled and she clutched them across her chest before releasing a sigh. Ava should be celebrating; she'd actually done it. Part of her wanted to scream with joy and jump on the tramp with Ish, another part wanted to fall into a heap and sob. But she wouldn't do either of those things, she would simply revel in the fact they were here. The enduring weight upon her shoulders lessened.

It didn't matter their new home was a far cry from the grandeur of the Cairo palace they'd come from. That fact didn't bother Ava in the slightest. Never having grown up with such wealth and luxury, this, here, felt normal. A proper family home. Or the beginnings of one.

Yes, the house needed work. Much tender love and care but it was still grand in a traditional, old-style way. Quintessentially Australian, the building was raised above the ground with timber battens to encourage airflow and cool breezes; the house they now called home had wide sprawling decks along each side and back, prominent exterior staircases and beautiful eaves and gables hidden under the dirt of years of age. The red tin roof was rusted and contrasted against the deep blue of the sky.

Nestled amongst acres of land, the house was built on a low grass crest. The closest trees were far enough away to be safe in a bushfire, but close enough for beauty and serenity. It was habitable until she could make the place their own but most importantly, it was private, on the outskirts of town with its secure gate and long drive to avoid prying eyes. Close enough for civilisation, yet far enough to be isolated.

The house was indeed a grand old lady that deserved love and Ava was just the person to deliver the attention it needed. A project would keep her busy and focused on their new life.

Unlocking her arms, she brought her hand back to her side and caught the sparkle of the large blue topaz ring on her wedding finger. Instinctively, she twirled it back and forth. She'd lost weight; she hadn't been able to loop the ring around her finger before. Practising, she pulled it off, the gold sliding easily over her knuckle. Her finger felt bare after the heaviness of the jewellery. Gosh, she loved that ring. But it caused a pain deep in her chest to open, like a chasm of hurt, filling up with the past. Of where she was now, of where they'd come from. Of love lost.

The sudden demise of her marriage still caught her by surprise. Something she'd had no time to process, instead she'd been occupied with fleeing to safety.

But to avoid the painful past welling up each time she saw it, the ring had to come off. Ava needed to learn to compartmentalise that part of her life and move on. Signifying an ending and a new beginning. Removing the ring would help. Plus, such an extravagant ornament was bound to catch everyone's attention, and that would lead to questions.

There'd been no qualms about selling her jewellery collection, but this one, her engagement ring, that was different, harder to part with. She resolved to worry about that later and pocketed it, no prevarication. She'd hide it somewhere safe in the house, until perhaps it might need to be sold, too. For now, the commitment to action made her feel lighter.

Ava breathed in deeply and focused on the present. The beauty of where she stood lifted her spirits. They'd be okay. There was a lot to do but, they'd do it.

The rumble of a car engine caught her attention. She sidestepped quickly and stood on kangaroo poo. Luckily the droppings had hardened, but the smell still wafted up from her expensive leather flats. Spinning on the spot she looked for Ismail.

The trampoline was empty. Where was he? Her eyes skittered to the back verandah; he wasn't there. Frantically her gaze raked the lawn and along the side path. A few kangaroos rested in the shade of bushes and low-lying trees but she couldn't see her son. Her heart thumped painfully. The vehicle inched closer; she could see it now following the fence line.

A bolt of blue darted into her peripheral vision. And then she heard that laugh she loved so much. Ismail whizzed out from under the trampoline, coming out the other side. She shot forward until she was by his side, only metres from the fence. The ute rumbled to a stop, the door opened and a man climbed out. His lips were moving and reciting what sounded strangely like poetry. He slammed the door shut and went around to the tray of his ute and started extracting tools. A broad-brimmed hat shaded his face. Dirt-smudged light blue jeans hugged tall and lean legs matched with a long-sleeved green shirt fitting snugly across very broad shoulders.

Ava clutched Ismail by her side; he wriggled so she gripped tighter.

'Mumma,' he whined.

'Shush.'

The man looked up. His face was ruggedly handsome in a country sort of way, his skin bronzed by the sun with a short beard of a few days' growth at most. She was just close enough to see the gold fleck in his eyes but they held a burning, faraway look in them. A sadness. His jaw tensed as he considered her while his forehead creased into a frown. Ava swallowed.

Had they been discovered already?

What rhymed with woman? Beautiful exotic dark-haired woman with arched eyebrows and a perfectly heart-shaped angelic face? No, that wasn't what he was thinking, that was what he was seeing. Damn it. Noah Hawthorn wracked his brain for the sentence he'd been constructing, the words running around the edges of his mouth. He'd almost had it and now it was gone. Off to the ether. Perhaps forever forgotten.

In the grounds of the old homestead stood a woman and a child. Her face was pale; the pallor exaggerated by the cascading jet-black, locks flowing past her shoulders. She was stunning, striking with her olive skin, slim waist and long legs shown off by her short summer dress. Too beautiful to be here. A city girl, he knew one straight away. It wasn't hard to tell, it was the grooming and polish you didn't see on country folk. The lack of fatigue, and wear and tear, the cleanness and usually, the confidence in their stance. Okay, oddly, this woman didn't have the self-assuredness.

Pleasure zoomed through Noah at the vision before him. She sure was worthy of a poem. But no time for that. He ignored the blissful sensation making his body pulse and shoved his equipment back onto the tray and cleared his throat. It was an invitation for her to explain. She didn't. Instead, she appeared as if she'd seen a ghost. He turned on the spot. Was there a snake he hadn't seen? A wild pig? Something to make her fearful? It couldn't be him, surely? And anyway, she was on his land.

'Um, not sure if you're aware but you're trespassing,' he finally said.

'I'm sorry?' Her arm dropped from securing the boy tightly to her side and the self-conviction that had been lacking, rose to the fore.

In a flash, his kelpie, Otis, jumped down from the tray and raced forwards before rising on his fore legs and placing large paws on the boy's tiny chest and licking his face. The boy squealed in delight until his mother tugged him away and behind her, partially hiding him.

Bit late for *that*.

'Otis,' Noah commanded the dog who obediently returned to his side to receive a neck rub. 'Sorry, mate,' he spoke to the boy, 'he won't hurt you; he gets a bit excited at meeting new people.' Noah held up his palm for a high-five in apology that the boy exaggeratedly clapped.

'This is private property and you shouldn't be here.' He crossed his arms in front of his chest as he addressed the woman again. 'But if you leave now there won't be any trouble.' He reached for his tools, dismissing her and ready to get on with the job.

'I'm terribly sorry for the inconvenience, but you're mistaken. So, if you wouldn't mind leaving, that would be great.' The woman matched his crossed-arm stance.

'Look, I'm sorry you're confused, but this ain't no tourist attraction so, I'd really appreciate you taking off. I need to fix this fence.'

'Why are you fixing my fence?'

'I thought we'd established that. It's my fence.' Something about this felt very wrong.

'Actually, it's my fence, my house.' She spread her arms wide. 'My land and you are the one trespassing. So, unless you want me to telephone the police, I suggest you leave.'

The police? Definitely a city chick. The police around here wouldn't be interested in this squabble.

'What are you talking about?'

'I purchased this house and land a month ago. We've just moved in.'

Noah dropped the hammer he'd been holding. It made a loud clunk as it hit the bottom of the tray and he gripped the edge for support. 'No, that's impossible. There's been a mistake. Who sold it to you?'

They both turned at the sound of another vehicle.

'He did,' Ava said and pointed as soon as she saw Mac Turner alight from his fancy un-countrylike BMW advertising *Bellethorpe Property Real Estate*.

Mac walked the short distance from the end of the driveway to the fence. Noah used the time to take deep breaths to cool his rising temperature. This had to be a silly blunder but he was confident Mac would sort it out.

'Noah,' Mac offered him a curt nod and then nodded towards the woman. 'See you've met. I'm just dropping in to check our new resident is settling in okay.'

Ava spoke first. 'Can you please explain to … to this gentleman that I'm the new owner of this property.'

Mac alternated his gaze between the two of them.

'Mac, we had a deal. You promised me. I've been saving up, wasn't going to be long now.'

'Look, Noah, sure. It was agreed you could have the place if no one else was interested. Except, Ava here was interested and paid the asking price with no negotiations. Quick sale, no conditions, no more waiting. You have to understand the owner has waited long enough, they wanted to get rid of the property.'

The woman was nodding, vindicated, he guessed.

'Mac, we're mates. That's a low blow…' He hung his head, unable to look at the trio.

It was suddenly hot. Noah felt the prickle on his bare neck where the rays of sun hit, heard the birds too loud in the treetops and his dreams dropping into a puddle at his feet. Looking at the old house, it wasn't much, but he'd imagined how it could be renovated into the perfect family home. The home that might have saved his marriage; instead, now, a home for him and his daughter, for their future. Except those dreams were being trodden on, squashed by a city slicker, no less.

'Good luck fixing the fence.' He strode back to the driver's door, slammed it shut and revved the engine before driving away and leaving dust in his wake.

CHAPTER
Two

'I'LL HAVE two punnets of strawberries please.'

'Oh, hello. Are you visiting for the weekend?'

Ava smiled in reply as the lady wearing a bright pink tee bagged up her goodies. 'No, we've just moved here.'

The lady's face lit up. 'Well, that's fabulous. Welcome to Bellethorpe. I'm Bridie Finch of Finch Berry Farm. I hope you love the strawberries. We're here at the markets every Saturday morning along with the other locals selling their fruit and veg.'

A flash of déjà vu hit Ava with a memory of country markets and fresh fruit. Of spitting watermelon seeds with her brother, Charlie and seeing how far they'd land.

She took the bag and placed it into her canvas tote. 'Ava Montgomery,' she offered. The name sounded strange on her tongue. 'These markets have been running for a long time.'

Bridie squinted, titled her head to the left with unasked questions. 'As long as I've been in Bellethorpe. Whereabouts are you living?'

Ava had forgotten about country life; everything was everyone's business. A timely reminder to keep her comments to herself.

'The house out on Kinross Road.'

Bridie's face screwed up in concentration. 'What, surely not the old place? Isn't it in a state after being empty all these years?'

Ava's laugh was nervous. 'It isn't so bad. A little reno project; I'm going to fix her up.'

'Admirable. Big job ahead.'

'Actually, I might ask your advice about that. I need help with renovations. Can you recommend someone?'

Bridie offered another broad, all-teeth smile and clapped her hands together; her luminous pink fingernails matched her shirt perfectly.

'Yes, there's only one. He's the best builder in the entire region. In fact, he's working at the far end of the street at my partner's restaurant this morning. We're building an extension, more seating space. Why don't you go and catch up with him? If you head straight down this road,' Bridie pointed. 'You'll see it on your left. I'd escort you but I need to man the stall.'

'Oh, no, that's fine, no need, thank you. I'll go and have a chat to him.'

Ava went to move away but Bridie stalled her by touching her arm. 'And I'll give you my phone number. If you ever need anything, honestly, please get in touch. We're family out here.' Bridie ripped out a sheet of paper from a notebook and scribbled her number before handing it over.

'That's really kind, thank you.' Ava accepted the number and turned to leave.

'Oh, and where have you moved from?' Bridie continued.

With her back to Bridie, Ava froze. Beside her, Ismail not similarly inhibited, piped up. 'London! And did you know it's winter over there and summer here right now?'

'Well, hello young man. Nice to meet you. From London, wow,' Bridie flitted a glance back to Ava who'd turned around. 'That sure is a long way. I've never been and fancy it being cold there and hot here at the same time. That's strange, isn't it? What's your name?'

'Ism...'

'Duke. His name is Duke. And we'd best be getting along. Thank you for the strawberries and the recommendation.'

Ava weaved in and out of the crowds, past the long coffee queue and people surrounding stalls filled with colourful produce. At the far end of the street, she followed the noise of grinding and hammering until she found *L'Amour* that had a front visage of romantic reds and deep maroons. With the door wide open, Ava observed a team of men wearing hardhats and earplugs and matching green collared shirts. A man passed by the entrance and paused. 'Hi. I'm sorry we're closed. Just doing some minor extension work this morning, apologies for the noise. I'll be operating take-out tonight if you'd like to come back?'

'I'll be sure to come back, thank you, but Bridie at the strawberry stall recommended your builder to me and I thought I'd chat to him whilst I'm in town. But if he's busy, I'll contact him another time.'

'Noah? Oh, no, I'm sure he can talk to you. I'll go fetch him. And how about a chocolate croissant while you wait, young fella?'

Ismail nodded up at his mother enthusiastically but Ava stuck out her hand to keep him by her side.

'Are you new to town? I'm sorry, I should have introduced myself. I'm Caleb Stirling and this is my restaurant. That was my wife at the strawberries.' His tone was soft.

Ah, no. Had she hurt his feelings? He was scary looking dressed in an all-black ensemble with tattoos covering his right arm. Even so, he seemed nice, but who did she trust? Ava was so confused.

As if Caleb could read the emotions flickering across her face, he smiled. Honestly, she hardly deserved his kind treatment.

'I'll grab Noah and the croissant and bring it out. It's no trouble.' He held up his palm to silence the protests she offered.

Ismail jumped on the spot. 'Yum!'

Ava kneeled low to speak to him. 'Remember here in Bellethorpe, we're using your middle name, Duke. People won't get confused because Ismail is an unusual name in Australia. Okay?'

Secretly, she was happy to be calling him Duke when they had company. Ismail, an Islamic name in line with her husband's faith, had never been her choice. She'd always shortened it to Ish, something her in-laws had never liked.

He nodded and her heart melted. 'Yeah, Mumma, I remember, sorry I forgot before.'

A man came through the door, 'Hi, I'm…'

She straightened up and her stomach swooped. It was him.

'…Noah Hawthorn,' he finished.

Caleb bounced up behind and delivered the treat to Ish. 'Noah, this is … oh, sorry, I didn't catch your name.' He addressed Ava.

Her smile was tight now. Bloody hell, of all the people. 'Ava, Ava Montgomery.' She held out her hand in introduction. Noah Hawthorn, the region's best builder placed his large workman hand in hers and shook it. His grip was strong and his eyes didn't deviate from her face as if setting up an unspoken challenge. Despite that, his hand was warm and felt nice.

Caleb made formal introductions. 'This is Noah Hawthorn, best builder around,' echoing her exact thought. 'I'll leave you to discuss details. Nice to meet you both.'

'I'm told you're a builder and can assist me.'

Another man appeared behind Noah. 'Oh, sorry to interrupt. I'm Alex Burgess, work with Noah. Mate, where's the shifter?'

Noah answered him and remained quiet until the fellow left.

'Sure, *Bellethorpe Builders* can help with your renovation needs. Unfortunately, we are booked up for months in advance. We currently have loads of jobs on the books, you know with the rush on building after the pandemic, so we'll have to get back to you regarding availability.'

'Oh, bugger. I want to get started as soon as possible. How long do you think until you're free?'

He shrugged and looked away into the distance. 'Three months at least.' He slipped her his business card and sauntered away. The cheek of him!

Ava plonked down next to Ish on a timber seat on the footpath outside the restaurant. Ish ate his croissant, the flaky pastry edging his mouth, other fragments drifting to the ground. She watched the crumbs in a trance and twisted her engagement ring—back on her right hand—around and around.

'Hey, don't worry about it.' Caleb, the restaurant-owner appeared by her side and she darted her hand out to reach for Ish and just as quickly dropped it. She needed to stop doing that.

Had he over-heard the conversation? Or did she look as discombobulated as she felt?

'This town takes a while to get used to. When I first arrived, it felt like I'd landed onto the set of a crime show.'

Ava blanched.

Caleb laughed self-consciously. 'Sorry bad choice of words even though that is honestly what I thought. But my point is, it can feel foreign out here and strange and the people overwhelming but then there's this moment, it arrives when you least expect it, and catches you by surprise, and without realising it, this place is under your skin and then, there's nowhere else you'd rather be. Just give yourself time to adjust.'

He offered a wave and strode off. She hoped he was right.

CHAPTER
Three

'DADDY!' That one word and his eyes misted. He placed his finger on the screen and traced the outline of her angelic child face. Noah tried to capture the exuberance of her cheeky, lopsided smile, instead, a shooting pain fissured his heart.

'Hey, baby girl. How are you?'

'I'm good.'

'Where are you sitting?'

'In my new room, see.' Emily moved her computer in a circle to show him a pretty and pink bedroom. There were plush curtains, a rug, muted lighting and girlish posters of rainbows and horses.

A wild animal was now batting its wings and scraping the edges of Noah's ribcage, desperate to crawl out, be free and unleash its fury.

'Tell me about your new home.' Was he interrogating his six-year-old or showing genuine interest? Sometimes he didn't know. It was so confusing. He wanted information of where she was, how she was living, her safety, but always aware of the fine line he wasn't allowed to cross.

'I have a pool!'

Did it have a legal fence with an automatic shutting gate? Were there palings she could climb over? Was she always supervised in the yard? And, oh, in the pool? Emily had only recently started swimming lessons. But…he didn't ask any of those pressing questions.

The ache spread across his chest.

Each word she spoke in her adorable little girl voice was a stab to his heart when all he desperately wanted was to enjoy these precious few moments. He knew, too soon, she'd be bored of speaking to him via the screen and become distracted by one of the many toys in her room. Or often, from her mother intervening.

Emily bumped the laptop so that it almost fell and sure enough, there was Lisa hovering in the background. Monitoring his every word lest he crossed that imaginary line.

'So, you're living in a big city now…'

'Noah.' Lisa's warning. Gosh he hadn't even been able to finish his words this time. But he heeded the threat. If he didn't behave the internet would miraculously drop and he wouldn't see his daughter for another few days. Not that spending time with her via the fancy new set up of Zoom was "seeing" her anyway. But, for the moment it was better than nothing.

A kitten meandered in front of the screen and Emily squealed. 'This is Smokey, he's my kitten. Isn't he cute?' Little pudgy hands gripped the tiny cat around its middle and held him up. New pets, new toys, a new house and family. Difficult to compete with when he had nothing but the "old" to offer. In his view, the old was pretty good. A country life filled with freedom, land, animals and opportunities to be outside, not cramped in a sardine-sized house in a suburban street with the only outside the local park and its solitary swing.

Where was Otis? He whistled for him. Emily loved that dog. He could do with some help.

The cat scooted, Emily chased after it, and left the screen behind. Conversation over. Lisa came into view and his heart moved to sit in his stomach. 'When can I see Emily?'

Damn it, he needed to practise his pleasantries. It was hard being nice to the women you'd once loved and had left you. Even after the passage of time, it still felt raw.

'Any time you want.'

He hung his head, biting back his words. Probably best to have this conversation via text, less chance of nasty exchanges. 'Okay, thanks. I'll come back to you with some dates.' He clicked end and the monitor went black.

Noah balled his hands into fists and then released them with a sigh. He reached for the notepad and pen he kept on the desk nearby and scribbled. Furious words that he'd probably be unable to read later.

Pain. Anguish. Fear. Gripping his heart like a vice, his pain ascending to new heights.

The words poured out of him.

There'd never been so many hours in the day after your family had left. Yes, he'd worked, but coming home in the evenings had been busy with a young child: baths, early dinner and story time. The hours had slid by until he and Lisa had both collapsed, exhausted, into bed, not long after Emily. Now without that routine, the evenings were interminably long and quiet.

And provided endless thinking time. In the depth of the dark nights, he tore himself apart with the "what ifs". Where had he gone wrong? What else could he have done to save his marriage and have Lisa stay? Was he not a good enough husband? Was he not a good enough dad? Surely, if he'd been enough, then Lisa would have stayed.

Wallowing in his own self-pity didn't answer any of those questions and tonight he had a community council meeting to attend. He finished the poem and put it away for later.

Noah jumped into his ute, uncertainty bubbling away inside him, burning just under his skin. How long could this go on for? Was Emily going to be permanently in Brisbane? The prospect cut like a cavernous wound.

Noah pressed the Bluetooth number on his speed dial so he could talk and drive. He needed to talk to another dad in the father support group; a group of like-minded parents who met regularly, their only common thread: a messy divorce.

'Hey, Noah.'

'Hi Andrew.'

'Are you okay? How's things?'

'I've just spent Zoom time with Em.'

'Hmm. How did it go? What's the latest?'

'Yeah, mate, she's fine and well. Happy, you know. She has a new pink room with loads of toys and a pet kitten. Life couldn't be better.'

'How long since you last saw her?'

'Couple of weekends ago because we haven't got arrangements in place yet.'

'Where is your wife living?'

'Brisbane.'

'Okay. Yeah, long drive. Did you let Lisa move there?'

'No, of course not. But her family are there and I guess, it makes sense...' His words petered out.

'Yeah, that sucks. What's Lisa saying about access?'

Noah told him that Lisa was being amenable to time whenever he wanted but the practicalities were difficult. The three-and-a-half-hour trip one way made dropping in after school or on Saturday morning to watch her dancing lesson impossible.

Andrew swore and Noah grimaced. Yeah, he understood; felt the same way to be fair but every swear word in the world didn't change his situation. His grip tightened on the steering wheel as Andrew got worked up. Eventually he calmed and they talked through a range of options. There just wasn't the option he wanted—to have Emily home with him.

Noah's chest hurt as his mind flitted back to the last weekend they'd spent together as a happy family. They'd taken Otis for a walk along the creek and had a great muck-about time, chasing a ball and tumbling in the grass. They'd come home muddy but with big smiles. Oh, how he wanted to be doing that right now; for things to be different; like it was, how it used to be before Lisa left. Unfortunately, she'd met someone else, but he understood, it wasn't about the new bloke, it was the lure of the bright lights of the city. Lisa was a city girl who'd given up her life and moved to Bellethorpe for the idyllic country experience; and done it for him. Like many city dwellers, she'd yearned for a hobby farm, a veggie patch and the rural trimmings. Except, like his father, some people couldn't hack small town life with its lack of resources and comforts. But as the years had passed, Bellethorpe had advanced. Okay, it didn't yet have a cinema but that would come. It was only two hours to the closest one anyway. In the country, that was a trip out for milk.

Noah could mull or he could try and fix the mess he found himself in. Andrew was still talking. Yep, he'd nut out what might work for spending time with Emily and talk to Lisa. Andrew was heavy on reminders of parental rights. He'd done that and each time it had ended in an argument, didn't seem any point going over the same ground again. Andrew said they'd put it to the group next meeting and get some more ideas. The other guys had gone through this before and could help.

Noah arrived at the town hall, cut the engine but took a couple of deep breaths to loosen his tight muscles. All he wanted was to spend time with his daughter.

And on top of everything he'd lost the house he was pinning his future on. A family home for him and Emily. Even if she didn't live with him full-time, it would have been their home, together.

Which is why he needed to attend this council meeting. To prevent something like that happening to others. The group of locals would make decisions about his beloved Bellethorpe without his input and make decisions he wouldn't agree with. He had to attend.

And that was half the problem. He loved his home here in small town Bellethorpe, where he was born and raised. Noah loved this place with a fierce passion, similar only to the love he had for his daughter. He was old-school country and proud and determined to keep his town great. But the weight of that commitment was also hard to bear.

In weaker moments, he wondered what it would be like to care less, be more spontaneous and light-hearted. Then he could move closer to Emily and life wouldn't be so tough. But the thought of leaving rural life made his muscles stiffen. Emily was born here ... this should be her home. But those thoughts only spun him off on an emotional rollercoaster once more that did nothing but make his blood pressure spike.

Inside the usual faces were in session. This wasn't a parliamentary meeting of local appointed pollies, but rather a group of concerned citizens and elected members attended too. Jacqueline Kennedy, the Mayor, never missed a meeting and she rose to greet him upon arrival.

'I hope you brought your A game, this one is going to be feisty.'

Noah's shoulders sagged. Another fight: he wasn't sure he had it in him tonight.

The group settled and the chairperson raised the agenda. A development company had sought approval to develop a multi-storey shopping complex. Noah considered the plans and listened to the arguments as to why this was a wonderful idea.

These meetings were getting a bit old. It was always about new, brighter and better things for the benefit of citizens. Why didn't anyone see that Bellethorpe was fantastic as it was. It had everything residents needed—fresh fruit and produce direct from the farms, plenty of local wine and major amenities. There was a good mix of community shops where residents could source whatever they needed. And if they couldn't, another option was never far away. And whatever they didn't have, they made up for in community spirit.

Someone spoke of tourism numbers and attracting more visitors to the region. Noah waited a beat before speaking up. 'We have multiple wineries that attract thousands of people each year and have our local accommodation booked out on weekends, especially during those long winter months. We also have other attractions like the Christmas tree farm, the fruit orchards and the national park isn't far away. Aren't tourists coming here to escape their city life? They don't come here to shop and if they do, they don't want the same stores. They want something different.'

The tension in the room heightened and a few members rolled their eyes. He knew he was often the odd one out. The group said he was anti-development, anti-anything that generated change. They said he was against change even if it was for the better. The debate raged and as always, ended with the development group being allowed to submit their formal plans for consideration. It did become a bit like Groundhog Day with the same discussions on repeat. If nothing else, Noah Hawthorn would keep the bastards honest.

Back home, the house was dark and chilled, but not with cold air, emptiness surrounded him, pervaded every corner. Noah didn't turn on the lights, but sat in the darkness, let his emotions whirl around him, alive and electric. He pulled out the earlier poem. Tinkered with it, tried out new words, other expressions. He scribbled notes by the light of his phone. Sometimes words were the only weapon he had that made him feel in control. Who knew that a simple builder from the country could do something else with his hands than make things?

Pain, grief, feeling sick
  It's always the mud that sticks
  Loud voices and harsh words
  Things that cannot be unsaid, comments absurd
  Resolution and agreement never seem possible
  Heading into a train wreck, unstoppable.

CHAPTER
Four

WIPING the sweat from her brow, Ava checked, for the third time, the whereabouts of Ish. She really needed to start calling him Duke; that way they'd both get used to it.

He was supposed to be tugging out weeds from the overrun garden closest to the house. A simple task given the entire bed was an undesirable mess of dandelions, crabgrass and other unrecognizable stalks. If there were any plants remaining, they'd have to be heavy-duty natives. Had to be best to start over again. She hadn't realised the move here would entail her learning such a broad range of new skills; she added gardening to the list.

Clearly having grown bored, her son threw a tennis ball into the air and caught it.

'Have you had a drink, mate? It's hot, isn't it?'

'Yeah, but not as hot as home,' he replied and kept tossing the ball.

Ava paused mid-snip, lowering the secateurs that were attacking one of the trees lining the drive. 'Home? You mean where we used to live? Where, um, Dad lives?'

He nodded.

'Do you miss it?' Her voice a tone too high.

'Um, dunno. Nah, probably not. It's pretty here.'

Ava released her breath. 'But I left all my toys and stuff there and don't see my cousins anymore but there are roos here.'

Yep, they'd left quickly, only taking what they could carry.

Ava kneeled and sat back on her ankles. 'It's going to be great here, though, isn't it? We have this yard for starters. When you're bigger we can think about a bike…'

That got his attention and the ball rolled away. 'A motorbike?' he squealed. Okay, yes, she was manipulating her son, but she desperately wanted Ish to like it here, have things to look forward to in this new life they were creating. And if all went well, they'd be here long-term. That was the plan.

Behind them the two horses who lived next door galloped along the fence line, neighing loudly as they went. Pulling up sharply, the animals tossed their heads wildly. Ava and Ish turned towards the commotion and saw a man.

Dropping the secateurs, she stood, wiped her hands down her old tee shirt and tried to ignore the fizz of fear bubbling in her tummy. For a property this secluded, there'd been too many unexpected surprises already and they'd only been here a few days! The man approached the horses who nuzzled their long necks into his body, demanding a scratch; clearly, they knew him. Ava's shoulders lowered from being hunched around her ears.

'Howdy!' he shouted and waved in greeting over the fence as he continued to pet the horse's necks with his other hand.

Ish looked to her for direction, his little jaw clenched tight. She smiled to reassure him and held out her hand indicating they'd walked over together. He clasped it tightly.

'Welcome to the neighbourhood. I'm Clive, your closest neighbour.'

'Hi, there,' she tried to match his hearty greeting. 'I'm Ava and this is my son, Duke. We haven't seen you around yet.'

'No, I don't live here fulltime, it's a bit of a weekend, holiday home. More like a retirement project but we don't get up here as much as we'd like.' The horses demanded his attention and he obliged. 'Lotta work you've got ahead of you.'

So everyone kept telling her.

'Yes, but one step at a time.' She wouldn't say she was already feeling overwhelmed and the list of tasks to do as a priority, too long. 'It's sort of silly being out here in the yard when I need to fix up the house so we can live comfortably, but I thought I'd just tame the mess so the house would appear more welcoming.'

He nodded. 'Yeah, sure. Particularly the entrance, I guess, it's spectacular, isn't it?'

She agreed. 'I love it. It was what attracted me to the house in the first place. This long drive with the trees lining it is a grand entrance in perfect symmetry. But yes, you're right,' she said, looking around, 'I might trim the trees along the drive and worry about the rest later.'

'You'll want to clear some of the paddocks for the young fella to play around in, too, I'm sure.'

'Hmm.' That was the problem, where did she stop?

'I can help. I have this fancy whizz-bang ride-on contraption that'd do the fields quickly. It's a snazzy new thing. Want me to run it over this afternoon? Won't take me long.'

Clive must have read the surprise on her face. 'It's a genuine offer. But I confess, I might want to ask a favour in return. Might be fun for you, though Duke.'

The knots in Ava's tummy were slowly untangling. She'd eventually adjust to speaking with strangers again, particularly so openly, so freely. After being unable to express herself for so long it was a weird, and yet welcome, change. She always used to trust her gut, now she wanted to learn to again. Clive was a friendly neighbour and if you couldn't rely on your neighbours, particularly in the country, who could you rely upon?

'Okay, we're listening. And yes, thank you, I'd absolutely love you to mow these acres of grass for me. That would be such a massive help. What can we do for you?'

'Do you like animals, young man?'

Ish nodded.

'Well, that's good. As I said, I'm not here all the time and I've had another young lad looking after these two,' Clive gestured towards the horses, 'but he's going to uni in Brisbane in a few weeks and isn't available anymore. Can you care for my horses when I'm not here? I'd give you a little pocket money, plus you can ride them whenever you want.'

Ish jumped on the spot. 'Please, Mumma.'

Gosh, she really had enough on her plate with the renovations ahead of her and with them simply settling in. But she'd chosen Bellethorpe and the outback for a reason. Well, lots of reasons, but one of them was wanting Ish to have the full country experience and a happy childhood. Just like she'd had.

'I used to ride when I was young.'

Ish looked up at her in surprise. 'You did?'

'Uh, huh. A lot actually, but I haven't ridden in years. Might be out of practice.' She leaned over the fence now and held out her hand to one of the horses. 'Would you like to learn, Duke?'

He jumped on the spot again, his smile imploring and his hands held in a prayer-like clasp.

'The riding equipment is in the shed down yonder; you can come and go as you like. The feed is outside the shed and there's a range of brushes.' Clive addressed Duke. 'If you brush them regularly, they'll be your best friend.' He paused and laughed. 'No, actually, if you give them any attention, they'll love you in return.' Clive chuckled at himself once more. 'This one here is Honey, and that one with the one white hoof, is Marmalade.' Clive provided brief instructions about their care.

'I'll see you in a jiffy. I'll go and get my mower.' Clive walked away and Ava lifted her face to the breeze; the harsh heat of the day gone.

Ish raced back towards the house searching for his ball. With a sigh, Ava surveyed all that was still to be done. Each time she ticked off a task, another materialised.

'Mum! Mumma! Come see.' Ish peered under the house at a section where a row of palings had come loose and fallen away.

'What is it?' She strode over and craning her neck underneath, Ava placed one hand on his shoulder and waited for her eyes to adjust to the dim interior.

'A dog!'

'What?' She moved him to the side to gain a better vantage. Sure enough, laying in a cool patch of dirt, was a dog, panting, eyes sad, front legs balancing the bright yellow tennis ball.

'And he's got my ball.' Ish reached out his hand, and Ava snatched it back quickly.

'We don't know if it's friendly. And he must belong somewhere, to someone.'

'…course he's friendly.'

'I think we should just leave him.'

'Can we keep him?' Her son sat back on his haunches, his hands in a prayer pose for the second time in as many minutes.

Ava prevaricated, again; she wanted him to have a normal childhood and as an only child he was often without company, and plus she'd be spending so much time on the house… but then she'd just agreed to care for Clive's horses. A hobby farm wasn't necessarily in her plans but maybe they could do it. Perhaps get some chooks too.

And she'd do anything for this kid. Make up for everything that had happened in his life so far.

'How about we try and coax him out and see if he's friendly and I'll ring the local vet. They can check him out and locate an owner. If he is someone's pet, there might be a little girl or boy crying somewhere right now missing them. We can't keep someone else's dog, can we? That wouldn't be fair.'

Ish's head bowed as he contemplated that. 'Yeah, okay.'

'I've got some steak out for dinner. I'll go and cut a piece and we'll see if we can encourage him to come and greet us. Don't touch him while I'm gone.'

Ava was gone only one minute, two at most. Upon her return, a large, roly-poly brown dog sat in Ish's lap. He petted the dog along his spine as it sat quietly.

Ava placed the bowl of cut up meat into his hand and he immediately held out a piece to the dog who lapped it up, licking his lips for more. Encouraging him around to the side of the house, Ava turned on the tap and they washed him down, gently and slowly. He didn't startle, seeming used to people. Underneath the grime was a deliciously chocolate-coloured coat that held a golden sheen in the dying afternoon sun.

Ish splashed at the dog and tickled him and laughed when the dog tried to lick the water droplets on his face. With a perfect bullseye, the dog's lips connected to his cheek and Ish broke into giggles.

This was why they moved here.

For this.

Ava thanked the world for the validation.

Later that afternoon as Clive mowed their paddocks, the dull hum of his tractor music in the background, the vet arrived.

'Hi, I'm Zac Coleman, the regional vet.' Ava introduced herself and Duke and he proceeded to examine the now clean and content dog.

'She's a chocolate Labrador and she's pregnant,' he said looking up at Ava with a rueful smile.

'Um … what?'

'Yep, 'fraid so. Usual pregnancies are about sixty-three days and I'd say she hasn't got long to go.'

'Puppies!' Ish fussed about the dog once more. Gently stroking her back and encouraging her to lay down on the specially constructed bed of blankets he'd made for her on their back deck.

'Unfortunately, she's not microchipped so I can't identify an owner. Might be tricky but I'll investigate. Are you okay to look after her in the interim?' Zac asked.

'Oh, yeah, of course. But she must have an owner, and a male dog friend, I guess. She can't have come far.'

'Good news is she's healthy, excepting the extra baby weight. You'll just need to keep an eye on her. Usually, they go into labour spontaneously and don't need any assistance. If you see her disappear and find solitude somewhere, likely she's in labour. But until then, Duke, don't get her too excited, no running around and nice gentle walks, okay?'

'Yes, sir!' Duke shouted and stood to attention.

Zac laughed. Ava didn't.

CHAPTER
Five

'WOWSER, you got yourself a great place here. All this land. Lots of open space. Must have cost a motza! House is a write-off though. Old. Ugly. Rundown. Out of date. Got loads of money, have you, to fix it up?'

Another new day, another stranger, another man on her property. Was she inviting trouble, making too many people aware of her existence? Given the knot in her stomach the answer was yes, definitely yes, but how did she renovate without help?

Only thing to do was trust her gut and, right now, it was ringing alarm bells. She didn't address any of the builder's questions but trailed behind him as he inspected the property.

He didn't seem bothered by the one-sided conversation. 'Yes siree, gonna cost you a pretty penny. Needs loads of work. The structure seems fine, but the stumps need replacing and the exterior palings. New roof, most likely new windows, doors, fresh coat of paint, obviously, and I'll have to do a thorough assessment of both sets of exterior stairs. And that's before tackling the inside.'

Ava swallowed the lump in her throat. Yeah, she knew that. The amount of work was obvious, but harder to hear it said out loud. So bluntly. So unkindly. The grand old lady didn't appear so grand anymore.

The inside would be okay. Yes, everything needed replacing: the kitchen, the bathrooms and the floors with the addition of new furniture, it was ascetic and excepting the heavy lifting of kitchen cabinetry and bathroom fittings, she figured she'd manage the redecorating.

It was the significant repair and replacement jobs that were outside of her ability. Hence the need for assistance.

An image of the blue topaz ring popped into her head and she instinctively went to twist it around her finger except, finally, it was safely stored away. She rubbed the obvious indent on her bare finger instead. If what this fellow said was true about the extent of the repair and cost, how long could she keep it?

Thinking of the ring transported her back in time to when Henry had proposed. They were at home in their shared apartment. He'd set up candles so the room had an amber glow, scattered rose petals across the plush carpet and soft classical music played in the background. He'd cooked. The occasion was quite unlike Henry who usually veered towards extravagant displays of affection. In tune with her needs, he'd made it just the two of them and it was perfect. But everything about her relationship with Henry had been magical; almost dreamlike. She'd been so in love and thought that their love for each other could have sustained them through anything.

The builder asked a question landing her back in the present, away from the romance of her former life. Ava screwed up her face. This guy churned her stomach. Those eyes that kept sliding to her chest; his builder's talk as if she were dumb. Plus, his macho and patronising demeanour matched with his salacious and unsavoury grin reminded her of another man from her past. A less pleasant man than her husband.

Heat warmed her body. She might have loved Henry fiercely but she hadn't travelled across the world, run away from her the man he'd become and her past life to be treated like this by another man. She wasn't prepared to tolerate it … but …

Builders were in short supply. As Noah had kindly pointed out,

COVID had seen the building industry collapse at first, and now, anyone who could hold a hammer was in high demand. Ava didn't have many options.

'Best to get some plans drawn up, not only of the work inside but also of the property to delineate where important pipes are laid and sewerage etcetera. I can recommend someone.' He pulled out a card.

'And you're available to commence work immediately?'

He stood too close and she smelled his unpleasant blokey scent. 'For you, I am.' His tongue swiped across dry lips.

Urgh! Damn it. She might have no choice but to hire this guy, but not today. 'Okay, thanks. If you can please send through your quote, I'll get in touch after I have some plans prepared.'

Ava followed him down the long drive to the gate and latched it before the dust had settled behind him. First priority: get a working lock for the gate. Access was too easy with the old clunker currently keeping people at bay. Next stop, the hardware store.

Striding indoors to drink a cool glass of water and wash away the sins of the visitor, Ava paused mid-step as the television blared with a breaking news story.

For months rumours have been circulating about the disappearance of the wife of the most rich and powerful man in the Arab community. The millionaire's spouse of ten years has not been seen in public at community events or engagements. It seems the mystery can now be solved, of her whereabouts at least. She has resurfaced in London and has filed for divorce in the Old Bailey commencing proceedings for property settlement and parental custody. Court documents reveal she is seeking safety and refuge alleging a life of harassment and distress including threats to her life, and those of her loved ones, mistreatment, abuse and being retained against her liberty in an environment she describes as hostile.

Ava's hands shook so much it took three attempts to flick off the television.

Rushing to the back door, she searched outside for Ish. He'd ventured into the yard to give the dog some mild exercise. Gripping the door handle and standing on tiptoes, she spotted him near the old, rusted windmill. Racing, her feet barely touched the ground, she reached him, crushed him in an embrace and lifted him off the grass. The dog wagged its tail at her sudden appearance.

'Let's get back to the house now, the bugs are out and the dog needs its dinner. Plus, we need to name her, don't we?' Only hours before she'd refused to name the dog in case it already had one.

Ish arched his eyebrows in question. Yes, Ava knew she was acting manic. Moreover, there was still hours of sunlight left and usually Ish played outside under her supervision until the last rays of light had disappeared.

'And we'll have a milkshake.' Now he definitely knew something was up. A milk drink before dinner? Never happened. Her son's mouth fell open as he reached for her hand and gestured to the dog to follow. In the weeks since they'd run, Ish had become adept at not only reading her moods, but at obeying. And at times like this, she was grateful. They strode toward the house. Once he was nestled inside with a cold Milo, Ava closed the windows, drew the curtains tight and bolted the doors. They weren't going out again today.

Noah pushed aside the other items on the shelf and searched for what he needed. Bugger. He knew that particular type of screw was outside the realm of renovation hobbyist, but he was sure he'd seen them stocked at *Hardware Heaven* before.

Karma was a bitch, right? This was the only tool shop in town. He'd been instrumental in preventing the expansion of a national hardware store into Bellethorpe only a few short years ago. It would have killed a business like this one; Trevor Fletcher, owner and operator, would have been forced into early retirement, well, perhaps not that early, already in his seventies, he'd been around these parts for as long as Noah retained memories of Bellethorpe. But that wasn't the point;

the point was that Trevor would be forced into a position against his will as a result of a big conglomerate coming to town.

Noah glanced around at the other shelves and noticed the empty gaps where products should be stocked. A little niggle at the back of his mind suggested he wasn't always right, and that made him uncomfortable. Studying the packets of screws on offer, he sized them up. Could he make them work? Nah. Whatever was right or wrong, either way, he now had a two-hour round trip to a larger hardware store to purchase a bag of screws he needed to finish a job.

Light conversation drifted down the aisle.

The new owner of his property walked down the aisle pushing a shopping trolley as if she was purchasing her groceries. The cute little boy walked beside her with his hand secured to the side of the cart. Except, it was no longer his property, was it? The idea was hard to get used too after years of dreaming.

Noah didn't usually run from situations but he didn't want to be rude and ignore her, so better to avoid a confrontation. It might be childish but he wasn't yet ready to forgive her. There'd be time for that when she hung around and contributed to their little township, until then she needed to earn her stripes.

Glancing over his shoulder, he saw the coast was clear. One more glance back, but no, it was too late. She was upon him and offered a tight smile.

'Noah,' she nodded and kept moving. Okay, he could offer polite pleasantries too and he smiled saccharinely in reply.

'Oh, and Noah,' she said just as he'd taken his first step towards the exit. He swivelled on the spot, turning back to face her. The boy looked up at him with soulful dark eyes that made him look older than his years. His eyes were matched with a head of dark, thick hair grown a little too long; it covered his forehead and flopped into his eyes. His skin was dark olive. Noah did a double take between the pair but couldn't identify any resemblance. Unlike his mother though, the boy's lips curled into a full smile revealing milky white teeth.

Where was his father? It was a fleeting thought lost as he turned his attention to Ava. Such a pretty name for an attractive woman. He couldn't deny she was striking even though he wanted to, very much.

Didn't want to think about her at all, actually. Today she wore more casual jeans and a pale-coloured long-sleeved top as if she'd planned a day in the yard. Yet, she wore ornamental boots that wouldn't withstand hard yakka in the paddock. Her nails were long and red but he noticed the nail on the left pinkie had snapped away and was jagged with a rough edge. And now that they were parallel, an intoxicating musky scent that reminded him of the exotic spice stall at the markets drifted across to him. He loved that aroma.

'I'm sorry you're not able to help me but I've located another builder who can, though. He sent through his quote this morning and can start straight away.'

'Who? There aren't any other builders in town.'

'He's not from Bellethorpe, from Amiens, I think he said.'

Noah shook his head. 'I know who you mean. You can't use him. He's notorious for overcharging and under delivering.'

'What? Well, what am I supposed to do? I need renovation help and you're not available. The one person I've found is not good enough.' Her eyes searched his. 'Look, I'm really sorry you thought the house was yours and you were planning to purchase it. I'm sorry I'm responsible for crushing your dreams. But however unfortunate you find this situation, the house now belongs to me. And it's not very nice to sabotage my attempts to restore it.'

Her manner was cool and aloof, and oh so irritating. He really was trying but it wasn't easy to recover from stolen dreams. His toes curled in his work boots.

'Yeah, I'm sorry about our misunderstanding, too. Mac knew I was saving to buy the place. It was a long-term, standing arrangement. Well, so, I thought. Until it wasn't. Until you bought it ...' He screwed his hands into tight balls.

She held up one palm. 'In fairness to me I wasn't aware of that arrangement. Mac didn't reveal there was any interest in the property so how could I have known? Plus, let's be honest. No seller is going to wait around for possibilities when there is a ready, willing and able buyer, prepared to meet the asking price. It's commercial reality, I'm afraid. I'm sure there are other houses.'

A headache pulsed at his temples. Bloody city folk. Yeah, other houses. Yep, there were loads of old traditional Queenslander houses on large acres of land for sale near the town centre of Bellethorpe. Why hadn't Mac had his back? But she was right. Money talked and unfortunately, Bellethorpe was becoming more like the city. Everyone was hurting and he couldn't really blame the owner, could he? The house had been vacant for years. Okay, it wasn't the owner's fault, and Mac was acting on instructions. And to his own stupidity, Noah honestly thought no one would ever show interest in the old girl. Wrong, he was very wrong. If it just could have been anyone other than a city girl fleeing to the country.

But really, what did it matter. His dream died the moment his wife left.

'We look out for each other in Bellethorpe and care about our own.' Noah studied her face, resisting the urge to drop his eyes lower and consider the rest of her. 'What do you do for work?'

She straightened to her full height and squared her shoulders. 'I'm an archaeologist.'

The laugh rolled out of him before he could stop it. 'An archaeologist! Impressive. Can't say I've seen too many old dead things around these parts recently.' He wasn't usually a smartarse. If his daughter had behaved in this manner, he would have pulled her into line swiftly.

And yet...did archaeology pay well enough to renovate a house almost beyond repair? He didn't know, but it didn't quite add up.

The boy was getting restless and swung his arms to and fro; Noah was too. Out of awkwardness, he started lifting the items in their trolley.

'What are you doing with this stuff?'

'Fixing up as much as I can myself.'

A flicker of admiration passed through him. He admired guts. 'What's this for?' He held up a lock.

She glared daggers at him with a look that could have pinned him to the nearby wall. She tried to swipe back the packet but being childish, he moved it out of her grip.

'It's for the front gate. There's a lock there currently but I want something more secure.'

'Why do you need to lock the gate from the inside?'

Her eyes darted left and right. 'Well, that's obvious, to keep people out. It's a secluded property and I don't want strangers entering without my knowledge … that's all.'

Odd. Noah wasn't sure what to make of that. He checked out the other stuff, all bits and bobs: some seedlings for a garden, a couple of small indoor plants, tins of sample paint.

'This one won't work. Follow me.'

The boy obeyed and skipped behind him. If not for her son, would she have followed?

At the lock section, he held out a more sturdy, appropriate mechanism that she glared at for a few moments before accepting.

Why was he helping her?

'Thank you.' He advised how to secure it, providing way too much detail but his words were getting away with him. Eventually she moved towards the check-out. Reaching behind him to grab the first item he saw, a toilet plunger of all things, he carried it and followed. At the register he stood by while she loaded her items onto the counter. The old lock remained and he went to remove it.

Ava gripped it. 'I'll keep it just in case.' And she stared at him, challenge in her eyes.

'You look familiar, love,' Trevor Fletcher said ringing up her goods.

There was no imagining the firm set to her jaw. So, Ava newcomer to town, had a bit of bluster. Impressive.

A sad, slow smile formed on her lips, only reaching the corners. 'Oh, really? I don't think so, we've just arrived in town.'

'Familiar I said, not that I know you. You look like a woman who used to live here many years ago and ran the clothing store. I remember because my wife used to spend a lot of her time and our money in there, you know, being the only women's shop in town. And the lady who ran it used to ship in fancy-types of clothes, like, and the ladies around here loved them.'

Ava's features softened and the smile lifted. 'Jane is my mother.' Noah craned to hear. 'My mother loved that store. It brought her a lot of joy over the years. She was devastated when we moved.'

Huh?

'I knew it!' Trevor beamed. 'Never forget a face.' He tapped his temple.

'I lived here when I was young. My father taught at the high school but he was transferred south when I was thirteen.'

'You are Jane and Damien's daughter?'

She nodded.

'The local ladies were gutted when the store closed, too. A couple of other women tried to take up the gauntlet but it was never the same and eventually, it closed and the women folk had to source their pretty dresses elsewhere.'

What? Ava used to live in Bellethorpe as a kid? They must be similar ages but he didn't remember her at school. So, she'd left and come back. Noah wasn't sure what to make of that either. Had he been too tough on her?

He glanced at Ava. She seemed lost to another time now, her gaze far away and dreamy.

'How lovely that you're back. How are they?'

It took her a moment to answer. 'My parents? They're well, thank you.'

Ava's features had twisted into something he couldn't read. Sorrow? Distress? Sadness? Or was it annoyance?

Noah leaned in, wanting to hear more, but Ava didn't elaborate. Instead, she packed her purchases into a canvas bag. 'Thank you for your help.'

Noah placed his plunger forward and swiped his credit card. Stuffing the receipt into his pocket, another piece of paper fell out. Ava, who hadn't moved away yet as she tended to the boy, retrieved it before him.

'What's this?' She smiled, a giggle emerging as she read. 'What's a squishy cuddle?'

'It's nothing.' He swiped the small square of paper out of her hand and tucked it into his pocket, shoving harder than necessary.

'Look, Ava, who do you trust in town?'

She regarded him quizzically.

'Bridie? Do you trust her?'

Ava nodded.

'Ask her about that O'Brien builder. She'll tell you the truth. She'll back me up that he can't be trusted and has several claims before the commission for his shoddy work. I'm not being vindictive. But get a second opinion. Bridie will agree and tell you to run a mile.' He tipped his hat goodbye.

CHAPTER

Six

AVA'S MOBILE rang just as she'd kicked the door shut behind her. Dumping her purchases, she checked the screen on the phone and her heart jumped into her throat. 'Ish, can you check Daisy? Give her some of those treats we bought?'

They'd agreed on a name that suited the chocolate lab perfectly. Daisy was a gentle, soul with a sweet face. So far, no one had claimed the dog and she had taken up a firm position in their hearts and home.

And she was a great distraction. Ava gripped the phone until Ish had raced away to tend to the dog.

'Jamila?' Ava spoke softly to avoid Ish overhearing. Jamila's distinctive voice was breaking up as she spoke in a rushed garble. It was the first time they'd spoken since Ava had arrived in Australia. There was so much to say, so much news to share.

'Are you okay? Are the kids okay?'

With the phone glued to her ear for the reply, Ava snuck outside and collapsed onto the back step. 'Okay, good, good. That's great. I'm so happy you're all right. It's making the news over here, did you know?'

Nodding, she listened. Yes, Jamila had taken legal advice and commenced divorce proceedings. Her lawyer was one of the best and she felt safe for the moment. She said she continued to look over her shoulder anytime she ventured out, or worse, if a plane or helicopter flew over. She described a constant vigilance that Ava could relate to. Her friend and formally her mother-in-law, described the veil of fear and intimidation that continued despite the sea of distance between her and her powerful husband. Yes, Ava understood. Australia was a world away so she hoped the increased distance improved her safety.

In other circumstances it would be amusing that Jamila, only ten years her senior, was her mother-in-law. She hardly ever thought of her in that context. The woman had been nothing but a confidante and close friend when Ava had moved to Egypt.

Ava stared out over her endless paddocks, the never-ending bush and listened; the wind whistled in the trees, birds chirped and there was the soft thump of kangaroos bouncing. She was protected here, wasn't she? More so than where Jamila was in London? London had a larger population but less places to hide.

'Jamila, if you need anything, please let me know. I can help. I'll do anything. I can never thank you enough for what you did for us. I'm forever grateful.' Was this her new mobile number? Was it safe? Yes, this was Ava's number, it was private, she was sure. Wasn't she?

With uncertainty hanging onto each word, fear of detection drove them to end the call prematurely with so much left unsaid.

Ava nursed the phone for a long while after she disconnected. The call had been unsettling while simultaneously reassuring her that Jamila was safe, for the present, anyway. The conversation was a reminder of where they'd come from, of what might be in her future. Neither of them was out of the woods yet. Jamila's journey was always going to be tougher, longer and more fraught with danger. Ava had gotten off easily. She prayed that Jamila's court proceedings would end swiftly and to her friend's satisfaction.

A blur of blue flashed past, along the road on the left ridge of her property. She couldn't see the car but heard the rumble of its engine. Time to test her handyman skills and lock the front gate. Was that enough to keep uninvited people out? She hoped she never had to find out.

Noah dropped home for lunch after his road trip to the next town for screws.

Pen in hand, he was scribbling a new verse when Otis barked right before a knock sounded at the door. It also came mid-bite on the chicken and avocado sandwich he'd just made. He was still chewing as he swung the door open.

'Are you Noah Hawthorn?' It was an authoritative and stern voice.

He nodded. Otis was dutifully by his side, his tail wagging. No guard dog there.

'You've been officially served with these court documents.' The man in his black trousers and white shirt with thin tie, walked away after shoving the papers into Noah's hands.

Weird. He ripped open the A4 envelope and scanned the cover letter. The bite of sandwich he'd eaten threatened to come back up.

What the heck?

He read the words again. Lisa had instituted proceedings in the Family Court for permission to move Emily to Brisbane ... because he'd refused to give consent. There was an affidavit attached to an application calling him to court. His body slumped into the chair and he pushed the plate away, his appetite gone. Otis sat at his feet, intuitive, and rested his head on his knee.

Noah poured himself a shot of whisky and devoured each word in the documents. At the end he turned the last page and folded the documents neatly back into the envelope, left the tumbler untouched and went out.

Minutes later he stood in the reception of Reid & Co Lawyers. 'I need to see the lawyer urgently,' he informed the receptionist, his voice surprisingly steady.

'We see clients by appointment.' The monotone and unemotional reply did not appreciate his entire world was falling apart. With her head down, the girl behind the counter scrolled through an old-school hard back diary checking for availability. 'Mr Reid has time at three p.m. tomorrow?'

The door swung open and Lincoln Reid entered the foyer area carrying a plastic tub of salad and a can of Diet-Coke.

'I need to see you please.' Noah had never had the need for Lincoln's services before but recognised him from around town and social events.

'And who might you be, young man?' The man tucked a news-paper under his arm.

'Noah Hawthorn.' Noah reached out his hand to shake but the lawyer's hands were full of his lunch.

The man sighed. 'And what's the urgency on this fine Tuesday afternoon?'

'I've been served with family law papers.' Noah avoided the man's eyes. 'I really need some advice.'

'Sienna?' the lawyer questioned the receptionist.

'You have a teleconference in thirty minutes. The Hardcastle matter.'

Turning back to Noah, he said, 'You have twenty-eight minutes and I'm eating my lunch while we talk.'

'Thank you.' Noah followed him into his office. It was poky and small and not what he'd imagined a lawyer's office to be. Beige walls, beige carpet and brown curtains with brown leather seats gave the room an unappealing mediocrity. Papers and folders were scattered from one end of the desk to the other.

'Yes, I know. It's a mess. I'm the only lawyer here. My niece is studying her degree and has agreed to cut her teeth and come out and help me when she graduates, but that's not for another few years. It's impossible to employ anyone out here. And when I do, they don't stick around.

'Anyway, nice to meet you. I'm Lincoln Reid, proprietor and lawyer at your service.' With a crack Reid opened his plastic tub of salad and dug his fork in. 'Let me see those.' He held his other hand out for the papers.

Munching on one, then two, then three mouthfuls, he read the material. 'Okay, your wife is seeking orders that your daughter live with her in Brisbane and spend time with you. It says she's tried to negotiate with you but you refuse to allow her to move Emily ...'

'She moved anyway.'

'Okay, we'll get to that. She says she has family support in Brisbane to help with Emily and that is where new partner works. There is everything the little girl could possibly dream of in Brisbane and your daughter has been enrolled in school there, ballet classes, gymnastics, swimming lessons and has made good friends. Plus, they live in a brand-new home in a newly developed suburb with available amenities.' Lincoln munched some more. 'Sounds idyllic, doesn't it?'

Was he being serious? Noah wasn't sure.

'So, what's your version?'

'My version?'

'Yes, your side of the story. Okay, I'll assist. Did you refuse to let Emily live with her mother in Brisbane?'

'Yes … but Emily was born here and has always lived in Bellethorpe. Lisa chose to separate and then doesn't wish to live here anymore. I don't understand why that means my daughter must follow her? If she wants to move why can't Emily stay here with me?'

'She can, of course, but you'd both have to agree. Lisa has now chosen to live in Brisbane and wishes to have Emily there with her. Emily has school, extra-curricular activities and friends but the clincher is family support for your separated wife. Did she move to Bellethorpe for you?'

'Yes.'

'Okay, that's going to be your biggest challenge. If your wife chooses to return to Bellethorpe, does she have any support here? Friends?'

'Me.'

'Other than you, given she no longer wishes to be married to you.'

Noah winced.

'Name me some of her friends?'

Noah wracked his brain. He knew Lisa had friends. In the early days she was always having coffee mornings at the French bakery and would often head into the nearest town shopping. There were catch-ups with other mothers from play group. He remembered she hosted occasionally. Once she played tennis at the club. When was her last game? More recently, he couldn't remember Lisa seeing Jill from the cattle property or Fiona from the gym. When did that stop? Sometimes she visited his mother. Noah should know this information, understood it was bad he didn't. 'I'm not sure.'

Lincoln let the pause linger. 'Okay, Emily is how old?'

'Six.'

'Has she started school yet?'

Noah nodded. She'd done one year of prep at the local primary. That was good, right? His spirits were dropping real fast. He could see how this looked. 'This is her home.'

Lincoln checked his watch. 'We have twelve minutes. I'll tell you how it is. This matter is proceeding to court where a judge will decide where your daughter lives unless you change your mind and consent for her to live in Brisbane. If you do not agree, you will have to argue why it would be in her best interest to return to Bellethorpe. The court will likely order that all of you are interviewed by a psychologist or family counsellor and they will help the court decide. That psychologist will provide their opinion on what is best for Emily through a course of interviews. Then if you still don't agree, the matter will go to hearing where you and Lisa will have to give evidence.'

Noah's head spun. Lincoln continued.

'I can act for you. I appear in the family court in Brisbane often as it's the nearest court of that jurisdiction to Bellethorpe but you would always be appearing there anyway, as that's where she has filed and where Lisa wants to live with Emily. You will need to pay me per hour and deposit an initial fee before I can help you.'

Lincoln stated the amount required and Noah blanched.

'Yes, it's a lot. Defending this application will cost you a lot of money. This initial deposit will get you to the first court hearing only. It will be chewed up in letters back and forth to your wife's lawyer and in the preparation of your evidence. You need to know this before you agree to fight. It will cost you both financially and emotionally. The scars from a battle like this are real. Don't do it for pride or to make a point, you must be committed to this course of action. Today, you're angry. Think about it for a few days and let me know what you want to do.'

The lawyer took three more large bites of his salad followed quickly by successive gulps of soft drink. 'Now I have another meeting, so you'll have to excuse me.'

Noah stood. 'Thank you, Lincoln for your time. Can you tell me one thing? What are my prospects of getting Emily back to Bellethorpe?'

Without hesitation, he replied, 'Less than fifty percent.'

―――――

The tumbler of whisky sat next to the scrap of paper on the table where he'd abandoned them. Noah read from the slip.

Squishy cuddles upon waking
Giggling, laughing until she's shaking

Squishy cuddles when it's time to start the day
Long held embraces are the only way

Squishy cuddles are all he thinks of upon return
Arms open wide, smiles ready, it's his turn

Squishy cuddles at the end of the night
Squeezing too hard until it's time to turn out the light.

He used to write Lisa poetry. Early in their relationship, he'd written verses most days before work and left them on the kitchen bench. Often, short and sweet, sometimes funny, always loving.

The whisky was warm as it rushed down his throat and the burn it provided was worth it. Noah poured another, swirled the amber liquid in the glass before tossing it back. It provided the exact relief he needed.

The poem was meant to be light respite but he no longer found it amusing. Nothing about pouring out his heart in matching rhyme could make this situation better.

Taking the bottle and the glass he sat on his back deck and whistled for Otis to follow. The deck wasn't fancy but had a chair and table and a spectacular view over the national park. The area was renowned for its rock formations and boulders. Granite to be precise. As far as he could see were large boulders, some balancing precariously as if they were about to tumble, others long and flat, handy for sitting upon. The rocky terrain was his favourite view. Not too far from here was a hike across large waves of rock face, through cliffs with other incredible rock formations. It wasn't dainty or neat, but bold and beautiful.

His aim might be off, but Otis wanted to play fetch. Noah threw a ball as far as he could. The dog dropped it at his feet only moments later. He threw it again. As a family, they'd spent many afternoons out here playing, often eating dinner on a picnic blanket as the sun went down. Emily loved ball games as much as Otis. He'd taught her how to catch, throw the footy and kick a soccer ball. They'd play team games, Lisa and Emily against him; there'd been lots of laughter. They were some of his best memories.

In the future he had imagined enrolling Emily in the kid's division of his touch football club. Or if she didn't fancy that, maybe little athletics. Now, he was unlikely to see her advance through any of these sports. At least he could still watch games on a Sunday when he wasn't working.

With another sip, he cringed as he remembered how he'd asked Lisa to stay. How she'd turned away, saying it was too late.

Lisa had been so full of life when they'd met and when she'd agreed to live in Bellethorpe. She'd relished the move and being extroverted had met more people in town than he had. He thought she'd cemented her place here and felt comfortable.

When she'd started grumbling, he thought it was just a phase, maybe baby blues and she'd feel better soon. Something else he was wrong about. She wasn't that unhappy, was she? Had she said? How had he missed the signs? Most likely because he was working.

With the birth of Emily, Lisa didn't continue her job and Noah had to carry the financial load. And he didn't mind but he worked longer hours and added in Saturdays, too. Whereas once, he would have been home in time for a glass of wine on the deck before dinner. Towards the end, he'd rush in, often late and tired. Lisa had been sullen, withdrawn, and the evenings quiet, until eventually there was nothing left to say.

He regarded the shack he called home. It wasn't the Taj Mahal by any stretch but he didn't mind it. Except, Lisa had wanted to move, longed for a bigger place, a yard, maybe some farm animals that they'd always dreamed of.

She'd only ever asked him once, and he'd refused, thinking she was joking. Move away from Bellethorpe? It was something he'd never consider. End of conversation. But then that was when his dream of owning the old house had come alive. He'd compromise and buy a large family home with lots of land where Lisa could nurture her veggie patch and have a brood of animals. Except, those things took time and money. He'd been saving ever since. A bolt of anger surged through him. Imagine if they'd purchased the place on Kinross Road and she'd left. Not only would he be stuck with a hefty mortgage, Noah would be caring for a menagerie of animals. He threw the ball again and treasured the relief of Otis chasing it across the field. *Ease up, mate.* That hadn't happened but maybe if they'd shifted, they'd still be a family.

But it was too late.

So, he should have known, should have realised what would come.

He was man enough to confess he'd stuffed up. But did that mean his punishment was not seeing his daughter? Lincoln had said the fight wasn't about principle or pride. It was hard to make it about anything else. Now that he'd lost everything, all he had left was Emily.

The support group said it was about father's rights. Each member of that group had a sorry tale to tell and most had no happy ending. The court system was biased towards mothers, they said. If that was true, why would he bother fighting? He was mentally fit for it, but the cost. Ironically the savings he had, of course, he no longer needed to buy his dream family home. Further irony, if he was successful, he'd never have the grand family home for Emily to live in. She'd have to return here because he'd have no money left.

Where did that leave him? He had the funds to pay the initial lawyer instalment. After that he'd be relying on weekly income and he understood the debt would outweigh his pay. Then, if he was lucky, and won, he had no family home because his savings were lost on the fight. It was pretty much a shit show whichever way he looked at it. But when Emily was older and asked him that question: why didn't you fight for me? The only answer could be, that he'd tried.

Otis nudged his foot reminding him of the game. Yes, game of ball. If only everything was that easy. Noah threw it once more and the dog belted across the grass.

A thought out of the blue made him sit up straight.

Who needed him and his building skills right now? Who had the money to pay generously for his work? Yes, admittedly, the same thought made the spirits suddenly taste sour in his mouth, but he was a genius. It was the perfect solution. Except of course, he would be working on the very house he'd hoped would one day be his, his and Emily's. But he had already accepted that dream was over.

He, builder, Noah Hawthorn would do the renovation work for Ava Montgomery.

There was endless effort required to fix up that place, might take months and be expensive, even charging his reasonable fees. She had mentioned cash up front, now that money could be his. Generously, he'd donate the plans he'd already drafted and suited the house perfectly. The plans were traditional and kept the house to its original grand style. If Ava was a modernist, she wouldn't be interested. But he imagined anyone interested in modern homes with their brick rendered facades and open living and clean and sharp lines, wouldn't have been interested in that house anyway. Sometimes an old house was an old house and there was no fixing up or modern cons that could change that.

With relief, he poured himself another drink. He had fixed his own problem. He could afford the lawyer and pay him on an ongoing basis; he would fight for Emily and for what was right. There was a way forward, he could see it now, feel it, grasp success.

Only hitch was, he had to get Ava to agree.

CHAPTER
Seven

AVA'S NERVES WERE A JANGLE. After her run-in with Noah at
the hardware store, and then her phone call with Jamila, she couldn't
quite settle.

Lost in thought, she gazed out the window, watched the horses run
free, their manes dancing in the wind.

They'd go riding!

'Ish!' she yelled. Her son came racing in, sliding on his socked feet.
'Want to go for a horse ride?' His answer was a squeal and he danced
on the spot. Ish made Daisy comfortable and tucked her up in some
blankets in a basket on the deck. They dressed in their oldest jeans and
long-sleeved shirts and headed out.

Ava had hoped her riding knowledge would come back once she
was in motion and she was right. The saddles and the right clips, the
length of the stirrup, the rug underneath, the bridle. She recited the
names for Ish and taught him as she went. Mounted upon Marmalade,
the boy sat diminutively in the saddle while she prepared Honey. Clive
had assured her they were both placid horses, but she tethered the lead
rope anyway.

The horse stables were on Clive's land, so they followed the fence
line until they reached a gate and entered their property. The gate was

down by the old windmill that was rusted, but majestic, tall and turning slowly in the breeze next to a pond covered with lilies in bloom. A track appeared ahead and she followed it.

The bush was dense down at the far reaches of their property. Mainly shrub that crackled under foot with its dryness, not unusual with the high temperatures of the Australian summer. With each step she forgot the pressures of real life that bore down upon her shoulders. Ava inhaled the country air and soaked up the solitude.

They were probably about fifteen or twenty minutes along the track when they came across a rock pond shaded by a canopy of tall trees. Large boulders lined the edge of the expanse of water and a slight incline created a series of tiny waterfalls.

'Wow!' Ish exclaimed.

'This is beautiful. Let's take a break.'

Ish jumped down without fuss and patted Marmalade's neck. The horse nuzzled into his side. Ava could see a friendship forming already between boy and horse. In just a few short days her son had a dog soon to be delivering puppies no less, and a horse. These small things made her heart swell. The making of a life. They'd be okay.

Sitting on a couple of flat boulders, they shared a snack and cool drink. 'It's almost as if this is a different place and we've left Bellethorpe, as if we've ridden for kilometres to find this spot. It's perfect, isn't it?' Ava said.

Ish agreed as he chewed on a muesli bar. Finishing the last bite, he removed his shoes and waded into the shallows of the pond. 'Oh, it's so nice, Mumma, come in.' Ava removed her boots and let the water lap at her ankles.

'Ish, that's so good! Surprisingly cold.'

He splashed water in her direction and she reciprocated. 'Enough, enough! I'm happy to cool off, but don't want to be soaked.'

'What's that do you think?' She pointed to various piles of dirt around the creek and down the track. Ish shrugged, not interested as he found something to hold his attention in the water.

Ava reached for the nearest mound and let the dirt trickle through her fingers. It didn't look natural and appeared out of place, like someone had been digging. It reminded her of tailings with its slightly silver, metallic shade. And occasionally when the sun filtered through the branches, there was the slightest hint of colour, a sort of pewter rainbow that bounced around the small area.

Further down the track were more heaps until the path hit a sharp curve and she couldn't see any more. The archaeologist in her pocketed a few specimens and enjoyed feeling the weight in her pocket. Ava didn't quite know what this place was, but she sensed it was special.

'Okay, buddy. Let's head back. We'll go riding regularly, I promise. There must be so many parts of our land to explore out here. Imagine if there are more of these gorgeous rock pools? I think we've found our own little oasis here.'

They rode back in silence and at a gentle walk until the horses caught sight of home and they commenced to trot. Ish shrieked as he bounced up and down in the saddle. It made for a quick trip. Back at the stables she taught him how to unsaddle the horses, even though he was way too short to reach, and the stirrups and buckles hit the ground as he carried the equipment. They rubbed the animals down, watered and brushed them and left them happily munching on fresh hay. Ava's heart swelled once more with contentment watching Ish skip ahead, fulfilled and happy.

'What do you say about Chinese take-out for dinner? I'm starving but too tired to cook. I can do a quick run into town.'

Ish was already pulling off his dusty clothes with Daisy in his wake. Thank goodness the old air-conditioner unit still worked, and she turned it on until she felt the cool cascade of air lowering the living room temperature. It worked, for now, but Ava made a mental note to get it serviced and soon.

Hearing Ish in the shower, she checked each window was closed and locked and double checked the front and back doors. The seclusion out here was great, but the disadvantage was they were isolated. However, the town centre was less than ten minutes away. Ava paused, bag in hand. For the briefest crazy moment she'd contemplated leaving Ish while she picked up dinner. Clearly a moment of madness. She was confident no one could enter the house with its security screens and double bolts; after all she'd overdone their security. And wasn't the country meant to be safe? Away from the crime of the big cities? But no, she put down her bag. What had she been thinking? There was no way she'd risk leaving her son home alone. Ava blew out a big breath.

After his shower, an annoyed Ish was bundled into the car along with Daisy for the short trip. Better to annoy her son than something happen while she was absent.

One huge advantage of living in a small town, there was always an available parking space. She snapped up the spot outside the Chinese restaurant and the flash of the illuminated sign trapped her gaze. Ava paused and memories from the past flooded in. On Friday nights in London, after a busy work week, she and Henry would often stay in, unless they had a flashy event to attend, and order Chinese. The sign flickered again and brought her back to the present. She wasn't in London now. Double checking the car doors were locked, Ava rushed inside, leaving Ish to cuddle Daisy.

With her mind trapped in the past, she didn't watch her step and ran straight bang into the large and broad chest of Noah Hawthorn. Her flat palms landed on his torso to catch her balance. Her fingers tingled at the touch of his warm and hard body … their faces were only inches apart.

He recovered first and took a step back creating space. 'Sorry.' His voice was the softest she'd heard yet, unsure and uncertain, not his usual curt and confident tone.

He blinked in quick succession and glanced downwards.

Oh, yes, her hands.

'Sorry 'bout that, should have been looking where I was going.' Her hands dropped to her sides.

'Ordering some Chinese?'

'Umm, yep.'

'Me too, I'll get us some menus.' Noah jostled to the counter and provided her with a double-sided plastic menu. There was a lot of choices.

'Anything you'd recommend?' she asked him.

He looked up and considered her for a moment. 'The sweet and sour is the best. I would also recommend the Mongolian lamb and cashew nut stir-fry. Plus, the springs rolls are great and the chicken satay sticks.'

'You know what? I think I'm going to order exactly that.' And a smile trembled over her lips. She was rewarded with a grin that was irresistibly devastating and Ava felt a lurch in her chest, a funny little giddy-up of her heart.

'Ladies first,' Noah gestured to the queue.

Now they had to wait together for their meals to be cooked and the silence was awkward.

'You know, I spoke to Bridie and she said exactly what you said she would. She was adamant that I cannot use O'Brien builders. Very emphatic. So, I won't...'

'I know we got off on the wrong foot, but my advice wasn't vindictive and I'm glad you know that. I would never recommend him to anyone and that's a fact.' Noah shuffled his feet, considered the lino floor in detail. 'About that...another job has fallen through. We were waiting on building approvals that haven't arrived yet and can't start as expected. I can do the work for you.'

The words hung between them.

'You can do my reno work and start straight away?'

'Yes, if you still want me to.'

There was no pretending this time. Her smile was wide, warm and genuine, radiating from the inside. 'That would be so great. I mean, I should really be telling you to shove it after the things you've said and the way you treated me, but I think you're aware that I need you.'

'And I need...' he began to speak as a loud crash of steel bowls and plates occurred in the kitchen.

'I'm sorry what was that?' Was he about to say he needed her too? Why would he?

'Ah, it's nothing. I want the job and am happy to help you. As you know I have a soft spot for the place and I want it to be the beautiful house it deserves to be. Oh, that reminds me, I did have some preliminary plans drawn up, only by me, mind you, but to the correct dimensions and in keeping with the old traditional style of design. I can bring them and show you. You might like to use them.'

'Gosh. That would be ... great. I don't know what to say.'

Order for Montgomery!

Ava stared at Noah, properly studied him for the first time. He wasn't wearing his hat tonight and it changed his entire appearance. Turned his rigid and usually stern face more handsome even under the harsh lights of the takeaway. Was it just the missing hat? No, she detected something else. His features were softer and his stance less combative than the times they'd met previously. His feet shuffled and he gazed down at the ground and up again. It was shyness, or perhaps uncertainty. And yet, when their eyes locked, he didn't look away. He had mesmerising grey eyes flecked with gold that were large and well-set apart. Everything about him was big and broad including his facial features with his wide and firm-set mouth and aquiline nose. Those unruly wavy curls on top were more blonde than brown. He was well-groomed and carried an air of authority that was charming and made Ava want to be around him. She sensed when he smiled she might be unable to tear her gaze away. This was a man who worked hard but was loyal and strident in his convictions. Someone to be trusted?

Order for Montgomery!

'Um, Ava, that's your order, isn't it?'

Oh, bugger, yes. Trapped in his gaze, she momentarily forgot her name. To be fair, it was her maiden name that she had only recently reverted to. It hadn't quite stuck, yet.

She giggled to cover her nerves at being caught daydreaming about him, in his presence. 'Sorry, yes. That's me!' she called, and a bag was thrust into her hand. 'Oh, this smells delicious.' Words of invitation formed on her tongue. They were both eating Chinese, they could eat their meals together, couldn't they? But then his order was called, the moment broken, her nerve frayed.

'So, sorry, just to be sure,' he bowed his head, 'is it agreed that I'll do the job?'

Ava nodded. 'Yes, absolutely.'

'Okay, great. And you mentioned something about cash terms?'

They were talking business. Thank goodness she hadn't invited him to eat with them. How embarrassing! Ava recovered quickly. 'Yes, sure. Can you invoice me?'

'Yep. Fantastic, thank you. I'll work something out and quote you.

An advance would be great to purchase materials and to cover the wages of my team. I'll do most of the work on my own, but for the bigger jobs I might call on my very experienced team of builders. You met Alex the other day. I'll give you some more details tomorrow. I'll head over first thing.'

'See you then.'

Ava jumped into her car and sped away. Not sure why, but something felt off and her gut twinged. Not a full twist, so that was something. Was it the handsome stranger and her almost *faux pas* or something else? Bridie, town crier and bearer of the knowledge of Bellethorpe, trusted Noah Hawthorn, so she could too, right? So, if the builder was trustworthy, what was it? Or perhaps it was too soon to trust anyone? Lack of trust was keeping them safe. After all, hadn't she learned the hard way? People said one thing and did another. Perhaps it was human nature. It would be okay. The renos would be completed, and she'd continue like she'd always done, on high alert, her only priority protecting herself and Ish. Tonight, that burden felt heavy.

CHAPTER
Eight

'KNOCK, KNOCK!'

Noah called out before he poked his head around the rear of Ava's house. The place was deadly quiet. First foot on the back stair and he saw her. Ava sat hunched over at the outdoor table. Crying.

He ascended the last few steps quickly. 'What's wrong, Ava? Are you hurt? Is Duke okay?'

Ava wasn't just crying; she was sobbing and struggled to catch her breath in between. Finally acknowledging his presence, she sat up, first wiped her hands across her cheeks and then patted down imaginary and wayward strands of loose hair.

'No, everything is fine.'

'Really? I know men are not very perceptive, but I'm pretty sure you don't cry like that unless something has upset you. What's happened?'

And man, while he was concerned, she was damn cute with her bright pink cheeks and swollen eyes.

Uncertainty swam in her eyes, but he saw a switch, the moment she decided to confide in him.

'It's so stupid! I've just dropped Duke at his prep orientation morning for school. I thought I was ready but he's so small and doesn't know any of the other children yet and, and … how can I be sure he'll be okay?'

Noah sagged with relief. 'That's not stupid. I think I was more nervous on my daughter's first day of school then she was. She woke, dressed and basically skipped away from me at the classroom with a cheery wave. I'm not going to lie, I was heartbroken. Me, her protector, and she was prepared to wave me off like the postman!'

Ava laughed and his chest puffed out a little. It was a sweet sound. The intensity around them broke and dissipated with the chuckle.

'You have a daughter?' Her left eyebrow arched.

Did he just admit that? Wasn't like him to let his defences down and talk so openly. The situation was relatable, he guessed.

He nodded. 'Yep. Emily was in prep last year and will be heading into year one this year.'

Noah gazed out into the distance with a slight rising panic. If Bellethorpe Primary was having their orientation day, then Emily's first day was fast approaching. He was annoyed with himself that he didn't know. With the living arrangements currently undetermined, he guessed Emily would be starting a new school in Brisbane. Another advantage to Lisa. His daughter should be here, in Bellethorpe, her home, returning to school. At each turn, Emily was being drawn further and further away from him.

After speaking with Lisa, she had agreed Emily could spend this coming weekend with him. School must commence after that. The glare of the sizzling sun made him squint and he refocused on the deck. He resolved to find out. He'd double check with Lisa next time they chatted; try to avoid an argument.

Would he go to her first day this year? Make the three-hour trip to and from Brisbane for a few minutes? Where once again, she might run off and not glance backwards? Yes, he would, of course he would.

Ava regarded him strangely, as if she could tell he was miles away. It's very hard to reveal only a little information. 'My wife and I are separated. Emily is currently living with her mum in Brisbane. I miss her desperately.' Bugger, his voice hitched on that last word. 'Your son has recently moved into a new area, a new house, tell me, has he adjusted okay?'

Ava reached out and cupped his hand. He froze. It was a gesture of solidarity between parents, wasn't it?

'He's adjusted better than me. We hold on to more memories, don't we? His only concern is the toys we didn't bring or, missing the donut we used to buy from the corner bakery where we lived. Simple things like that. Where we as adults, hold on too much more.'

Noah nodded.

Did Emily call Brisbane home? Her new bedroom her preference? What did she think of Lisa's boyfriend? An ache shot through his chest. Covering up his distress, he removed his hand and went to sip his coffee and remembered he was holding a take-away cup for Ava. He offered it. 'Make us both feel better?' She gratefully accepted.

'It's a standard latte, nothing fancy.'

'Nothing fancy is wonderful, thank you.' She took a deep sip and used the paper napkin that accompanied it to wipe her face dry.

Then she startled, eyes wide like saucers, looked down, around. 'How did you get here?'

'Um, I drove. The gate is locked, so I parked the truck and walked up.'

Her shoulders relaxed. 'Okay. If you'd let me know I would have opened it for you.'

He shrugged. I don't have your number.'

'I'm not very organised this morning, sorry. Given you'll be working here, I'll give it to you.' She recited it and was already on the tenth number when he tugged his phone out of his pocket. 'I'll punch it in,' she offered.

Noah unlocked the phone and handed it over. His favourite image of Emily beamed up at him before fading.

'Thanks. There'll be tradies coming and going, so might be best to leave the gate unlocked and open.'

She flinched and chewed on her lower lip. He wished she wouldn't do that; it made his insides start somersaulting. But, more importantly, what was she frightened of? He scanned his surroundings expecting someone might jump out at them. Was it country seclusion? Well, don't get him started … if you can't hack the country, don't live here, or, alternatively live in town. There were other options. But what if it was more …

She sipped the coffee and moaned in an exaggerated fashion. To cover up? 'So good, thank you.'

'So, how did Duke go? Did he settle okay before you left?'

With thoughts of her son, she offered him the full throttle smile, the one that crinkled the edges of her sparkling eyes and caused her cheeks to broaden. It was beautiful. His somersaulting stomach was joined by a rush of blood to his extremities.

'He was great, so good and here I am blubbering like a baby. It's a blessing when they let you leave isn't it? Even when they know it's a new and strange place. I guess travelling across the world makes you a little resilient, right?'

'Across the world? Where have you come from? Where's his dad? Is he coming soon to help you renovate?'

Oops, too many questions. The beaming smile dropped and her mouth took on an unpleasant twist. 'He's living overseas at the moment.' She brought the cup to her mouth and sipped twice. 'Are those the plans?'

Overseas? What did that evasive answer mean? He stared at Ava and she returned the look, as if daring him to ask another question that he sensed she would refuse to answer. Her eyes diverted to the rolls of card tucked under his armpit. He'd let it go for now. 'Yes, let's take a look.'

A dog scratched on the glass sliding door seeking to be let out. 'You have a dog?'

'Yes. Duke found her under the house, resting in the cool dirt. Do you recognise her? She must have an owner, but the vet can't locate anyone and she's pregnant.'

'Pregnant? Wow!' Noah performed a low whistle. Seconds later, soft footfalls thudded up onto the deck.

'Oh, yes, you have a dog, too. I'd forgotten.' Ava laughed and Noah cursed that he enjoyed the sound so much.

'Where was he?'

Noah rubbed Otis' neck vigorously, roughing up the dog. 'He was down the side having a kip. He comes on site with permission, so I wanted to check with you first. Could be nice company for …?'

'Daisy. And apparently she needs to rest. Otis looks like he wants to play.'

'He always wants to play but he's very obedient and gentle and will be wonderful with her. Keep an eye on her.' He ordered the dog.

True to Noah's word, Otis led Daisy to the far reach of the timber deck and together they collapsed down, their noses touching.

'So sweet. He's welcome anytime. But these plans?'

Noah spread them wide, keeping the edges flat with his palms. He allowed Ava to consider them first before jumping in. One end of the card flipped up and her hand grasped the corner the same time as his. Their hands brushed and she gasped. There was no bolt of electricity, that was the stuff of fairy tales, but the touch of her warm, smooth skin sent shivers of desire pulsing through him. A magnetic force built between them, had been building since they met; an intense shared connection. He wrenched his hand away, confused and chanced a look at her under his lashes. Her eyes were fixed on where their hands had touched. He swore his hand prickled with sensation.

'What's this?' Ava pointed to some buildings to the left of the house.

'At the moment they are empty sheds. Not sure what they were ever used for. Storage, I guess. As you can see, I intended these to be workspaces for me, building small projects, cutting up and finishing work. But I think we can tweak those for your work. Do you need some custom and personalised space at home?'

'My work?'

'Yeah, do you ever need a place to examine relics or keep items or somewhere just for you to perform your work?'

'Oh wow. I've never had my own space and those sheds are huge!' Girlish excitement crept into her voice. 'That would be magic. I have a whole pile of old academic books at my parent's place that I'm sending for. They can be stored out there and maybe tables for sorting or storing items I'm working on and shelving. There is always a lot of stuff.'

'You didn't want to move to be near your folks? Did I hear you say they moved south?'

Ava released the edge of the plan and it curled up, the corners snapping together. 'Yeah. Tassie. It's pretty cold there.' She paused. Opened her mouth to speak, shut it. She was holding something back. 'I loved my time in Tassie, went to uni there, but coming back, I only had thoughts of Queensland.' Another pregnant pause.

'Okay, then.' He filled the silence and they exchanged a smile, a truce of sorts.

'These plans are fantastic, Noah. Obviously, it's drawings and dimensions mainly but I can tell you are committed to the era and traditional style of the house. Me too. I want it to be the grand lady it would have once been. I want us to source authentic pieces, where possible. If the floor needs replacing, I'd prefer original and recycled timbers and the same with the doors and windows. I actually don't know a lot about these heritage homes but I'm happy to learn and will be guided by you. I'm sure you've fixed up plenty of these.'

'For sure and I know the places to obtain original parts and there's a few shops in Pozieres that will stock the fittings. Like antique door handles, light switches and even things like towel rails and those little features that are important.'

'Thank you. I don't know what I would've done if your plans were to knock out the main walls to create open living spaces and to modernise with steel appliances and those fancy kitchen taps. I don't even know what they're called but you know the mixer taps with the long hoses that would probably reach the bathroom.'

'Oh, I don't think you'd have had any trouble telling me where to go with my plans.'

She acted coy. 'As I said last night, I'm genuinely sorry that we got off on the wrong foot. It must have been such a shock to learn that the house you'd been dreaming of was no longer yours. I'm sorry about that. Can't promise I still wouldn't have bought it if I'd known, but...' She shrugged.

'Thank you, that means a lot. And it makes for an easy start. I'll spend this afternoon getting together the materials we need and I'll start tomorrow.'

'Okay, so you'll need some money?'

'Oh, um.' His mobile phone rang. Lisa. Shit. 'I'm not sure what the timber and stuff will cost up front, so I'll come back to you with the info.' The phone continued to trill, echoing in his ears. Why was he refusing the money? Because he liked her? Hang on. Things were heading off track. And now Lisa was ringing and she'd just served him with court papers...

'I've got to go. See you bright and early in the morning.'

'Mumma, Mumma, I can't find Daisy!'

Ish had dumped his school bag and gone looking for Daisy, first thing, only to find her bed empty. Had she been in her bed before she'd left to collect Ish from school? Ava couldn't remember. In fact, she couldn't recall the last time she'd seen her. The dog could have wandered anywhere, her mind had been a bit of a mess during the day.

'Let's search the house first.' They split up. He checked the bath-rooms, and Ava the bedrooms. In the kitchen he opened the cupboards and peered inside.

'Nothing,' he announced.

'Let's check outside.' Together they searched the perimeter of the house and the back of the sheds. They trudged over to the fence and contemplated checking the horse stables, but Daisy usually didn't wander that far.

Racing back to the house, they saw a paling on the grass at the spot they'd originally found Daisy.

'I fixed that. Quick!' Ava grasped his hand and they rushed over. In the cool and dark interior, Daisy whimpered. 'Hey, Daisy, are you okay?' Ava murmured to the dog and stroked the fur she could reach under the house. 'Can you see any puppies yet, Ish?'

Ish craned his neck each which way. 'No.'

'Okay, you stay here and talk to Daisy, keep her calm, and I'll ring the vet to see if we should move her.'

Only moments later, Ava was back with a blanket. 'Ish, the vet said we can move her somewhere calm and quiet and warm. So first, we'll lift her onto this blanket, okay? Can you help me?'

It wasn't easy. Daisy had chosen to bury herself under the house. It looked comfortable but no one wanted to deliver their little babies onto the dirt. In the end, their efforts were in vain, and, with the encouragement of a liver treat, Daisy stood and walked slowly towards the back staircase. She paused, one paw on the first rise and glanced back.

'You can do it, girl.' Ish gently held her bottom to prevent a fall. The next paw went up and the next until she'd climbed the short steps. Ava fluffed up the pillow and blankets in her basket and patted the ground. Daisy approached and plopped herself down.

'Can you see if she'll take a little water?'

Ish raced away to refill the water bowl and came back, holding it to the dog's nose. She lapped a few sips. 'Now offer her some small treats.' One by one Daisy ate the pebble-sized treats from his hand. 'We have to make sure she is comfortable and keep an eye on her, okay. She needs you tonight. You up for it?'

Ish nodded and sat on the deck, one hand on Daisy's back, the other holding his knees to his chest. 'You can tell Daisy about your orientation at big school while I start dinner.'

Before Ava had stepped inside, she heard Ish reciting the school rules: you must sit cross-legged on the mat, put your hand up to speak, and not talk when the teacher is speaking. He mentioned a boy he'd met, a new boy too who hadn't lived in town long, his name was Samuel. Ish said it made him feel better because the other kids knew each other already and they hadn't even attended school yet. Ava clutched a hand to her heart. This was more information than she'd gotten out of him on the short drive home. He told Daisy it was a good day; yes, he'd had fun; yes, his teacher was nice. He would be happy to start there when school commenced. She paused to listen to more, but he went on to tell Daisy that one child had a vegemite sandwich—how disgusting! —and another had jam. Once he'd detailed about four sandwich fillings, Ava headed to the kitchen.

Later, after dinner, they sat together on the back deck, on the timber flooring right beside Daisy, and played snap. The stars shone brightly in the sky and the evening temperature was mild. By bedtime, there still weren't any puppies. Ish had fallen asleep, his head resting on Daisy's lower body and Ava carried him to bed, tucked him in and watched him sleep.

With his bedroom not yet ready, he slept in her room. Tonight, lids fluttering in his sleep, his lips slightly parted, he spread across her double bed like a starfish. Sometimes, when she couldn't sleep, she'd gaze at him and was amazed that this was her son, that she had created him. It never failed to cause a bolt of something straight through her chest. Pride? Love? Hope? It was more a fierce protective love that she would do anything for him. The feeling scared her at times. Particularly now. What length exactly would she go to if she had to protect him? A strange tingling rippled beneath her skin. Looking at him it was impossible not to think of his father. Ish had inherited his father's dark features, thick hair and that gorgeous sun-kissed skin. Occasionally, moments overcame her and fear for the future gripped her around the middle like a vice. Ava breathed deeply in and out, watched Ish. For the moment, he was safe, he was here. Her heartbeat slowed. Shutting the bedroom door, she grabbed an extra blanket, a yoga mat and a book and sat leaning on the wall next to Daisy who was now mercifully asleep.

CHAPTER
Nine

NOAH RANG Ava's mobile three times while he stood at her locked front gate. No answer. They'd agreed yesterday that she'd keep it open. He wasn't one to jump to conclusions, but should he be worried?

Being stranded at the gate was frustrating this morning because he was ready to start work and his gear was in the truck. Attempting to get hold of her one last time, he whistled for Otis and made the trek up the long drive. First sight of those morning kangaroos and Otis was off at full pelt. His chances of catching any were poor, but it was amusing to watch.

Noah stomped up the back stairs to avoid surprising Ava. Needn't have worried; she lay on the ground next to the dog's bed curled into a ball, purring quietly like a cat and fast asleep. One hand was stretched towards the dog, but not quite touching. She wore long dark exercise pants and a loose pale tee, bare feet with her hair loose and fanning her face. She looked peaceful despite her position on the floor.

Daisy whimpered and looked at him, her tail wagging wildly. Next to her were puppies! One, two, three, four, five, he counted.

'Ava,' he shook her shoulder. 'Ava.'

She startled. 'It's okay, it's morning and you've been asleep, and look,' he said, pointing. Her eyes were shrouded with sleep, but he kept watching and was rewarded with the surprise and delight of what she saw.

'Puppies!' She sat up. 'Oh, Daisy, you clever girl. You did it all by yourself and here I was available to help during the night.' Jumping up, she headed for the back door. 'I've got to wake Ish; he'll be so excited.'

Ish?

But he didn't have time to contemplate the name change. The boy ran out, his hair mussed and his smile crooked. 'Oh,' he squealed. 'There's five! Two brown and three yellow. Oh my gosh.' He knelt at Daisy's head and patted her along the nose. The dog lapped up the attention. 'Can I touch one of the puppies?'

'I don't know, I guess, maybe try and see what Daisy does.'

Ish reached out with one finger and stroked the back of one chocolate puppy. Daisy watched undisturbed.

'I'll ring Zac and see if he can come and check them out, see if everything's okay. I'll put the kettle on too, coffee?' She directed the coffee question at him.

'Yes please, thanks Ava. I stopped at the hardware store on my way today and couldn't get to the café.'

When Ava returned, she'd changed into denim shorts showing lots of leg and had pulled her hair into a neat ponytail. Her face was fresh and clear. She handed him a mug. 'The vet will drop in this morning.'

Noah accepted the cup of deep blue with gold edge. 'A Pharaoh, huh? Interesting.'

Ava paused, glanced down, a darkness passing across her eyes. 'I used to have a collection of these really authentic cups made in Egypt with a special motif on each. They were lovely to drink out of. Not touristy like these....' Her voice lowered. 'That one is Cleopatra one of the most powerful female Pharaohs. Mine is Nefertiti, another female Pharoah. They are my favourite. I'm obsessed with ...' She glanced at her son but he was focused on the dogs. '...Egypt. Their relics, well anything Egyptian. I had a large collection....' She paused and seemed to order her thoughts before appearing to recover. 'But these aren't bad. I particularly like this one.' Holding up her own, she showed him the image of the Pharaoh wearing elongated head wear.

Noah couldn't help it; he laughed. He guessed there were stranger things to collect.

'Hey!' Ava tried to slap his arm but he shot out of reach.

Otis bounded up onto the deck after his roo pursuits and pulled up short at the sight of the puppies. He sniffed the basket and plonked himself down at Noah's feet, keeping guard on the newborns.

Drinking the last remnants of coffee, Noah put down his mug. 'I'd best get on with things, even though you could easily spend hours watching those gorgeous little creatures.'

Ava agreed. 'What are you tackling today?'

'I'm checking the foundations. Need to inspect the stumps; I think from a cursory glance one or two might be rotted and need replacing but maybe all of them. I'll keep you informed. Also the front and back stairs, but if I need to take them out of action, I'll give you plenty of notice. You need a solid foundation first before working on anything else.'

The easy smile she offered him kept him pinned to the seat until she glanced away and he uncurled himself reluctantly from the chair and rose.

'Oh, I almost forgot. I need to unlock the gate.'

'Sorry, Noah.' She grabbed the keys from the kitchen bench and handed them over. 'And you mister, need to feed the horses.' She addressed Duke.

He hadn't taken his hands off the dogs, either reassuring Daisy with gentle strokes or cradling the puppies, still with their eyes screwed shut. 'So many animals, Mumma, it's like we live on a farm.'

Ava laughed. 'Yes, a hobby farm, at least. We should think about getting some chickens, at least they lay eggs.'

The boy jumped up. 'Yes, can we please? That would be awesome!'

Emily would love the puppies. She loved Otis. Was she missing her old pet or did she prefer her new cat? Should he offer to take one of the puppies for her, make it her very own dog? But he just as quickly squashed that idea. What good was a pet to a child that rarely lived with him? And the last thing he needed was another responsibility, particularly one that wasn't a working dog. Otis was easy, Otis followed him onto every work site and therefore was never left alone.

A lab would be a different story. Reconciling the situation, he agreed that he'd bring her over to see the puppies in the next few days when she was due to visit.

Tuning back in, Ava was talking to Duke. 'Yes, we'll get some chickens but only if you do your chores.'

He groaned in typical little boy fashion with a grin on his face. 'I'm going!'

Ava rose and stretched, her tee rising up to reveal her stomach. Time concertinaed and all Noah saw was the pale, creamy skin. It was over in a flash and her arms were at her side, clothing back in place. He'd stood moments ago but found himself rooted to the spot, transfixed by her and the family scene in front of him. Noah shook his head clearing away the cobwebs quickly gathering. He stepped back and crashed into the chair. 'Um, I'll get to it.'

She regarded him quizzically. Yeah, he would too, because he was acting weird and he felt strangely discombobulated. 'Otis, come,' he said more tersely than intended.

Okay, time for her to get started too. Today she was commencing work on Ish's room. Bunking in with her had suited perfectly when they'd landed in a strange place with only each other for company, and a rundown old house. But sleeping together could not continue. And the way to get Ish into his own room was to make it special.

So, his room was first, despite the kitchen and the bathrooms that made her grimace at the state of their disrepair. At least they were functioning and had hot running water. The reality was there was so much work to be done, starting with anything was enough.

Standing in his bare room with the veejay walls, faded cream paint and the panel above the large and solid timber door, memories rushed in. She stared at the fretwork. These weren't new to her. Their childhood home had had patterned panels, too, but these were distinct Australiana with an emu and kangaroo holding a coat of arms on a desert floor with sprigs of brush. It could either be tacky or unique but she liked it, so went for unique.

Their house had been near the school where her father had taught. The school that Ish would soon attend. Driving home the other day, she'd wandered through their old area and was gutted to discover the house had been demolished to make way for a new estate. The blocks of land were spacious but the homes were low-set, brick and modern. Even Bellethorpe couldn't avoid development it seemed. It made her think of her parents. Tugging out her mobile phone she rang, listened to the dial tone until her mother picked up.

'Hey, Mum, it's me.'

Her parents had been delighted at her return to Australia and then disappointed she hadn't settled in Tasmania. It had been a difficult conversation as she'd revealed little and they'd struggled to understand the reason for her return, alone. They knew she was safe in Queensland; knew she had something to hide. Eventually they stopped asking. Above all else her parents couldn't know where she lived. Anyone trying to find her would go to them first.

Placed on speaker phone, Ava chatted with both her parents. They caught her up on local news, and about Charlie and his wife Lizzie and children who lived nearby. She clutched her belly, giving herself a hug. Ish had cousins he'd never met. She made a promise: he'd meet them one day soon. When things were different, when life was settled.

Looking around the room, she noted the work required and rang off providing assurances to be back in touch soon.

The bare room was a blank canvas. It had the original wardrobe built into the wall, so that was one less thing to worry about. Unless ... she opened the doors and it seemed in order. The room only needed a lick of paint and furniture.

The grate of the sandpaper along the timber boards was strangely gratifying. It was like her work: methodical and satisfying as you worked toward a goal. Ava was on her third wall and many pieces of sandpaper later when she tried to prise the window open. It was stuck fast. On top of the timber, double hung window was a narrow ledge. The sleeve of her long work shirt jagged on something, and objects cascaded to the ground landing with multiple clacks against the Tasmanian oak flooring.

Jumping down from the stepladder, Ava wiped her dusty hands

down the back of her jeans. Kneeling low, she scooped the items in close to her. There were ten or so, all tiny in size and width and appeared to be small rocks.

She rubbed her fingers over the various pieces, removing layers of dust. Some sides were smooth and others, rough and open and ragged. Sitting with an inelegant plop onto her bottom, she gathered some spit between her thumb and pointer finger and wiped one edge to reveal a kaleidoscope of dazzling colour. Quickly she wiped the others to reveal similar hidden patterns.

A tingle of excitement grew in the pit of her tummy.

She was not an expert on rocks, even though they touched on geology in her studies, but she was pretty sure these were opals. That alone was special. Holding one close, she went cross-eyed. She was pretty sure there was more to this than a pretty gem.

Was it possible…?

Noah knocked and entered. 'You okay?'

'Um, yeah, sure.' She took another look at the pile of rocks and gathered them together in the palm of one hand. Pulling a tissue out of her jean pocket, she wrapped them carefully and placed them into her back pocket for safe keeping.

'I've nearly finished giving the walls a light sand and then I'll wash them down. I got distracted by a few trinkets I found.'

Hopping up, she wiped her hands again.

'I'm impressed. Doing your painting prep properly. You'll use sugar soap, to wash it down? I have plenty in the truck.'

'Yep, definitely, but I have some, thank you.'

His gaze searched the room. 'What about primer?'

'No, I don't have undercoat or paint yet. What would you recommend?'

Ava took notes on her phone. She was still typing away when she noticed he'd finished speaking. Looking up, his light eyes had turned dark and broody.

Her body flooded with warmth. 'Um, how are the stumps?'

Noah seemed to return to the present. 'Yeah, good, two down. I had a look at the front stairs and they'll need replacing. I'll rip them out today, just letting you know.'

'Okay, thanks.'

He started to move away. 'Oh, Noah.' He paused, turned back. 'Could you help me get this window open?' She gestured towards it.

'Sure.' He pushed and pulled to no avail, then took out a tool to jemmy it. Eventually it loosened and opened.

'Sorry, a bit of damage there.' He picked up the card of sandpaper and smoothed over the diverts he'd made. 'Good as new. You might want putty in there to make it even.'

They discussed gap filling in between the veejay boards. Ava wrote this down too.

'I can help if you'd like. It's a lot of work,' he said.

'That's really kind but you have your hands full outside. I'll take care of painting. I don't mind hard work.'

Noah gave a curt nod and left.

An hour later, Ava left the washed walls to dry, gobbled down a ham, cheese and mayo sandwich and quickly made another that she took to Noah.

'I'm heading into town to buy the paint. Do you need anything?'

'No, not after this sandwich, thank you.'

Before heading anywhere, she made sure Ish had eaten his sandwich and checked on the puppies. The vet had given the babies a clean bill of health, including Daisy. At the moment, Ish jumped on the tramp, his uneaten crusts on the plate and the dogs were asleep, the puppies curled into Daisy's side.

'Mate, did you apply sunscreen?'

He shook his head. 'Come off then, I've got to head into town anyway.'

'I don't want to go. I want to stay here.'

She sighed. Noah approached from behind. 'It's fine, leave him. You'll get your stuff done much quicker.'

'You don't mind?'

'Not at all.'

An internal tussle was in full force before she waivered. She guessed she'd have to leave him eventually. Her face must have revealed her uncertainty. 'Ava, it'll be fine. I'll keep working and no doubt he'll keep playing.'

She nodded in agreement. Noah was a parent; he would know how to take care of her son. 'Duke, put your sunscreen on!' she screeched before heading for the car.

Outside it was another glorious summer's day, the sun bright and hot. She'd worked up a sweat and the moisture on her skin felt good. A gentle breeze was up and Ava chose to wind the window down and relish the coolness against her arms.

How best to decorate Ish's room? He'd never had a bedroom furnished specially for him before. A bolt of panic passed through her. What would he want in his room? What did he enjoy? It frightened her that the answers didn't come readily. Since their arrival in Bellethorpe, he'd fallen in love with animals. He liked the trampoline and Lego. She thought he liked planes. Cars, yes, he was fascinated with Matchbox cars.

Pondering this dilemma, she passed the cutest shop with a bright red bicycle outside and flowerpots in a variety of colours. Ava hit the brakes and found the nearest park; she was excited to check this place out.

Entering *Café Antiquities* was like walking into Aladdin's cave. It was a veritable treasure trove of new and old goods. The aroma of coffee hung in the air, adding to the appeal of the whole scene. She'd grab a coffee and browse.

At the counter, the man taking orders beamed at her. 'Ava Montgomery. It's been a long time.'

'Mr Shoebridge! You were my school bus driver.'

'Indeed, a very long time ago and before your family moved.'

The woman standing at the coffee machine, watched on with fondness and an emotion Ava couldn't pick. Mr Shoebridge kept talking. 'Are you back visiting?'

'No, I have returned to live here with my son.'

'Oh, how wonderful! Whereabouts are you living?'

'That place out on Kinross Road. Do you know it?'

'Do we know it? Of course, we do.' He turned to the woman

behind him and they grasped hands. The intimacy caused a lump to form in Ava's throat. 'Did you ever meet my wife? This is Sheila. Sheila, this is Ava who was one of my students on the bus route all those years ago. She's just moved back to town.'

'Welcome back, Ava. Can we get you a coffee?'

'Oh, yes please. A cappuccino would be lovely. You have the most gorgeous store!'

'Thank you. Have a quick browse and we'll holler when your coffee is ready.'

Ava walked around the mountains of goods piled high, lining the walls, sitting on desks; it was a plethora of novelties all in one place. An antique lover's dream or perhaps an archaeologist's? Only made better if she'd been the discoverer.

Along the back wall she found a collection of Matchbox cars, ones she was sure were no longer manufactured. Next to them was a model aeroplane kit. Turning the other way, she bumped her head on a constructed fighter plane hanging from the ceiling. It was painted in traditional khaki greens and reds. She collected the cars and model plane kit and would ask Peter if she could purchase the finalised version hanging from the ceiling. It would look fabulous in Ish's room.

She wandered back to where there were a few random and mismatched tables and chairs with some comfy sofas scattered around to find Peter holding a mug and searching the store. 'Oh, that must be me, thank you.'

He held onto the cup tightly and regarded her with a tense expression. 'Um, this is a cappuccino.' He turned back to Sheila who was busy at the coffee machine grinding beans and frothing milk for the next drink.

'What sort of coffee did you order, dear?' Peter spoke to her as if they hadn't met. 'Um, a cappuccino.'

Peter checked the coffee he was holding. 'Oh, yes, this is a cappuccino. But, I'm ...' He hurried back to Sheila's side.

They returned together, Sheila holding the mug. 'Sit here, Ava.' She was seated at the closest laminate table with an old vinyl seat, then Sheila addressed Peter. 'Peter, this is Ava, she is living at the house on Kinross Road, remember, you drove her to school on the bus?'

Ava watched as his vision cleared, his eyes going from foggy and inert, to alive and present.

Sheila leaned in. 'Dementia,' she said quietly.

Oh. But the old Peter was back, chatty and lively. 'I remember the old guy that used to own that place. Do you remember him?'

'Um, no, but I'd love to learn more.' she said instead.

Her eager response pleased Peter. Over her shoulder Sheila called out. 'His long-term memory is perfect!' The words were light-hearted and spoken in jest, but Sheila's smile was tight and the expression on her face spelled heartache, all the while pulling another coffee, accepting another order and supervising customers in the shop. Ava didn't know whether it was a help or a hindrance that Peter sat with her, talking.

'Well, you know about the history of the area and its returned servicemen?'

'No, I don't but I should.'

'So much history!' Peter became excited and his voice animated. Peter reminded Ava of her father, of the man who had shared his own love of history and of what had become their shared passion.

'The region offered to home returned servicemen from World War I. It was a scheme developed by the government of the day. Upon their return from the war, these men could choose to live here and they were provided with land and housing. It was a win-win, of course. Our regional area benefited with a greater population and increased productivity because they were encouraged to farm, plant orchards and the like. The heritage centre has lots of information about that, you should pay it a visit. It's very interesting,' he added. 'Plus, each year we celebrate an annual Bastille Day festival in their memory.'

Ava quickly made the connections. The names of the nearby towns where the soldiers were resettled had the names of the French battle-fields, she'd noticed that, and now the famous French festival was connected as well. She got it.

'I do know that your house was part of the scheme. The solider, I think his name was Edwards, he died in the early seventies, I think, but the house went to his son. Sad story, the son was married and had children but they died in an accident. He lived there alone for many years after, became a bit of a recluse. But one thing I remember is that his father was a blacksmith and the son became a blacksmith too. And in his later years, he made the most beautiful silver and opal jewellery.'

Opal?

'Was he the last owner?'

'Yes, when he died, oh, quite a few years ago now, the house was left to a distant relative but they never lived there or took any interest in the property. It sat empty for years until it was put on the market. And now it's yours, of course.'

'Hello, Peter, how are you?' A loud voice boomed, and a firm hand landed on his shoulder. He flinched. The lady didn't remove her hand and waited what seemed like an eternity to Ava. 'It's Jacqueline, Peter,' and she beamed a smile at him until recognition dawned in his eyes and he jumped up and offered a kiss to her cheek and they embraced each other.

Releasing Jaqueline, he went to introduce Ava. 'And this lovely young lady is...she is staying at...' His face clouded in and his eyes went downcast.

Ava jumped up. 'I'm Ava Montgomery, recently moved into the old place on Kinross Road.'

Jacqueline beamed the most dazzling smile in her direction then, and Ava felt enveloped in its warmth. 'How wonderful. I've heard of your arrival and have been meaning to meet you. I am Jacqueline Kennedy, the mayor of Bellethorpe.' The mayor spoke as if she held a loudspeaker and her voice boomed through, loud and confident. She was dressed in casual corporate wear with slim-legged white pants and court high heels that extenuated her height. Layering her pale blue cotton top, was a flamboyantly multi-coloured scarf.

'Ava?' The woman with Jacqueline spoke up.

'Bec?'

'I thought it was you.' She leaned in, Ava presumed for the double-cheek kiss, but she instinctively stepped back. It was a mistake. Bec stalled, uncertain.

Ava went to twirl the ring on her finger. Damn it! She'd never get used to a bare ring finger.

'Bec! It's so lovely to see you.' Ava touched her on the arm.

'You know each other?' Jacqueline enquired.

'We went to school together … were best friends,' Bec informed her.

'Ah, yes. I heard the rumour that you used to live here, Ava. You're returning home, permanently, we hope.'

Ava didn't fill the silence that swelled around them.

'What are you interested in, Ava? We have many committees in town and we always need help. Now, what's the date, Peter? It's mid-January, isn't it? School is resuming soon, we have a wonderful local school, Bellethorpe Primary, do you have children?'

'Um, yes, a son, he'll be starting the year there in prep.'

'Wonderful. They always need help in the tuckshop and changing school readers in the library and with their fundraising. Oh, and then of course, how could I forget, the Summer Festival is coming up soon. It's to mark the end of summer and is a lovely community event. That's what Bec and I are discussing today but, would you agree, Bec, most of the work is done?' Jacqueline flapped one hand. 'Doesn't matter. I'm sure we can find something for you to do.'

Ava's head was spinning. Jacqueline was too much. Thankfully, the mayor's mobile phone rang and she was called away. Ava stared at her former best friend. It had been gut-wrenching to leave all those years ago, and even though they'd kept in touch with letters for a while, their contact had dwindled away. Now, a life later, how could she possibly ever tell her friend where she'd been, what had happened to her?

'Honestly, it's great to see you. Such a surprise! We'll have to catch up for a cuppa.' The words sounded false even to Ava.

Bec nodded. 'I'd like that.'

Jacqueline called for her and she waved away.

Peter had stood there silent during the exchange. She hadn't finished her chat but the moment was gone. It was obvious Peter was lost again. 'Thank you for the coffee. I'm going to buy these items for my son. Could you help me with the plane hanging from the ceiling?'

Whilst she'd enjoyed meeting Sheila and Peter and had loved hearing the history of her house and the town, Ava's heart felt heavy leaving the store. Nothing was ever simple, was it? She only wanted decor for Ish's room, not to make friends or connections. And in-store, her past and present had collided and she was torn between her deepest desire to form roots here in this town and make this place their home, and of the need to escape her past. This knife edge she balanced upon was slippery. As uncomfortable as it was, distance was key.

Spotting old vintage teacups on her way out, she thought of her Egyptian mugs which obviously appeared silly to other people. But there was a time when she thought she'd be just like those powerful leaders. Strong. Do important things. As a teenager and when she was friends with Bec, everything had seemed possible and she'd had no doubt she'd grow to be a tough woman like them. She was a strong woman, until she wasn't. Her greatest regret was becoming someone she wasn't. Of allowing her dreams to be trodden on, for her life to become unimportant and stand in the shadows of a man. Even worse, to be controlled. How could she have let that happen? Out of every-thing that had occurred, in that she was the most disappointed. She'd let herself down and now she had to remember exactly who she was and what she stood for. One thing was certain, she wouldn't ever let anyone else dictate the terms of her life again.

Putting on a brave face with a wide smile, she waved at Jacqueline and Bec who sat in a comfy sofa in the quiet front corner of the store. She had a sense well-meaning Jacqueline Kennedy might best be a force avoided, unless of course one required her help. That woman was canny and Ava wanted to keep her secrets, and she feared under the mayor's scrutiny, Ava might just crack.

And Bec, well, her heart fissured a bit more. She missed having a female friend, missed Jamila; a confidant to spend time with, to laugh and share small anecdotes. Seeing Bec reminded her of all that was lost. But she couldn't make friends. Couldn't get close to anyone. She'd been a fool to think she could slip into Bellethorpe and blend in and people would leave her alone. She had to make it work though, their lives depended on it.

CHAPTER
Ten

NOAH PULLED up at Ava's gate. It wasn't locked this time, but he dialled her number anyway. Rather than letting the Bluetooth play through the car speakers, he retrieved the phone and held it to his ear as it rang.

'Ava, hi, how are you? Sorry, I'm a bit late today. I have Emily for a few days. Is it okay if she tags along with me? She won't be a bother, I promise.' He held his breath.

'Okay, great, thank you. We're at the gate, see you in thirty seconds.' He rang off, his relief enormous.

Noah had come straight from collecting Emily that morning and couldn't bear to be parted from her. It was his first visit in a few weeks, and the feelings at seeing her again were raw. The warm and fuzzy emotion after she ran into his arms and they'd enjoyed a squishy cuddle lingered. His heart had melted with her cheeky grin. In that moment, Noah understood that any pain he suffered in negotiations with Lisa were worth it. Nothing could beat the feeling of being with his daughter.

Up at the house, Ava met them on the back deck. He carried Emily's backpack, a bag of food, toys and two coffees.

'Here, let me help. Honestly, you don't need to bring me coffee every day, but,' she held up her hand, 'I do love it.'

Her radiant smile sent his pulses racing and his body temperature rose. With a free hand, he puffed out his shirt to create some air.

Had they become friends without him noticing? Noah swallowed. Or more? Their chats bordered on flirting and he had to confess, he quite liked it. But today, perhaps with Emily here, the intimacy of it caught him off guard. His eyes lowered and caught a glimpse of Ava's lean legs in tight leggings that left nothing to the imagination and her tumbling, sleek dark hair that always looked like she'd just left a hair salon. Even in her house gear, she appeared glamorous. She was a natural beauty. He didn't think he'd seen her wearing make-up yet, but her skin always glowed. While she seemed to have lost her city-clean appearance, she was always immaculately presented. Poised was a good word to describe Ava Montgomery.

And damn attractive, but he tried not to focus on that.

She sipped her coffee and he swallowed again as he watched her rose bud lips open... *Oh, boy.*

Ava clutched the cup in her long and lean fingers and he imagined them trailing down the bare skin of his back. Her head tilted in question. Oh, yes, waited for his reply. 'It's no trouble,' his voice came out croaky and he cleared his throat, 'Plus, today I wanted to get some treats for the kids.'

Emily, dressed in very practical tee and shorts, tugged on his arm. 'And this is Emily.' It was ridiculous, but his chest puffed out a little. Finally, he could introduce his little girl to Ava.

'Hello, Emily. I'm Ava.' At that exact moment, Duke screeched past the glass door, sliding in his socks. Ava called out and introduced him.

'That's a funny name!' Emily laughed.

The boy turned his face up to his mother, gauging her reaction.

'I think it is a very cool name and you, young lady, should not always say what you think.'

She immediately bowed her head. 'Sorry, Duke. I do like it, it's just unusual, that's all.'

'Want to see my new room?' he asked her, now not worried what she thought of his name.

Ava nodded in that direction. 'I finished it. Want to take a look?'

Noah agreed.

'You don't mess around, do you?' he joked as he entered and inspected the paintwork and ran his hands down the wall. 'This is fantastic. You've done a very professional job.'

This time her smile was shy, the corner of her lips barely curling, and she didn't reply. But he wasn't joking, it was a top job, he was impressed.

'My room is pink because it's my favourite colour,' Emily announced. The coffee burned his throat a little. Emily's room at his house wasn't pink.

'I could paint this any colour I wanted, Mumma said, but she really didn't want me to choose blue. So, I chose silver, see, just like the colour of the moon.'

Emily gushed over it and the model aeroplane they'd affixed to the ceiling.

'Duke, you could have had blue, but not because you think you had to choose it because you're a boy. That's all I meant.' Ava explained.

Ava must have caught his frown. 'I don't want him growing up living a stereo-type. You know, he must like blue, never wear pink, be good with his hands, be the man of the house, be the one in charge…'

Noah's frown deepened. He was smart enough to understand this wasn't about the colour blue, but what was it about?

But Ava kept going. 'You would never tell Emily, would you, Noah, that her only job in life was to grow up and get married and have babies, would you?'

'Eww,' both kids exclaimed.

'Um, no, not at all.'

'Well, it's the same issue. It's about teaching them that men and women are equal and we can grow and aspire to be whatever we want without gender labels.'

O-k-a-y. 'You're the perfect role model for that Ava, with your job as an archaeologist.'

Her look was sharp. 'What, because it's a man's job?'

'Um, well, I thought, well … it's an unusual job. That's all. Not that it's a man's job….' Geez, he was really ballsing this up.

'What's an archaeologist?' piped up Emily.

'She digs up old stuff,' Duke informed her dryly.

'Cool!'

Ava laughed and the tension was broken.

Inspection over, the kids rushed from the room talking of puppies.

Noah held up the coffee. 'Peace offering?'

'No sorry, it's all good. I get carried away sometimes. Want to see the puppies?'

The puppies were super-cute but he was already running late after his mammoth trip to Brisbane and back that morning.

'Did you collect Emily from her mother's this morning?' Could she read his mind?

'Yes, an early start.'

'Gosh, I bet. You can take the day off if you'd like, spend the day together? You don't need to be here all of the time.'

The kindness in her voice almost let him spill his guts but he stymied the words with another sip of coffee.

He would love nothing more than a fun and relaxed day with Emily. Quality one-on-one time. What a dream. How to say that he needed to be here, though, keep this job progressing, on track, get paid. All so he could fight for more days with Emily. It was ironic, wasn't it? His girl was here and he couldn't spend time with her. But most parents worked; he wasn't special. And he wouldn't work tomorrow—he usually would work Saturday—and he'd spend the weekend with her.

'No, not at all,' he brushed her off. 'As long as you don't mind her hanging around?'

'No, not at all,' she threw back at him. 'In fact, you're probably doing me a favour. Looks like these two are going to be great mates.'

They both observed the children to be tickling the puppies on their tummies and gushing over them.

'You get started. I'll yell out if we need you.'

'Thank you,' his voice was deep with emotion and he avoided Ava's eye. As he walked away, the kids were yelling out name suggestions for the puppies.

Throughout the day he saw them feed the horses, have endless turns on the gigantic trampoline in the yard and at one point, they delivered biscuits. 'Did you make these yourself?' he asked them only to receive a nod.

'These are the only two left!' And they giggled, running off again to their next adventure. Seeing Emily having such fun assuaged his guilt a little.

Ava watched the two children playing and couldn't help imagine what it would be like to have a daughter. Of course, if these two were siblings, they'd probably be bickering as brothers and sisters were prone to do.

She might be feeling melancholy that she didn't have a daughter, but she was also grateful. The culture her son had been born into was bad enough for a boy, but for a girl ... Ava's body shuddered at the memory of Henry's teenage niece who had lived in the palace with them, wearing clothes she had borrowed from an American friend. It was an innocuous ensemble of a denim miniskirt with its hem above her knees and mid-drift top. She'd been so innocent and proud until she'd been punished and told it was immodest and ordered to remove it immediately only for it to be burned in a hostile ceremony led by Henry's brother, Ahmed, in front of the entire extended family.

The first time Ava had been directed to wear appropriate clothing she'd been incensed.

But not for the first time she reminded herself she was safe in Bellethorpe. Her son would not be raised to believe men were the superior gender, the worthy sex. She would never again be directed on what to wear.

Yes, she'd brushed away her thoughts on this topic in front of Noah, but she felt very strongly about the role of men and women in society. Freedom of any sort was not something she would ever take for granted again. Civil liberties for everyone needed to be maintained. And as far as she was concerned, that started with not re-enforcing gender or any other sorts of stereotypes. Ish had helped bake the biscuits. He would learn to cook and perform other tasks often considered "girls work".

This made her think of Jamila. How was she? Was she coping? Safe? Not a day passed that Ava didn't think of her.

Having been born into a similar cultural hierarchy, albeit a less strict and more forgiving one, Jamila was aware of what she married into. Ava, however, fiercely in love with her husband, wasn't blindsided, exactly, it was more like an insidious mould that grew slowly and spread until it could no longer be controlled. But Jamila's situation was serious and she worried for her friend. To numb these feelings, Ava reached for the dirty clothes basket. She'd put a load on while the kids were occupied with building Lego.

Something knocked the stainless steel of the tub as she threw in her jeans. Oh, the rocks! Tugging the pants back she out extracted them. They glittered and her stomach fizzed like shaken lemonade. Grabbing the nearest towel, she wrapped them up and rushed outdoors to place them on the table.

Along the way she retrieved the brand-new toolkit she'd ordered online, one of her first purchases after settling in. Opening the beautiful leather tie-up satchel, a wave of melancholy hit her. This kit was beautiful but not her original. Her first dig kit had been a present from her parents upon graduation. It remained in pristine condition due to its lack of use after she'd moved overseas. Didn't mean it didn't hold a special place in her heart, though and she wished she could use it now. She brushed her hands over the smooth leather, it didn't matter; this kit was probably better. Ava wondered what would happen to her tools and the other belongings they'd left behind?

In the kitchen she grabbed a bowl and the household vinegar. Despite it being the afternoon, she turned on the outdoor florescent lights.

There were ten objects in total. First, she placed one into a shallow bowl of vinegar. It was a household trick, but it should work. No more than two minutes and the acetic acid should dissolve the carbonates which are a component of sedimentary rock. Her legs jiggled as she waited, and she examined the other items. Perhaps they weren't all rock. A couple had odd-looking bits to them. She resisted considering them more closely, one at a time.

Another bowl of warm water to the ready, and her trusty soft-bristled toothbrush, she let the droplets roll off the object to dry a little. Colour was immediately obvious. Bold with an underlaying dark base. Ava turned on her headlamp and began brushing into the cracks that were distinct on one side of the stone. This one had a strange shape, like a crescent moon or a croissant. Quickly a centimetre squared section of bright lime green revealed itself. The base was clearer, somewhat translucent and the green area was surrounded by less vibrant mottled colours.

She sat back in the chair and held it up. It was a pinecone. Ava had discovered an opalised fossil of a pinecone, she was pretty sure.

Not able to help herself now, she picked up each one in turn. One might be a shell if the distinct curved sides were any indication. One had a sharp, spiked edge and it had a metal-like quality. She tugged it gently and it held fast. Could it be a tag? A hard-edged rim? Or, her mind turned back to her conversation with Peter Shoebridge. Could it be the remnants of a piece of silver jewellery?

A black crow cawed as it took flight and the noise startled her. The bird launched itself off the paddocks of dry grass and became a black dot in the blue afternoon sky. The glare had lessened and the intense heat of the day was waning. The crow flew towards the bushes at the rear of the property. Were these finds related to the piles near the rock pool? Or was her mind stretching too far?

Steps thudded up the stairs and Ava covered the items.

Most of her equipment was back in her satchel by the time Noah arrived at the table. Ava greeted him and shone the headlamp right into his eyes. 'Oh! Sorry.' She removed it and patted down her hair.

'That looks interesting.'

'Hmm. Taking some time to examine a few rocks that I found.'

'Wow, rocks, okay.'

'Yeah, all right, that sounds boring, I agree, but these are fossilised rocks which means there might be old things inside them. To explain it simply.' She shrugged.

'Hence the additional light?'

'Yep.' Awkward silence. 'Actually, you've lived in Bellethorpe your entire life, haven't you?'

'Yep.' Was she mistaken that his back straightened?

'Do you need to head off?'

He paused, searched the yard for the kids who were still tearing around with too much energy. Now they were engaged in a game of tag with Daisy who was feeling better after the birth of the puppies.

'Want a drink? Glass of wine? I assume you've finished for the day?' It was a normal offer but the moment Ava asked him, she rebuked herself. Noah was too quickly penetrating her defences and getting under her skin. She needed to keep her wits about her. Better the devil you know she figured.

Too late, he said yes.

While Noah washed his hands, Ava poured their glasses and prepared a cheese platter. Placing it on the table, a wave of nostalgia washed over her. Not for times gone past, but for the normalcy of the act. She hadn't done this for ages.

'Cheers,' she offered. 'For your hard work so far.' Despite everything else, she remained focused on getting the house finished.

Noah gave her an update on the day's progress. Things were moving slowly.

'Did you want to buy this place for any special reason or only because you liked it?'

'I wanted it to be my family home. I loved the location, the size, the land. It's perfect for raising a tribe of children and animals, horses, etcetera.' As if realising what he'd said, he blushed.

'Okay, so you aren't related to the previous owners or anything?'

'No. I didn't know the owner. Wasn't it some distant relative that didn't live here? They'd not even visited as far as I'm aware.'

'Yep, apparently. You know Peter from *Café Antiquities*?'

Noah nodded and slathered a cracker with goat's cheese.

'I was there yesterday and he told me about the history of the town and the house. This house was part of the returned soldier's program.'

Noah filled her in on what he knew about the scheme and it was pretty much what she'd already learned. Ava informed him of what Peter had divulged. 'I didn't know about the son. He lived here, of course, when I was growing up. But no one ever saw him or talked about him either, from memory.'

'So sad…'

The kids raced up the stairs. 'We're hungry!'

Noah cuddled Emily to his side, an embrace like he'd really missed her.

'Lucky, I have snacks then.' Ava offered them chips.

'Mum, can Emily stay for dinner?'

'Yes, please, Dad, please!' the girl begged.

Ava and Noah looked at each other. 'That's fine.' She said but her stomach twisted. 'I was making mac and cheese. I get pretty lazy cooking for two, but if you're staying, we might barbeque some steaks and have salad.'

Either a storm was brewing or the air around them became electric. Noah gazed at her with such tenderness, her insides went from twisting to flipping about. Her body betrayed her with its excitement, damnit. But it also made her apprehensive … she was supposed to be keeping her distance, right?

'Thank you. I hope we aren't intruding.'

'Not at all.' Emily and Ish were jumping up and down. 'Daddy, come and play with us. Can you be it?'

'That's a great idea. Why don't you play with them while I make a start and I'll yell when I need some help?'

'Wait,' Ish reached for Emily's arm before she could run away. 'Dads don't play games, they're too busy for that. They have to run businesses and palaces and do important things, not like mummies. They have lots of time to play.' He tilted his head to the side in confusion, his eyes narrowed.

'What?' Emily said. 'Of course daddies play! They are the best at playing. Mine plays all the time!' she smiled broadly showing off a missing front tooth.

'Duke,' Ava reached for him but he shrugged her off.

'Hey buddy,' Noah said, 'I've got plenty of time to play with you both before dinner, there is nothing I'd rather do.'

Ish nodded but Ava's heart tore in two. She stood quickly so that she could release herself from the weight of Noah's questioning stare.

What was he doing? He counted to ten as the kids ran to hide. Noah Hawthorn only had one plan and that was work hard, make money and fight for his daughter. Oh, and keep his hometown free of unnecessary development. But Emily came first.

Staying late after work and eating with his client was not part of the plan. But … Emily. She'd had a ball playing with Duke. Animated, alive, normal, like her parents weren't separated and living in different cities and fighting over where she lived. So maybe staying for dinner was for her.

As dusk drew in, Ava called them to join her, and poured him another glass of wine and he found himself relaxing. He cooked the steak on the barbeque and they ate together, laughing, joking and having fun.

'Thanks so much, Ava, for today, and to you too, Duke for keeping Emily company. What do you say, Emily?'

'Thank you, I had a great time.'

'Honestly, I'm really grateful. You got me out of a spot.'

'What else are you going to do with your dad this weekend, Emily?'

'Oooh, we're going to see the alpacas! It's going to be such fun. Last time I was there, they had babies and those babies will be bigger now.'

'Alpacas? Wow. Are they nearby?'

'Yeah, it's a bit odd, isn't it? There's an alpaca farm just outside of town. It's attached to a winery and the kids just love it.'

'Duke, wanna come?'

Ava and Noah both simultaneously replied with excuses. 'I think your daddy wants to spend some time alone with you, he's missed you.'

'Ava and Duke have better things to do.'

'No, not fair. Duke really wants to see them. Don't you, Duke? What are you doing tomorrow?'

'Nothing, so we can come.'

Ava looked at Noah and he shrugged. 'It's a great way to get to know the locals and see the sights.'

Ava didn't reply. Was she being polite? Did she want to go? He couldn't tell. But it would have been rude not to include them now, and besides, Noah couldn't think of one single excuse as to why he didn't want to spend more time with Ava tomorrow.

CHAPTER

Eleven

NERVES AND FEAR danced for space in Ava's tummy. Maybe a little bit of excitement thrown in, too.

Problem was she'd be lying if she said she wasn't thrilled at the prospect of seeing Noah today, but trying to understand what that meant exactly had her fraught with anxiety.

Mixing with the locals and seeing the sights and further integrating herself into this little community, added the fear factor and was exactly what she shouldn't be doing. The pact she'd made with herself to keep a low profile was swiftly going awry. Now she and Noah and Emily and Ish were friends, and today they'd meet more locals. So much for running under the radar.

Trouble was she wanted to be part of this community.

And she also wanted to be invisible.

Noah pulled in his ute beside her and her nerves racked up a notch.

Not for the kids, though. Both barrelled out of their respective cars and shrieked in excitement at seeing each other.

'Hi.'

'Hi.'

Unlike their parents.

Noah was freshly showered, his hair still damp causing the long waves to curl on top. Out of his work gear, he wore deep blue jeans with a red collared shirt and leather boots. Honestly, he could have walked out of the pages of a magazine fashion shoot. And as he stood near, she caught his scent, all woody and earthy and the underlying tone of tangy citrus. Pure heat swept through her and the ground shifted beneath her feet.

He leaned in and kissed her on the cheek. His smooth, warm lips connected with the very corner of her mouth which opened slightly at his touch. He remained close for two long excruciating heart beats.

They stood awkwardly but the kids rushed towards the fence to watch the alpaca. Ava turned her head in their direction but when she spun back, Noah still gazed at her. His look swept her up in a warm blanket: sensuous, inviting and safe. She filled with want.

He broke contact first. 'It's a proper alpaca experience. You can walk them on a lead around a paddock, enjoy a picnic while they graze nearby, paint them, loads of things. I thought we'd have a picnic today. Does that sound okay?'

'Sounds incredible.'

Rounding up the kids, they approached the couple near the entrance.

'Noah, nice to see you.' The men shook hands. 'And you too, princess.' Emily giggled. A lady with pink strands of hair framing her face introduced herself to Ava. 'I'm Adele. Welcome to our alpaca farm. Is this your first visit?'

'Yes. How can you tell?'

'Because you're standing back just like the first time I ever saw an alpaca.' Adele rubbed the neck on the brown and white one standing close to her. It made a weird noise and Ava stepped further back.

'I've got it restrained. It won't move.' Adele held up a rope as proof. 'They make those noises all the time. Try to scare people, I think, but the sound doesn't mean anything.'

The man, Blake, had the kids organised and ready to walk two smaller and what she hoped, were friendly alpaca. He addressed Ish. 'This one is Cupcake and he's very pleased to meet you.' Ish took the rope held out to him and turned to Emily, his eyes sparkling with excitement. 'Let me guess,' she squealed. 'This is Pikelet!' Blake shook his head.

'Chips?'

'Ice cream?'

'Lollipop?'

'Lamington?'

She gave up.

'This is Hotdog!' The group of them cracked up laughing. 'Any trouble, give me a yell.'

'They seem nice,' Ava said as they wandered behind the children through the plush grounds. Emily seemed to know where she was going.

'Yeah, Blake's a great guy. Owned this place for a while now. The vineyard is successful and Adele organises weddings on the premises. Adele has only lived out here for a couple of years, I think.'

'A newbie like me, then.'

'You're not new though, are you?'

Ava lowered her head and kept pace with Noah.

'Nothing is a secret in a small town.'

'Is it meant to be a secret?'

'No, not at all ... but it's not exactly something you advertise upon arrival.'

'But you must know people from back then?'

'I haven't kept in touch with anyone ... but I did run into a school-friend the other day. It was great to see her.'

'Yeah, people don't really move on that often in Bellethorpe. We must have been together at school?'

'Do you remember me?'

'No,' he laughed. 'I was a silly boy back then. I wouldn't forget you now.'

Her heart did a funny little giddy-up.

The kids had taken them down to the banks of a gorgeous creek where the water flowed gently over rocks and boulders. A few other guests were relaxing and enjoying picnics in the shade.

'Did your parents not like living in Bellethorpe?'

'No, not at all. My father was offered a head teacher role interstate. It was a wonderful opportunity for him.'

'I can't imagine ever leaving Bellethorpe.'

They perched themselves on adjacent rocks. 'Really?' The tone of incredulity gave her away.

'Yeah, boring, I guess. But it's where I want to live. So why leave?'

'It's beautiful here, sure. But there's a big wide world out there. I mean, I was thirteen when we moved. I didn't want to go, but then I grew to love Hobart. It's beautiful too. So, if you've never been anywhere else, there might be somewhere else you love just as much.'

She thought he didn't hear her, as he went silent for a moment.

'And your parents love Tassie?'

'Yes. Plus, my brother, Charlie has settled there, it's home for them now.'

'And yet, you chose here. That's a long way from your family.'

It wasn't a question, but Noah clearly wanted more.

As she deliberated over what to say, Blake strode over with picnic blankets and baskets. He tied up Cupcake and Hotdog.

'If you let them off, they'll gobble up your lunch, okay? Leave them tied up until the food has been eaten. Promise?'

'Yes, sir!' Ish replied. A bolt of discomfort shot through Ava at the authoritarian reply Ish had been required to give his father and other male members of the household. It belonged in the past, in another time, not here.

Reminders of Henry were everywhere. And just like that she was transported to another warm summer's day in an English park, not long after they were married. A picnic like this one, people lounging on blankets and children running around on the green space. Everyone in London was happy when the weather was nice. Her memory painted the moment as perfect until Henry had taken a call from home. That conversation was the first mention of his father's illness, of a need for him to visit the city of his birth. Ava had shown the appropriate family concern, but nothing more. There had been nothing to worry about at that point. They lived and worked in London and had no intentions of leaving. Upon reflection, that was the beginning of the end.

Blake gave Ish a pat on the head. 'Here's a basket for a special young lady and gentleman.' And he set them up on their own plaid rug and revealed the contents of their lunch.

Engrossed in watching the children, Ava hadn't noticed Noah pour her a glass of wine. 'This is the Estate's signature wine.' After he'd poured his own glass, he held it up and they clinked glasses. 'It's been really nice to meet you, Ava.'

Their eyes connected and her tummy fluttered like there were hundreds of birds in there.

***

Noah sipped his wine and the icy cold liquid raced too fast down his throat.

'This place is glorious! The creek, the grounds, it would be magic to get married here!' Ava blushed and Noah couldn't take his eyes off her.

'Tell me, what do you love about living here?'

Good diversion and he was thankful for it. Things were getting a little steamy. He tugged at the collar of his shirt. 'My mother is here, she's the only family I have. It's lovely having her close by. But it's a connection to the country, it's where I'm always drawn to, where I always want to return to, where I always want to be.'

That reminded him, he really needed to work on his poetry some more. He'd neglected it of late.

'Oh, that's lovely. To feel that pull, that's special. I didn't realise how much I missed Australia until we returned. I've lived in a few places now, places that I've loved, but I'm looking for the place we can call home.'

She was? Had she told him where she came from? Obviously not Tassie, he remembered it was overseas. He couldn't remember and wracked his brain. Ava was looking to settle in the country? Here in Bellethorpe? A myriad of emotions rushed through him at once.

'It's very quiet. It would be perfect if there was say, a movie theatre or shopping complex, a few more resources...'

Ah, there it was. You could never take the city out of the girl.

'Our appeal lay in our community spirit, the townspeople, old traditions, the land, the outdoor and rural opportunities. We do not want to be like the city.'

How long would Ava last? Lots of city folk dreamed of the country, the romanticised version, not the real one. Would she last until the renovations were complete? Would the house be valued so high then, he wouldn't be able to purchase it? The thought crashed down on him. If she did leave, he'd be in debt and have no money left. Probably no ability to get a loan, either.

'Duke! Come and put some suncream on if you've finished your lunch.'

The kids obediently ran over, and Ava slathered Duke over his face and arms. What was he thinking? He needed to do the same for Emily. Playing silly buggers, she resisted but eventually succumbed. He couldn't send her back to her mother sunburned.

Duke haphazardly applied cream to his mother's bare shoulders before he raced off to play in the shallows of the creek.

On Ava's back was a clump of unrubbed in cream. 'Um, you've got a spot on your back.' Noah pointed, but of course, Ava couldn't see.

'No, is it bird poo?'

'No, it's suncream. Here, let me.' He wriggled across the rug and their knees connected. Shifting, he sat behind her and with only two fingers lightly touched the glob of lotion.

'You'll get burnt, there isn't really enough cover, and it's so hot today. Do have the tube?'

Ava offered it over her shoulder. The tube made on embarrassing spurt noise as he squeezed some onto his hands. Noah raised them ready for contact and they connected to her bare skin revealed in the thin-strapped, low back dress.

Ava stiffened at his touch.

'Cold hands,' she said by way of excuse. His hands weren't cold.

Her skin sparkled in the sun and was warm to his touch. What started with two gentle fingers became two firm hands. The feel of her beneath his fingers tantalised him. Noah caressed across her shoulders, over her knobbly blades and back down into the dip of her back. One dress strap was in the way and he tugged it to the side where it slipped to her elbow. Her heard a small gasp. All of a sudden, he realised she wasn't wearing a bra and he dropped his hands as if her skin burned him.

Ava's chest rose in an exaggerated fashion and he followed her rhythm. He glanced across at the kids playing happily and wished his hands were still upon her soft and smooth skin. Instead, he lifted the thin cotton strap of her dress and placed it back onto her shoulder. It stuck there, the cream like glue.

His imagination went a little crazy then visualising his hands exploring other parts of her body …

Ava shifted and the spell was broken. His legs had cramped and he stood to stretch them out. Neither spoke and he refilled her glass and sat next to her, ensuring no part of him touched her. Noah wasn't sure how long he could maintain his control.

Risking a glance at Ava, her features were locked with her lips in a thin straight line and her jaw clenched. Her focus was over his shoulder.

Glancing that way, he watched a family set up a picnic. There was a lot of noise coming from the group of fifteen or so.

Ava remained transfixed. He touched her arm and she zeroed in on him. 'Do you know them?'

'No.'

'What is it, then?'

'What do you notice when you look at that family?'

Huh? 'They have a lot of children?' Noah was confused.

'No.' She spoke through gritted teeth. 'Look, the father and sons are on one blanket and the wife and daughters are serving up the food. See the husband is sitting back barking orders for his lunch.'

Noah sat back and took a better look. Yes, the family was segregated, they would not have fit on one blanket anyway, and the wife was serving her husband and the daughters were helping. The man wore a turban of Indian tradition, but Noah didn't sense this was a cultural rebuke. Perhaps Ava was right, but … what did it matter?

'And that bothers you, Ava?'

'Yes. There are other women, too. Do you think they are aunts or his other wives?'

'Wives?' This was getting weird. 'Isn't polygamy against the law?'

'Yes, but that doesn't mean it doesn't happen…'

Noah didn't know what was going on but the entire mood had shifted. He took a risk and placed his flat palm over hers, 'Ava?'

'I'm sorry,' was all she said in reply.

CHAPTER
Twelve

NOAH STRUGGLED to control his red-hot rage. Trapped in the driver's seat, he tried to regulate his breathing as he gripped the steering wheel so tight his knuckles turned white. He glanced at the speedometer. Shit. He released his foot from the accelerator. No point killing himself. No point being so angry that he never made it back to Bellethorpe and never saw his daughter again. Thank goodness he was alone so no one could see him like this.

'Noah, tell us about your experience today.'

The usual three-hour trip back to Bellethorpe had flown by; his angst spurring him forwards, home, to his destination. He'd gone straight to the father support group, fortuitously, their regular meeting was on tonight. Noah needed to talk, tell his story, get the poison out of his system.

'Today was the first hearing to agree on interim orders. The judge said we should have reached consent before this but the issue is about where Emily lives long-term. This was just the first step, or so my lawyer tells me.'

Noah considered the small circle of men in attendance. They leaned in, interested, ready to offer words of support and encouragement. Their eyes were burning, their hands clasped tight, some hostile expressions. For a split second, Noah relaxed his features, fearful he resembled them—angry and ready to fight, fight for the cause.

'For the time being, Emily remains living with her mother in Brisbane…'

The men burst out angrily.

'Unfair.'

'Unjust.'

'Ridiculous.'

'She took your daughter and gets rewarded.'

Noah listened and his anger simmered again.

'What time were you awarded?'

Noah hung his head. 'I can see her as often as I want, mid-week, weekends etcetera. I tried to make it clear to the judge that I'm miles away and can't just drop in. The judge nodded and I thought he understood. But I was still awarded two weekends a month and I'm to pick her up and drop her back.'

The group shouted over each other until the chairman quietened them. 'Let Noah finish. Tell us how it ended.'

'I can telephone each evening. We are to see a family report writer who will give their opinion about what are the best arrangements for Emily in the longer term. After those appointments we return to court for a final decision. I do have Easter and the half the next school holidays, so I guess that's something.'

'Child support?'

'Full child support.'

A few men jeered; others sat silently. Noah observed them and his temper dissipated. These fathers all felt they had been vilified, treated unfairly and unjustly by the family court system. Each had sought shared care; some had been successful. That didn't seem an option for Noah with the distance between homes too great. On the trip home, he had felt screwed over too, but watching these men, the fight suddenly left him. He was tired; it had been a long day. Despite how he might feel right now, he'd never give up on Emily.

Before long the mood settled.

'What did your lawyer say?' asked the chairman.

'It was to be expected. There are processes, he said. The court doesn't like parents making their own decision about where children live, but in my case, the age of Emily, that she had been cared for by Lisa until she went to school, that they were close, that Lisa's family lived in Brisbane, they were all important factors. Unfortunately, though, the longer this arrangement continues, the more likely the court will make it permanent. What else can I do?'

The men were generous with their suggestions but some bordered on ridiculous and he shut them out. His heart ached thinking about his daughter far away in Brisbane.

The conversation in the room had moved onto action. What could they do as a collective group to advocate change? Noah didn't know much but he sure needed his lawyer today. There was no way he'd have been able to eloquently express his position to the judge who had appeared intimidating with his grey wig and black robe.

So, having an empty bank account had been worth it. His savings were extinguished; the money gone quicker than his vacuum cleaner cleared his dirty floor.

For the first time in his life, he felt helpless, out of control and as if the stakes were raised against him.

At home, he took Otis for a long walk, but abandoned it halfway. Today it evoked too many memories. It was a walk he often took with Emily where she'd make endless discoveries: beetles on leaves, insects in the air, birds singing in the treetops at dusk, and her little feet jumping across the rocks in the nearby creek. Resting back on his deck, he watched wild kangaroos scattered across his patch of grass. Much like Otis, Emily sometimes chased them too. These were scenes that usually provided him such comfort, tonight it seemed as if memories were everywhere.

A tsunami of emotions swirled inside Noah. People could laugh at him, could joke that he'd never travelled, but this place was where he belonged. This is what Emily would miss if she stayed in Brisbane. This outdoor lifestyle that country life provided. The lifestyle *he* could provide. He knew it was where he belonged. Isn't this where Emily belonged, too?

He reached for the pad and pen where words swept across the page.

. . .

Single, alone and devastated
Heart sick, crisis created
House too quiet, loneliness is real
It's impossible not to feel
Lost now, uncertainty abounds
His wounds real, know no bounds.

The second line didn't work and he scratched it out, once, twice. No substitute words came. His mind blank. Perhaps a better sentence would come to him with a fresh, new day, tomorrow.

Molly and Dolly, the two brown puppies nipped at Ava's feet but she stared at the computer screen. A message from Jamila still had the effect of stopping time. On this occasion, it was an email from a new account. Ava read that she'd secured a listing date and the matter was proceeding through the English court system. That was huge. Unlike Ava who could disappear without publicity, Jamila's case generated great public interest as her husband was the patriarch of one the most wealthy and powerful families in Egypt. And then she'd left him. Without consent, without anyone's knowledge, stealing away in the stealth of darkness with the children. Ava had too; she wasn't passing judgment, but her case was different.

Ava had married the less important brother. But if not for Jamila, she'd never have had the confidence or means of getting out. Ava glanced at the few loose photographs beside her; the few she'd grabbed and shoved in her bag when they'd left. Rummaging around for something else, she'd found them yesterday in the spare room where she'd shoved them out of sight. A wave of melancholy hit her straight in the chest. Photos of a happy family doing normal things. Of her husband with his dashing good looks posing with newborn Ish.

These were the entire memory of Ish's childhood with Henry in one small, pathetic pile.

She showed them to Ish this morning, but he'd only glanced briefly and run off to play. Okay, she'd tried. It had to be important to talk about his father, hadn't it? All the photos had done for her was dredge up old memories and, for a time, made her feel sick. Sick for the love she had for the man she married and how badly it had gone wrong. She batted away those feelings now. Regardless, Ish did have a father, so Ava vowed to try again with him another time.

Shooting out a quick email reply to Jamila, she didn't delete the thread as she usually would, and then slammed the laptop lid shut and put the photographs away in a box and sat back. Her legs jiggled and she felt a nip to her ankle again and laughed.

'You are naughty puppies.' She scooped them each up in turn. The puppies had grown and were crawling around now. They'd added another lovely element to their home. Ish adored them and took his responsibility of caring for them seriously. Ava would never forget —if they'd remained in Egypt, Ish would never have had a dog, let alone a dog with puppies, or if he did, the task of caring for them would have been relegated to a servant. Or they might have been destroyed, unless they were valuable. Ava shivered.

She adored the dogs too. The house had a sense of home with their mewling noises and even with their messes. Looking around with a sense of satisfaction, she again confirmed she was doing the right thing.

Ava paced the circumference of the house unable to sit still. She paused at the kitchen. She'd intended to start pulling out the old cabinets in preparation for the new to be installed. Together with Noah, they'd agreed it would be renovated next. But Noah hadn't shown up these last two days. Was it because of how she'd behaved at the picnic? At the sight of that man dominating his little family, her world had shrunk and she became that small, unimportant woman once more. It had been a horrible feeling, moreover, she'd taken great offense at the treatment she'd witnessed.

Ah, she didn't want to be thinking about these things all the time.

Another look at the kitchen and she could simply get started. But then she spied her riding boots by the back door. She'd go for a ride!

Saddling up Honey, Ava noticed the large satellite dish on Clive's roof. Funny. Their internet was patchy but reliable, really, for the country. Why would her neighbour need such a powerful connection?

With the wind in her hair, Ava's troubles disappeared with each fast gallop. Or at the very least, blew away in her wake. Ish was at a play date with the boy he'd met at school orientation. She'd agonized over letting him go but he'd been insistent and she wanted him to have a normal life, right? She had to get used to them being apart, but it was the first time since they'd fled, and well, it was tough. There had been so much change and adjusting was hard. Plus, he was off to big school soon and she'd have to get used to being alone and releasing him into the world, a safe world she hoped.

She rode fast and as her mind freed her senses came alive.

Unlike the other day when it had taken them at least twenty minutes to reach the pond, today she arrived in only minutes. She pulled Honey up gently in the most glorious spot that was illuminated by the sun's bright morning rays. The pond glistened, casting shadows onto the land. Without dismounting, Ava let the horse drink generously at the water's edge. Colour sparkled in her direction; she hadn't been dreaming the other day. Jumping down, she loosened the horse's harness and wrapped it around the nearest tree branch.

Ava walked away from the water towards one of the mounds. She trailed her fingers in the pebbly dirt. Behind the pile was a makeshift bunker she hadn't noticed the other day; it was like an old-fashioned lean-to. For shelter? Standing at the frame, she couldn't see inside, it was too dark but her eyes gradually adjusted. The structure went back a metre or so, the timber stumps leaning dangerously to the left. Something scuttled at the side and she jumped back, her heart thumping. Nothing but empty space and dirt in there. The corrugated iron roof was covered with branches and leaves, twigs and seed pods. Someone had once taken time and effort to build the little hut. But why?

Ava chose a spot to sit and moved aside the debris from the base of the first mound. Like the shed, fallen leaves and branches covered the pile. It wasn't dirt, but rather more pebble-like rocks of various sizes.

This was definitely the result of a digging. But what had the person been digging for in this spot? What had they found?

Wishing she'd brought her kit with her, Ava ran her fingers through the first pile. Sparkles of colour occasionally bounced up at her and reflected in the sun's light. Holding a pebble up, she saw distinctive blues and greens hidden within the rock. Wriggling over to the water, she dunked it once, and quickly and slid her finger over the specimen. The clear section revealed a deeper set of colours. Putting that one down to dry properly, she applied the old-fashioned spit test. Yep, it stuck to her finger. There was something here, she knew it. The coincidences kept building up. Were these simply opals? That in itself would be an incredible find, but she sensed more. Were these fossils, too? And given the depth of colour, she knew it was possible they were opalised fossils.

Under her shirt she wore a white singlet so she ripped off her long-sleeved cotton tee and spread it out on the dirt. Methodically, she sifted through the material, occasionally finding something she declared worthy of further investigation and placed it onto her pale pink shirt. After she had collected some specimens, she paused holding one up to the light. She examined it closely, held it one way, and then the other. With the distinct shape of a shell, ridges were prominent on one side.

Ava jumped up and spun around as a twig snapped behind her, going off like a gunshot. Her heart raced as the clip clop of hooves signalled an approaching rider. Bending down, she quickly spread her tee shirt over the small pile she'd put aside.

Honey nickered and moved towards the sound rather than away from it.

'It's a beauty, this spot, isn't it?' Clive called out. He was on Marmalade, and on her land, but she guessed she was riding his horse and rules were laxer in the country. A little part of her was indignant at her precious time being interrupted.

Nonetheless in response to his hearty greeting, she smiled up at her neighbour as he stopped near her.

'Have you ridden around these parts much?' she asked.

'Oh, yeah, I've covered a fair bit of ground.'

'Is there anything significant about the land I should know?'

'Not that I'm aware of, besides it being beautiful and a special part of the world. But as I said, I've only ever lived out here part-time, so I'm not always around or up to date with the latest news. What do you mean exactly?'

'Did you know the previous owner?'

'No, he died before I took over my place. A few years before, so we never met. The entire time I've been coming to Bellethorpe your property has been vacant.' Clive turned sheepish then. 'That's sort of why I've ridden these trails, had free reign and no one cared whether I was trespassing or not. So, I must apologise, I'm used to taking the shortcut through your land to reach mine.'

Ava was grateful. 'No need to apologise, you're very welcome. You've been so kind letting us ride your horses.'

'It's a mutually satisfying arrangement.'

'Clive, what do you teach at the university?'

'Anthropology. I'm into the linguistics side of it myself.'

Anthropology, the study of people and cultures. It had to be a sign. Deep in her gut, Ava thought she could trust Clive. And, let's face it, she needed help.

'Is there an archaeology department at your uni?'

'Oh yeah, of course. It's popular and there is some exciting research coming out of there. An interesting field.'

He was looking at her oddly, wondering where this line of conversation was heading but he was placating her, and she appreciated that.

'Clive, I've found a few things and it's outside my scope of knowledge, but I'm convinced it's important, significant, but I don't know enough.'

He murmured for her to go on.

'What do you think of these?' Ava knelt and uncovered her finds. Clive hopped off Marmalade and sat next to her. With a gentle touch, he collected one rock and held it up for examination and did the same with three pieces. Ava respected that he didn't rush in with an opinion straight away; he seemed to be a man who carefully considered things.

'This is definitely outside my scope but what do you think? With this colour, is it opal? Is there more to it?'

'Yeah, I think so. I reckon it's opal. And look around you, someone has searched for something. These seem to be tailings, don't they?' Clive relinquished the gems and covered the surrounds, investigating each pile. He found the lean-to; Ava didn't intervene with her views, simply let him observe.

'It's not a professional set up, so maybe a hobbyist? Or did they start and get interrupted? It's hard to tell. I need to talk to someone with knowledge...'

'Whoa, hang on. We don't know what we're dealing with yet.' Ava stood and guarded her territory. It was her find, her land. What had she done? She was getting nervous now at the prospect of involving other people and having strangers nosing around. But she needed help and that is exactly why she'd asked.

Clive regarded her intently. 'I know people in the archaeology department, people of integrity, whom I can trust. If I ask them to keep it to themselves, they will. What about I ask them to do a reconnaissance visit? Simply check things out? I might need to take an example. Otherwise, it's a big ask.'

The archaeologist in Ava knew that was the best approach. But her chest tightened, her breath went shallow. Involving other people scared her. For many reasons—what if she was wrong? No, that didn't worry her. What if it was something, something significant and she had uncovered it? What then? And what would that mean? The idyllic and quiet life she'd been building in Bellethorpe could shatter. But, of course, she was getting ahead of herself. The excitement of a potential find could do that. There wasn't a choice, was there? She had to know. There was only so far her limited knowledge could advance the investigation.

She nodded, slowly, reluctantly. 'Promise me, Clive, for the moment, you'll keep this quiet. Until we at least know what we're dealing with.'

The man agreed and stared once more at the piece of dazzling rock in his hand.

CHAPTER
Thirteen

AVA LAID her shirt flat on the outdoor table and rubbed her hands together. They were dirty; her fingernails lined black and particles of dirt clung to each crease of her knuckles. Filth from the dig and horse riding; it was gross but made her feel like she'd done some real work.

Without bothering to wash her hands, she carefully considered her specimens; it was a beautiful time—the discovery, the unknown, the possibilities. Thoughts spiralled through her mind; one idea rolling over into another. What had she found?

Ah, the excitement! A semblance of her former self crept in.

Until she heard a car pull up. Her heart beat double time until she remembered she'd left the gate unlocked for Ish's return. When would she stop having a physical reaction to unexpected events?

Reluctant to tear herself away from her work, she rose and went out to greet him. The back door of the car opened and Ish jumped out. 'I've had the best time. Thanks Mrs D!' he shouted before racing inside.

'Thanks so much for having him.' She chatted to Sam's mother through the front passenger window, keeping her filthy hands behind her back. It was a quick chat as Sam's mum had to rush away to an appointment. Suited her perfectly. Returning to the deck Ish played with the dogs and she made lunch. Listening to Ish talk about his time with Sam, she kept glancing at the rocks, her mind coming up with a range of potential scenarios. It was so irritating she didn't know what she was dealing with! Patience had never been her virtue. Best to move onto something else.

'Okay, kiddo, want to help me pull out the kitchen?'

'Yeah!'

Showing off their muscle as a team of two, they enjoyed the splintering of old timber as it lost its secure footing against the wall. It was hard yakka and Ish stood behind her and helped her tug out the fittings. Together, the cabinets around the sink came out quickly and were dumped into unruly piles. Halfway through ripping out the tall cupboards lining the long wall opposite the beautiful open bay window, there was a crash and jangle of something hitting the floor.

Something small and heavy rolled into the four corners of the rectangular room. Ish chased after them and collected a handful of coins. 'Aw, gross, Mumma!' he exclaimed holding up his hands that were now black. The coins were filthy.

'Wow! Ish, look,' Ava examined them in turn. 'These say *liberte, egalite, fraternate*. They are French coins.'

'Cool. This one has a hole through its middle,' he said as he held it up to his eye.

Ava scraped away the dirt to reveal the number five on the one she held. 'And the date is 1912! Incredible. This one is a bit tarnished but larger than the others and has some sort of leaf on it. It's worth *two francs*.'

'How much is that?' Ish asked.

'Like two dollars sort of.' Holding up another one it was stained gold with *ten cente* written in the middle and decorated with some sort of emblem around the edge. 'These must have belonged to the original owner. What a find!' She jumped on the spot. 'Can you get some hot soapy water and clean these for me?'

The smile on his face dropped. 'Do I have to?'

'Either that, or you can clean up this mess?'

With neither choice holding appeal, he wandered out. Ava replaced her dust mask and peered in the remainder of the cabinets still attached to the wall. The corner of yellowing lino that lined the base of the cupboard stuck up in one corner. Ava lifted it and circled a small section into a roll and threw it onto the floor. She'd dispose of the mess properly when the room was a bare canvas.

Reaching back inside her fingers dragged on something else, hard and sharp

-edged. Pulling over a chair, she climbed higher to get a better view. Gently, she pried whatever it was from the bottom of the ledge. It was a small and rectangular postcard displaying a gorgeous image of a young woman wearing a large bonnet and holding a bouquet of flowers. The next was a woman pulling on a shoe, standing half-dressed in a bedroom. Both were black and white and faded with age.

Poking her head further inside, she extracted a few more. Rifling through them quickly she saw they were romantic poses of couples in a garden and on a swing wearing old-fashioned formal clothing. The women were in long dresses and the men in suits with stiff collars and heavy coats.

From the far back, Ava retrieved a handful more, those depicting images of war. Men in uniform holding guns, walking through valleys and fields, marching through villages.

It was a motley collection and Ava plonked down onto the chair to consider them properly. They were all French if the language was demonstrative of their origin. She flicked over to the back of some of them, hoping to find descriptions but they were blank. As she fanned though the postcards she sneezed in quick succession; the dust rising from the cards and penetrating her mask.

Her thoughts returned to the previous owner, the soldier. What was he doing with these cards and why at some point did they end up lining his kitchen cabinets?

Coins and postcards … what other treasures would she find hiding in these walls?

Ava moved her gaze around the kitchen and into the rooms beyond, as if the past might jump out and surprise her. An odd turn of phrase that she wished she hadn't used. History was everywhere, wasn't it? Remnants of people's lives left behind, puzzles to solve and this place was certainly working out to be a doozy. Outside and in. She could never have imagined the secrets she might be unlocking … well that she hoped she was unlocking. And now she had a keen desire to learn as much as possible about the original owner.

From now on, she'd need to be more careful to ensure nothing of historic value was ruined or lost.

Ava had a sudden urge to tell Noah of her finds; the thought came out of nowhere. But then, she had no friends and no one else to talk to, so was it really so strange? He'd always seemed interested in restoring this house to its former grandeur. Would that extend to knowledge about its inhabitants and the mystery within the acres of land?

But he wasn't here for her to gauge his interest. Two days had passed and he hadn't shown up or called to say he wasn't coming. Not that he had to. In fact, she'd told him he didn't have to come every day, that he must have other stuff to do sometimes. It appeared he did.

Ava was torn. Should she continue with the kitchen—she was desperate for work to commence on a fully functioning kitchen—or go where her heart was calling her, the history centre and try to find out more about this soldier. Or, at the very least, see if she could contribute to what she imagined was an already established collection of artefacts from the region and the history of their returned soldier scheme.

'Ish, want a milkshake in town?'

He raced back in. 'Yeah!'

A short time later, Ava stopped outside the Bellethorpe Historical Centre in a small building attached to the Anglican church. Ava didn't need to try the door to know it was locked. The sign advised it was open one day per week but didn't say which day! Bugger. What a disappointment. She was desperate to speak to another history buff.

'Do they sell milkshakes here?' Ish asked.

'Nope, but I know a place that does. Chocolate or strawberry?' And they hopped back in the car for the short trip.

Unlike her last visit to *Café Antiquities*, this time it was quiet. A lone customer sat by the rear window sipping a latte.

'Hello, love. You look familiar,' Peter said as she approached the counter. 'And who's this fine young man?'

'Peter, this is my son, Duke.'

'Duke, hey. That's an unusual name. Is it because you're royalty?' He laughed at his own joke. But of course, like most five-year-old's, Ish had no idea what to say.

'I'm not sure about that, but he does love a strawberry milkshake. Could we order one please?'

'Are you new around here, love? Or are you just visiting?'

Sadness weighed down her shoulders that Peter didn't remember her. Sheila appeared behind him. 'Ava, hello again. How lovely to have you back. And with your son.'

Peter's brow furrowed in confusion.

'This is Ava, darling, she's living out on Kinross Road. She visited the other day and you told her about the returned soldiers.'

The creases in his face cleared at the familiar topic. 'Oh yes, the returned soldier settlement. Did you know that this region housed—'

'Peter, be a dear and make the milkshake and I'll get Ava her coffee.' Sheila offered Ava a wan smile.

Ava glanced over at Ish. He had spotted the box of toys in the corner and was playing with them. 'Actually, you might be able to help me with something. I went to the history centre and it was shut, said it only opens one day per week. Do you have any idea which day it opens?'

It was obvious Sheila knew the answer but she allowed Peter to assist. 'Yes, you need Hilary Goldsmith. She usually opens on a Saturday trying to exploit the tourist trade and get a few people through, but I think the schedule is pretty flexible.'

'Oh. I was hoping to have a look and a chat. You see, I've found—'

'I can give her a call, or you can take her number. Hilary is always up for a chat.'

Peter stopped the blender and busied himself writing numbers on a small slip of paper and passed it to her. Behind him, Sheila joined in. 'Hilary will be more than happy to speak to you. Give her a ring now.' Sheila glanced at her wristwatch. 'I can't remember if today she helps in the old people's home or maybe she's at the craft group. I think Tuesdays she's at the support complex. But anyway, she'll be up for a cuppa.'

Before Ish had slurped the last of his milkshake, Hilary had agreed to meet them at the centre. 'Thanks so much, Peter and Sheila. Hilary is heading over from the quilting group and will give me a quick tour. Cheerio.'

'Oh, quilting. Of course. See you love.' Peter gazed at her with a blank expression.

'About seven hundred soldiers made this area their home after the Great War,' Hilary said.

'And yet, there doesn't seem to be much history on them.' Ava's words petered out. About an hour later, she sat with the local Bellethorpe resident in their history centre.

Hilary leaned back and scrutinised her. 'We've done our best. Everything got lost after the war, and then we entered another war. Life in a small community was busy and tough.'

'I'm sorry, Hilary, it wasn't a criticism. History is lost all the time unless there are people dedicated to the cause, like you.'

Hilary's chest puffed out at the compliment. 'I do my best, dear. But this collection, of which I am the sole curator, only survives on donations. Most people throw away rubbish without realising its significance, of course and then it's lost forever.'

Ava glanced around at the meagre history centre. It was one tiny room, with an eclectic collection of bits and bobs, some of which she even doubted would be authenticated. The clear glass cabinets with their laminate rims were half-empty and the rest was, well, she couldn't tell. Old jars or vases maybe that had been dug up in someone's garden, some posters on the walls, and a few medals hanging from a dummy in the corner resplendent in military uniform. On closer inspection, Ava recoiled at the thick layer of dust atop the long sleeves.

It was ridiculous to compare it to the British Museum. That establishment employed thousands of people, sometimes with one person being responsible for only one artefact. Not to mention the heat and dust and environment the items in this centre were subject to. No climate control here.

'Have a look at these, Hilary.' Ava extracted her phone and pulled up the images of the coins and postcards. 'I found these in our old kitchen. The cards were stuck under some lino and the coins in the kitchen cabinets. They must belong to the original soldier owner. I was hoping to find out more about him.'

Hilary took her glasses from the top of her head and placed them on her nose. 'Oh, these are lovely,' and she held the phone up close to examine the images. 'In the kitchen you say?'

'Yes. Peter from the antique store told me a bit about the soldier. Must have been his. You don't have a register?'

The woman's face lit up. 'Yes, we do!' She raced over to the corner filing cabinet and rummaged around for a scrapbook and then brought back to the table. 'Here it is.'

Ava opened the first page. And the second. It was a collection of newspaper articles, more general than on specific soldiers. She flicked forwards and the haphazard collection of articles continued. Pieces of paper stuck out at odd angles catching each page as she turned.

'We had a fellow a few years back who was cataloguing information for us, but you know, he … passed away and well, I haven't had time to pick up his research again, but I do intend to.'

Ava held back a sigh. This place wasn't going to be of much use in her search for information. Maybe she needed to focus on renovating her house and forgetting about mapping out the history of the area. But what about unravelling the mystery on her land?

CHAPTER
Fourteen

CLIVE STOOD at the back fence, waving to catch their attention as Ava pulled the car to a stop. Ish slammed his door shut and raced over to pet the horses.

'Regarding that matter we were talking about yesterday—' Clive said.

'Oh, yes.' Ava leaned her arms along the top railing of the fence. 'Did you have any luck?'

'I spoke to a few people and they expressed interest but are cautious. They need a little more information before making any promises. I told them you are an archaeologist of great experience but not with rocks. They suggested you email them. I presume you took photographs? Send them and provide loads of detail. I'm sure you know what to say. Enough to pique their interest, yes?' Clive patted his nose in a gesture of solidarity and mystery. He pulled out his mobile phone. 'Give me your email address and I'll send their details to you.'

'You'll keep my details private, won't you, Clive?'

'The email address or your potential discovery?'

'Both.'

'Of course, Ava.'

'Okay, it's all lower case, bookofthedead1992@gmail.com.'

He gazed at her over the glasses perched on his nose and punched into his phone. 'Is that something I should have heard of?'

'Only if you are an Egyptian artefact and culture freak, like me.' She smiled.

'Well, you've got me there, I know nothing.'

'We used to live in Egypt!' Ish piped up, clearly listening to the conversation while brushing Marmalade's mane.

Clive shot a glance between them. 'Is that so?'

'Yeah, it was really hot and we lived in this fancy palace with our entire family. And there was lots of rules and this one time—'

Ava tugged Ish on the arm. 'We've got to go, thanks so much, Clive. Once you send the details, I'll contact them.' Turning to her son, she said, 'Come on you, we need to check on Daisy and her puppies.'

Safely on their deck, Ava gazed towards the fence joining the properties. Clive was still standing there watching them. A rush of goosepimples exploded on her arms and legs. Clive had told his colleagues at the university about her being an archaeologist of great experience; that worried her. She hadn't told him specifically she was an archaeologist, let alone what experience she had. She'd asked about the archaeology department and advised it was outside her scope of her experience. Perhaps he'd made an assumption? And was the experience part an exaggeration to pique the interest of his colleagues? She guessed that was possible.

Or…it was Noah. He was the only person she'd told about her work. Had they spoken? Was it the community grapevine working overtime? But why would Noah tell anyone about her job?

A droplet of moisture formed in the cleft between her breasts and rolled slowly down her chest.

Otis jumped from the tray of Noah's ute and commenced chase, and like every other day, the kangaroos scattered fast. Today, the gate to Ava's property was not only unlocked, it was open. Strange, but convenient. The rear sliding doors of the house were open, too, so Ava and Duke were home.

'Hello!' Noah sang out and deposited the take-away coffee on the only space left on the outdoor table. She sure liked her rocks. He picked one up and noticed out of the ten or so in a long line, some were smooth, others rough and all pretty colours. Was there gold in them hills? Wouldn't that be convenient, solve his troubles. Except, of course, it wasn't his property. Today he didn't want to be reminded of that.

He still harboured a bad mood after court the other day. Like a lingering headache that wouldn't disappear no matter how many drugs you took, he couldn't shake it. His hope lay on a good, solid day's work to shake his melancholy. Unlikely, unless his life suddenly changed, his wife returned and his daughter lived in the same house as him. Wishful thinking, well about Emily, anyway. Lisa … he didn't want to think about her.

One step into the house and his path was blocked. Debris of old cupboards and their doors, planks of timber and ripped up lino littered the floor. Dirt and dust lay on every surface. Zigzagging around the pile, he found the kitchen in a mess. Who started a job and didn't finish? If you were going to rip out the guts of the room, you didn't stop halfway. Annoying but it wouldn't take long to finish.

Ava was obviously trying to help. Or maybe she got impatient. Couldn't blame her given he'd been AWOL the last couple of days. She'd probably done him a favour. Time was of the essence and he needed to push on with the job, get it done, get the next payment so he could pay his lawyer another outrageous amount of money. Another reason for his foul temperament.

No, this was good; he'd have the rest of the remaining cabinetry out in a jiffy and work could move along swiftly. Popping in his ear buds he pumped the music loud to drown out his thoughts and used his crowbar to strike. The physical smack of tool against timber was satisfying.

A hand touched his upper arm and Noah flung back in fright, the tool flying across the room while his elbow connected with something hard. The music still blared in his ears and he tapped the bud twice for silence.

'Noah! Stop!'

What? He turned. Ava lay on her back, legs askew over a discarded section of pantry. 'Ava! Are you okay? Sorry!'

'I'm fine.' Even though her words were strained. 'You've got to stop.'

Noah frowned. Was he missing something? *Stop what and why?* He knelt low, his tool belt in the way and placed his hand on her leg. 'Ouch. Let me help.' Lifting her until she was upright, he placed his hands at her waist to steady her wobble.

Noah closed his eyes; repressed the urge to squeeze her in tight to him, and rest there a moment. Her touch was warm and welcome and it made not only his skin sizzle but every other part of him too.

She lifted her head and their eyes connected; and he swore a zap of something hit him square in the chest. Man, in this moment, he wanted her and wanted her bad. Her touch drove him crazy, starved as he was of female affection. Her eyes seared, scorching him. His hands gripped Ava tighter, unconsciously not wanting to let her go.

But then she grimaced and his bubble of lust burst.

'Are you hurt?' His eyes roamed her body checking for abrasions. 'You have a cut on your shin.' His hand rested there, stopping the trickle of blood running down her leg. 'Let's patch you up.'

Placing her into the deck chair as if she'd sustained serious injury, he retrieved the first aid kit he kept on site. There'd been one too many incidents with reckless builders in his time so he always had the basics handy.

'This might sting a little.' Noah dabbed at the open cut to wipe away the blood and washed it out with water. He raised her leg onto his and held it in his hand. Her skin was warm and smooth but dusty from the debris of the house. He glanced up; her eyes were wide and her lips parted. Best to focus on the wound. Once clean, he patted it dry and placed a heavy-duty gauze over it. It was too much for a simple cut.

'All done.' His voice was deep and husky as if his words struggled to form. She was too close, clouding his vision, making his movements clunky.

She went to rise and he helped her, his hand back on her hip. They stood close; Ava's eyes darted to her waist and back to his face, regarding him. Time paused, noises around them receded and neither spoke. With one finger he traced the curve of her lips, moving along her jaw and across her cheeks, tracing her luminescent skin. Her breath came out sharp and short, her eyes flickered with his touch but shot open as he reached the creamy expanse of her neck. Her chest rose and fell. His fingers trembled and he pulled them away as a hot, intense flare catapulted through his body and filled him with longing. He returned his hands to his sides, holding them rigid before dropping his gaze.

Ava's fingers curled into his and their eyes met.

'Thank you.' Her voice was soft. 'That'll teach me for not cleaning up.' Her smile was tight. 'But I need you to slow down. Yesterday I found things in the cupboards so now we need to remove everything carefully to make sure there isn't anything else hidden in there.'

Noah was rooted to the spot, conscious of her fingers entwined with his; it was intimate and did nothing to quell the fire in his body. He cleared his throat. 'What sort of stuff?'

Her eyes remained connected to his. 'Um, old French postcards and some coins. Relics from the war and I need to preserve them. And there might be more.'

Old things in the cupboards? His frown must have given him away. Lifting their joined hands, she said, 'Come, I'll show you.'

The way he was feeling, he'd go anywhere Ava wanted.

The coins were laid out next to the rocks. Funny, he hadn't noticed them before.

'See.' She held up one gold coin. His hands felt empty after she let go. He took the coin and read words written in another language. Ava handed him another, and then another, her smile growing wider and wider. His shoulders relaxed a little and his desire abated.

'I'm learning you get very excited about old stuff. Honestly, if I'd been working on this kitchen, this stuff would have gone to the tip. I have no idea that it's valuable.'

'It's not the monetary value that's important, it's the history. Some finds allow us to retell history or patch together parts that we know little about. And as it turns out, this town that likes to flaunt it heritage, knows very little about the soldiers they housed.'

'Is that right?'

'Are you making fun of me?' Her lips twitched as she spoke.

'Not at all. You make it sound very interesting, unlike the history that I was taught at school. Boring with a capital B.'

'I know. Schools lose the interest of kids early on. But it is fascinating!'

'I'll take your word for it.' Noah paused, savouring this moment between them. 'So, what next? How do we tackle this?' A slight crease returned to his forehead as he considered the delay. 'We need to get your old kitchen out so you aren't inconvenienced for too long and we can install the new one.'

'Yeah, I'm sorry if this holds you up. But I must check everything before we dump it. Probably best I do that before you rip anything out? Or if that's not possible, when it's out? What do you think?'

'Sure.' His stomach cramped at the potential delay but he didn't give anything away. 'Only the back wall remains, the cupboards above and around the cooktop.'

'And the floor.'

'Yes, and the floor.'

'I know it's a cliché but people always hide things under the floor.'

'Okay, sure. This is making my job a lot more exciting.'

Ava stood close to him, hands on hips wearing only a sport tank-top and short bike pants. The way the stretch material clung to her body left nothing to his imagination. Her arms and legs were toned, like she exercised often. Her skin was nut-brown, her long dark hair was pulled high into a ponytail. It bounced around and over her shoulder each time she moved. His body burned once more.

'What have you been doing this morning?'

'Oh.' She paused. 'Duke and I took the dogs out. The puppies can't walk far but we carried them down the paddock. They loved it and now they'll sleep for hours they're so tuckered out. And then we picked a few veggies from our new patch. It's really taken off. Unexpected, given we've never grown vegetables before. And, oh, did you know we have chickens now? We're feeding them the scraps and hoping for eggs, but not yet.'

Noah's chest tightened and his breath caught; Ava was settling in.

She was making a life here, establishing a home. He might have been wrong; she may not be the city-chick he'd thought. It didn't matter anyway; he could never ever afford this place now. He was well and truly skint. The original grand plan of taking over when she upped stumps back to the city was never going to happen. Those dreams were long lost.

Why then did his chest expand with a sensation that felt strangely like hope. Did she see the beauty in Bellethorpe? But he was being ridiculous. What did it matter to him? The only thing that mattered was doing this job to get the money he needed to fight for his daughter. That was all.

Ava started collecting the discarded furniture and threw items outside on the grass. He watched the lean muscles in her arms tense with the movements. She was a hard worker and that was a problem as her list of admirable qualities just kept growing. She was focused and enthusiastic and she continued to surprise him. Now she retrieved a chair and mounted it with surprising agility. Standing on tiptoe, she reached inside the cupboard on the wall searching for further items. The chair wobbled and he rushed forwards and grasped her around her waist.

Argh! He needed to stop this. This time he felt her tiny waist and the skin underneath where her tee crept up. He swallowed and his body pulsed with need. This was too much. Her curves were beneath his fingers and he imagined her body crushed against his, feeling all of her, her head burrowed into his neck, the smell of her hair in his nose. He wanted that and it scared the hell out of him.

Ensuring she was stable, Noah dropped his hands, and stepped back. Touching her was a bad idea.

'Nothing there.' She jumped down from the chair but didn't face him. Did she feel it too? 'How can there be nothing else?' Her disappointment was crushing. But not for long. She spun around. 'Floor next?' Those dark almond-shaped eyes peered up at him and all Noah could do was nod.

CHAPTER
Fifteen

AVA IGNORED her awareness of Noah's every move, his touch upon her skin, his smell, his intense stare.

It was easier to focus on the work. Kneeling on the floor, she picked up one corner of lino. 'Argh, this is disgusting!' The floor covering was an old-fashioned yellow colour with a green swirl that she was sure would have been lovely once. Now, well, yeah, it was out of date, not helped by the fact that there was probably one hundred years of dust and dirt under there.

Ava donned her dust mask and held another up in silent question to Noah. He shook his head. She didn't lecture. His call, but her sinus passages were better off not blocked with dust. And what a great way to hide the emotions she was struggling not to express.

Mask safely in place, she peeled up another small section. 'I knew it!' Without waiting for him, she rolled the corner further, revealing the floor beneath covered in newspapers. 'Quick, Noah, help me get rid of the lino but don't step on the papers.'

The lino was stiff and unmalleable and it took great effort to remove it. 'I'll need to cut this with a knife,' and he extracted the tool from his belt and sliced. Ava hovered, holding her breath.

As the floor space was revealed, Ava covered her hands over the mask imitating her mouth and turned to him, eyes bulging. 'What a find! I'm going to pull each piece up and put them somewhere safe. I'll need to be careful, sorry to be a pain.'

He shrugged. 'I'll grab a drink of water.' Ava watched him saunter away, the belt around his hips jangling with its multitude of tools. Her eyes diverted to his cute backside snug in his denim jeans. *Hot damn.*

'It's a broadsheet, perfectly preserved, except for the dust of course. They've laid page after page down over these floorboards. There might even be a whole paper here.' She talked out loud to herself.

Not saying anything upon his return, Noah stood at the doorway and lifted the edge of one corner of paper to examine the floor underneath.

Ava kept reading. 'Oh, you'll never believe this. This page is dated 1919 and there's an article on the Spanish flu. How ironic we're reading this after suffering through our own pandemic. You know they say the two are very similar. Thousands died back then and they didn't have the science or innovation we have … incredible!'

Noah was busy running his fingers along the floor. 'You might be in luck. These timber boards look in pretty good shape. There's nothing nicer than the original boards sanded back to perfection.'

'Oh, that will look so good.'

'Is there anything else I can help you with?'

'Uh, ah, no. This won't take long. I'll try to get them up and you can keep working.'

'Okay, great. I'll get the rest of this room out today and prime it for the new installation. The floor will be done last so that's no bother. I'll get the team in to do the kitchen over the next few days. Working together, it will be completed in half the time. Is that okay with you?'

'The team? Oh, yeah sure. Whatever you think best.'

'It will take less time and be more economical in the end, plus you'll have your kitchen back quicker and I can move onto the next room.'

'Sounds like a great plan.'

'Ava?' Still kneeling on the floor, her nose close to the ground, she didn't look up. Distracted, she carefully manoeuvred a piece of the paper to avoid it tearing. Triumphant, she first heard, and then saw, Noah's boots shuffling back and forth.

'You were saying?' Sitting back, she gave him her full attention even though she was desperate to read the date on the sheet she'd just rescued.

Now he held up a piece of his own paper. 'I have an invoice.' He avoided making eye contact. 'Most people pay as we progress through the work. Um, it's easier for me too, you know cash flow and all that. And certainly, when the team is on the ground, I have to pay their wages for the work they perform.' A distinct red flush crept up his neck.

'Of course. Give it to me and I'll pay immediately. I'm so grateful for everything. You've been spot on with your plans and ideas. Your help and guidance have been invaluable.'

Plus having the company of Noah Hawthorn had been wonderful too, but she didn't say that. Instead, she held her hand out for the invoice.

Noah grimaced as Ava took the invoice and retrieved her phone out of her back pocket. 'It's a lot of money, Ava, I'm sorry. The stairs and stumps were expensive to replace and then there's labour … I've been here most days…'

Ava barely glanced at the sum before arranging the transfer on her mobile banking app. Who paid that sort of bill without even raising a sweat? Paying even half that amount would have him scouring his bank accounts and working out payment plans.

And here he was sweating on getting paid, but that was a different story.

'And there's a lot more to be paid yet.'

'Yep.'

'Geez, Ava, are you a closet millionaire?'

She put her phone back into her pocket. 'Don't be silly, of course not.'

'It's just that I haven't seen you working since you arrived in

Bellethorpe, and you're spending a lot on the house…' Noah managed to hold back the other words he wanted to utter this time, but he was curious how she could afford the significant renovations. Nothing like reality to douse those burgeoning flames still flickering low in his groin.

She weighed him up with a glance. 'It's not any of your business.'

'No, it's not. You're right. But I'm pumping a lot of time and effort into this place and I need your reassurance that I'll be paid. I can't afford for the project to go bust.' Challenging her was safe territory, way more comfortable than the uncontrollable desire of moments before. So, even if he wanted to stop, he wouldn't; he needed to know.

She sat back with a thump and a myriad of emotions ran across her face. He sat back, too. Had he unintentionally touched upon something? He knew nothing about this woman, where she came from, who she was. Despite telling his brain not to be stupid, it went off on tangents, flying a little out of control with ideas.

'I saved some money before I moved home. It's enough, please trust me. You'll get paid for the work you're doing, I promise.'

'You sure must have saved a lot.' Gosh, it must be nice not to have financial worries.

'What do you mean? If you need some help, I can give you a loan.'

Oops, damn it, did he say that out loud? 'What? No. I would never accept a loan from you.'

'Why? Because I'm a woman?'

He rose, paced back and forth. 'No, I mean, yes, no. I just have a few bills with the lawyer's fees…'

'Oh, Noah. I'm sorry, I haven't asked how you went.' Rushing to get up, her legs cramped and she stumbled. He reached his hand out to help but she ignored it. 'How did it go?'

Ava's brow furrowed and her beautiful, moist, pink lips closed into a straight line. The pain he kept buried, now sat like a hard lump in his chest. It hurt. 'It was to be expected at this stage. I was stupidly hoping for a miracle. Emily remains living in Brisbane for the moment and I see her twice a month and can telephone whenever I want.'

'Twice a month?' her words were a whisper. 'That can hardly be in Emily's best interest…but that's not the end, right? There's still hope?'

He wouldn't meet her eye. 'Oh, yeah, of course. I won't give up.'

Her lips were a hair's breadth away. Her scent of sweat mixed in with dirt and the tiniest hint of strawberry. Did she taste like strawberry? A rush of heat passed through him and his self-control slipped once more. He wasn't sure he could hold back anymore, didn't want to. Placing one hand to her waist, he rubbed his thumb over the bare skin revealed between her shirt and shorts.

Oh…the feel of her. Her silky-smooth skin. He sought out her eyes and found them smouldering in his direction. That was the encouragement he needed and he took another step forwards until their bodies touched. It took all Noah's control not to groan as her soft breasts pressed against his chest. He rested one hand at the nape of her neck, kissed her throat and behind her ear, rolling his kisses down to the hollow of her neck, around and up along her collar bone until their mouths crushed together. She tasted exquisite, just like he'd imagined. His hand moved to her lower back. Their teeth clashed and he slipped his tongue in and out, desiring to taste all of her just as he'd craved. Shifting her head to another angle, they caught their breath but then reached for each other again. Cupping her bottom, he fondled the soft flesh through the barely-there cotton. He wanted to keep pressing against her, feeling her skin, breathing in her smell, touching every part of her.

'Mumma! I'm hungry!'

The voice preceded Ish running into the room. 'Wow, this looks so different. Can I have a banana?'

They jolted apart and stood stock-still.

'Sure, help yourself,' Ava said but her eyes remained glued to Noah's. Their chests heaved in unison.

Noah turned and left the room.

CHAPTER
Sixteen

IN 1919, the horse, Artilleryman won the Melbourne Cup and the treaty of Versailles was signed ending World War 1.

Ava sat in the dim spare room reading the pages of the broadsheets spread out in front of her. Quite metropolitan for its time, the local paper, *The Bellethorpe Times* had covered both international and local news in the early twentieth century. A photograph of the prize-winning cake from the 1919 Brisbane Exhibition took pride of place on the first page. When they had lived in Bellethorpe before the move south, Mum and Dad had taken them to the Ekka, as it was known. She and Charlie had been most excited about the sample bags with their treats and the Ferris wheel ride they'd been allowed to go on twice.

Ava didn't read every article in entirety but skimmed the contents out of interest, taking care not to damage the fragile pages. She had gently wiped over each page with a dust cloth and laid them flat one atop the other and place them under a heavy, framed painting. The spare room would be their safe place until the papers found a permanent home elsewhere. Even the few items she'd found in this house would double the collection at the history centre. The local museum could be a better option and she mulled over how she could help. A project for another day, but until then, these items were safe here.

Touching her fingertips to her lips, her nerve endings tingled and she thought of Noah. Their gentle and sweet kiss had deepened in urgency quickly. Was Noah's need as great as hers? She'd surprised herself by wanting more, seeking their kiss to continue. Her body still ached for his touch. What would have happened if Ish hadn't interrupted? Yes, she wanted the kiss but had she lost her mind?

Inviting a relationship would be disastrous. How could she build the foundations of anything? For a start she was still married and Henry didn't know where she was. No one in this town knew she was living a life of subterfuge; let alone poor Noah. Any moment she expected Henry to arrive and then what…He'd haul them back to where he thought they belonged, wouldn't he? No questions, no explanations. Despite the love they'd shared there would only be repercussions and retributions. Regardless of what her husband might wish to do to her, she'd never allow Ismail's future to be compromised. He could not grow up in the strict regime that his father stood for. That was not negotiable and she'd do anything to avoid that. Wracked with guilt because of the life she was living, Ava knew in her heart that telling Noah the truth could be fatal for both of them.

There was so much to worry about. The money she'd transferred to Noah and his discomfort. He seemed to think she was wealthy, and she guessed she had given him that impression, but her insides had been squirming as she'd made the transfer. Reluctantly she left the newspapers, retrieved her laptop and gazed out the window at a blazing orange sky while it powered on.

She pulled her gaze away and logged on. It was as she suspected. Her funds were dwindling. The move, the house, the renovations had made a massive dent. She needed to find a job but hadn't planned on returning to work yet. She really wanted to finish the house first.

Closing the laptop, she went to the old timber bureau she'd picked up at a garage sale and slid open a drawer at the bottom. From the front the timber appeared to be a decorated panel, but it was deceptive. Inside was a small secret, compartment. Large enough to hide her ring. Pulling it out of the case, her heart hitched as it always did when she looked at the sparkly gem. She'd finally adjusted to not wearing it and her fingers didn't wander to that bare spot anymore. But ...the ring remained special, was symbolic of all that she shared with Henry, of their love. A reminder of deliriously happy times, when they loved each other deeply and were a united front. Selling other items of her extensive jewellery collection hadn't been so painful. They were beautiful pieces acquired over time but did not hold her heart in its grips like the topaz ring. Together they'd chosen the band, the gold, the jewel and accompanying diamonds. It represented a time in their life that was full of promise.

But she was in charge of their future, had to do anything to secure it. Now faced with return to work sooner than intended, or an injection of much needed funds, she had to put her sentimentality to rest.

But how?

Her gaze returned to the setting sun and the vista over her lands as she contemplated. She caught sight of Clive's house. Clive! Yes, he'd help, she could trust him. And honestly, what other options did she have?

Now the strong orange glow of the sun had muted to pink and amber. Ava checked Ish was still playing with the dogs in the lower paddock and walked quickly to the fence before she lost her nerve.

Ducking between the palings and moving past the horse stables, Ava approached Clive's house for the first time. The out-of-place dish on his roof sat on what was otherwise quite a nondescript low-set brick house. Not at all country-traditional or farm-like.

She rapped on the door still able to hear Ish's giggling on the breeze. Clive opened and he immediately stepped back in surprise, glanced behind him and appeared flustered. Was it that surprising that a neighbour should visit? Perhaps his wife was here too and she'd interrupted? Didn't people drop in unannounced in the country? She could trust Clive couldn't she or was this a mistake? Too late now.

'Ava, hello, how are you?' His tone was friendly enough but not his usual joyful self. He remained half-hidden behind the open door.

'Hi Clive. Sorry to bother you. I have a favour and hope you can help.'

'Is everything okay?'

'Um, yes, of course. I just want some advice.'

He nodded, seemingly reassured.

'I would like to sell something. Would you be able to recommend somewhere?'

'What sort of thing?'

'This ring.' She tugged it out of her pocket and held it up. Clive's eyebrows arched.

'Yeah, I know. Can you advise me of anywhere around here?'

Clive glanced behind him again before stepping out and shutting the door, double checking it was closed. Odd...maybe his wife was asleep?

He took the ring and examined it. 'It's beautiful.'

'Yes, it was very special to me.' She caught herself then, laughed out her nerves. 'But very unsuitable for country living.'

'Sure. There aren't any places in town where you could sell this, but there would be in Brisbane. Are you heading to the city anytime soon?'

Ava shook her head, avoided his eye.

'I can make some enquiries next week when I'm back at work if you'd like?'

'That would be great, Clive, thank you, I'm grateful. I'm not planning on heading to Brisbane anytime soon,' and she returned the ring to her pocket.

'I'll come back to you as soon as I can. Oh, and Ava, have you heard from the uni? They said they replied.'

'Oh, I haven't checked my emails. I'll do that straight away.'

'I hope it's good news. Cheerio!'

At the fence Ava glanced back. Clive remained at his door before slipping back inside after a brief wave.

Should she read anything into that interaction? Clive was always friendly and happy to chat. She was being silly; she had no reason to doubt Clive. Perhaps like her, he was having a bad day? He'd been nothing but reliable, good company and had given her a sense of protection out here on her isolated property. She shut down her intuition that something felt off.

After their last chat she'd written a letter to the university attaching photographs and setting out what she thought was significant information on her finds. Ever so briefly she'd forgotten about it, but now her tummy bubbled with excitement. What would they think?

Before retrieving her laptop again, she checked on Ish. In the dying remnants of the day, he ran around the spacious yard, a smile on his face, playing with the dogs. Moving here *had* changed their lives. She had to keep to the plan, had to pull it off. She felt for the ring in her pocket. Giving it up was a small price to pay.

Ish squealed with delight as Daisy performed a trick at his command. He slept well here since they had been in the country. London, the short stop they'd made after fleeing Egypt, had been fraught with uncertainty, but here, with his active outdoor lifestyle and constant stimulation, he zonked out most nights. Ava hoped that meant he was adjusting to their new life well.

Opening her emails, she clicked on the message from the university. Holding her breath, she read the content and smiled. Yes, they were interested in seeing her finds. They agreed with her suspicion that they might be specimens of opalised fossils. And she was right about the pine cone! Not bad for an archaeologist with no experience in these sorts of digs.

Thank you, Ms Montgomery, for informing us of this discovery. We are keen to see the items in real life and suggest travelling up to your property next week. It is also important to visit because, as you would appreciate, often there are more significant finds on the site or its surrounds, where samples are found. With any luck, this might be a great new discovery. If you could please reply with confirmation that our suggested arrangements are suitable and provide us with your address.

Great new discovery! This response was better than she'd expected. Her gaze instantly went outside to the site.

Shooting off confirmation, Ava scanned the remainder of her inbox. Given it was a new address, there was little spam and the mailbox wasn't congested yet. Scrolling, she paused on one message. An unfamiliar name and handle. Her heart immediately jumped into her throat. Could be random? With fingers hovering, she clicked it open.

Jumping up, her laptop crashed to the floor and the lid banged shut. She raced to the back door and screamed. 'Ish! Ish!'

She ran to the spare room and raced over to the curtains and shut them. Went to the empty kitchen and pulled down the blinds, and then the same with the remaining rooms. The back sliding door didn't have any coverings to block out prying eyes. Instead, she turned off the lights to reduce visibility.

An owl hooted outside, and she jumped. Twigs scraped on the new Colourbond steel roof and guttering. With alarming volume, every sound crept its way into her head and rather than enjoying the normal bush orchestra, these noises taunted her. Had she locked the gate? Unable to remember, she resisted the urge to race down the long drive. She double checked that each window was bolted and the front and back door.

Ish scurried up the back steps. She pulled him into her chest and held him hard and close before dragging him inside. Bless her child that didn't ask any questions. Ava slammed the glass panel and locked the door. Only when she was satisfied someone couldn't infiltrate the house, she sat tensely with Ish by her side on the couch.

She dragged in a breath and put a hand to her chest. Could someone locate your whereabouts from an email address? She found her phone in between the cushions and was about to Google the question. What if her phone was hacked? Or traced? Or bugged? Whatever the appropriate description was. Henry had both the resources and skill to do that. It was a new phone she reasoned and had not been in her possession when she'd fled. So, it couldn't have been tampered with, right? But what about the email? How did he get it? Nothing made sense. She had been so careful. Except … she put the phone down.

She'd given her email to Clive and the university, two strangers. Clive assured her it'd be private and the university, why would they pass her details to her husband? How would any of these people even know her husband? Nothing made sense.

But still the fact remained that she had received an email from

Henry to an address that she'd only recently set up and barely used. A new address with a cryptic handle.

Ava couldn't answer those questions right now. She had to read the email, even though her lunch now burned her throat. Turning towards their makeshift kitchen, she turned the kettle on, but gagged at the thought of the fragrant chai going down her throat.

Flicking off the switch, she picked up the kettle and dumped it back down on the bench. Okay, no tea. Racing back into the living room, she put on the television for Ish. Turning to him, the boy sat rigid, silent tears streaming down his cheeks. 'Oh, Ish, honey.' She sat down and embraced him. They sat like that silently together for a short while. 'How about some time watching the Disney channel?' Thank goodness she'd invested in the streaming service. Just for times like this. For times when she couldn't get her thoughts straight and she needed Ish occupied and safe, and most importantly, distracted. The blaring music of Guardians of the Galaxy boomed out and spiked her adrenalin even more.

Giving him the remote she collected her computer from the floor and sat at the dining room table. She puffed up her cheeks with air and blew out a deep breath as she flipped the lid. Her sweaty hands made the top slip and shut with a bang. Finally open, the screen flashed, then went dark as she waited too long to punch in her code. If she clicked on the email, would that send him anything? Her location?

The nightmare was starting; she'd been foolish. She'd taken for granted that they would be safe in this sleepy back hollow of a town. And this is what happened when you let your guard down. What an idiot, she'd been

Dear Ava. Polite, formal. Closing her eyes, she took a couple of deep breaths not sure she could read the words.

Disappointment

Surprise

Deception

The words jumped out at her in a jumble. He'd signed off with Hamid. Not long after their relocation to Egypt, he'd reverted to his formal family name instead of the Henry she'd once known and loved.

I could have offered you a wonderful life. You just needed to adapt and be

happy in the luxurious circumstances I provided for you. We could have been a family. Where are you? When can I see my son? Are you returning?

Did that mean he wasn't aware of her location? She wanted desperately to believe it. When a man tells many lies, how can you possibly decipher the truth? Ava slammed the lid shut. What the hell was she going to do now?

CHAPTER
Seventeen

AVA ROLLED OVER, desperate to clutch even one minute's more sleep. After last night's shock, she hadn't slept a wink. Ridiculous, she knew, but in the darkness of those early hours, her mind played tricks and everything became distorted; every sound became an intruder.

Now it must be a new day—not because the sun came through her curtains, she'd shut them so tight that wasn't possible—but Noah had arrived and she could hear male voices talking and joking, with the clink of tools being emptied out of trays. He wasn't alone. He had the team with him to install the kitchen. Just as they'd discussed. Before they'd kissed of course. Before her husband had made contact. Ish's soft feet thumped down the hall and she heard the back sliding door open, the dogs bark and the outside world enter. Pulling up the doona, she covered her head.

Could she stay in bed all day? Not enter the real world, even for just a short time?

Noah's voice bellowed. 'Howdy Duke and Daisy and who is this? Flopsy, Mopsy and Cottontail?' Her lips curled into a smile, that was funny and they would have been great dog names. But within moments, her mouth dropped, reality crashing back down. Ish laughed in reply and the voices receded as they moved through the house.

Throwing off the cover with a dramatic sigh, Ava reluctantly rose and dressed. With her heart beating like a drum, she entered the kitchen. A group of men worked on various tasks and already, one cabinet was in.

Noah spotted her and handed over a take-away coffee. 'Morning.' His greeting was a husky whisper and despite her frazzled nerves, the sound resonated deep within causing little shock waves to radiate outwards and ripple along her skin. He stood in front of her and kept eye contact despite the noise around them. His presence, his voice, his close proximity had her heart galloping.

'Thank you.' She accepted the drink with their eyes focused only on each other. A layer of mist formed and she blinked. *These coffees… Noah…him…here…*

The weight of this simple and kind gesture after her restless and stressful night was too much.

Alex Burgess approached, the man she'd met on her first day. 'Hey, Ava. Nice to see you again. We'll have this kitchen in as fast as we can and be outta your hair.'

Thankfully he didn't wait for a reply as it appeared she'd lost any ability to form words. Instead, she offered a tight smile to his departing back. Her focus remained on Noah. His stubble was longer today, and she was so close she could see where each hair grew. If they kissed right now, she'd feel that roughness against her cheek. He took a sip of coffee. And she'd taste his latte.

Noah recovered first and introduced the rest of the crew. The small kitchen space was crowded, a radio was playing loudly and the some of the men were singing along.

The room closed in around Ava and she struggled to catch her breath. Her chest tightened. She got out of the crowded room and the relief was instant.

'Ish!' He dragged himself in from the deck with the puppies in tow. His hair was sleep-tousled and his face still creased with sleep. Her eyes filled with tears that she batted away. He'd been quieter since last night. He knew something was up, but he didn't ask. 'Have you fed the chooks?' She ruffled his hair as he got close but the suffocating feeling continued; it clawed at her neck. She needed to get out, away.

'I might head back to the creek this morning. Will you come?'

Ish looked around and back to her. 'Mumma, can I stay here and watch the builders? I can look after Daisy and the pups.'

'You might be in the way. They've got a fair bit of work to do today.' His face crumpled. Was he missing male company? Was he missing his father? Is that why he wanted to stay? Henry had spent little quality time with him, so that would surprise her. Should he stay? With her nerves well and truly frazzled, it might be for the best. But would he be okay? There was a team of strong capable men in her kitchen but would they keep him safe?

Ava was torn. 'Noah?' He was in the middle of lifting a cabinet and balancing it while another fellow connected it to the far wall. She waited until he'd finished and he wandered over. 'If I go for a ride and Duke stays here at the house, will you keep an eye on him?'

'Of course, sure.'

He must have gauged her uncertainty. 'Honestly, Ava, go. You get such little time to yourself. Go and we'll keep him busy. I'll find a little project for him. Who knows, he might like building with his hands.'

'He isn't allowed to leave the house and must stay near your crew, right?'

He looked at her strangely. Yes, it sounded stupid and honestly, she was losing her mind with worry and uncertainty and craziness. She wanted what was best for them and to keep them safe but if she didn't get out, she might just self-implode.

'Yeah, of course. Otis is here too, and he can be in charge.'

A dog. That wasn't exactly the reassurance she needed. 'I'm going down to the most far paddock. You have my number, ring me and I can be back in a jiffy.' Noah stayed still as if there was further conversation to be had; Ava sensed he wanted to say more, or perhaps with his twitching fingers, maybe he wanted to do something else. A shiver raced up her spine.

Not here. Not now.

Ava rode Honey too fast trying to out chase the thoughts in her head and the fear that clutched her throat. A calm of sorts descended once she reached the pond. It always had that effect on her, and today she was grateful. The peaceful serenity of the bush, the majestic bird call and the crackle of twigs from low-lying animals you never saw, only heard.

Today she chose the far side, a place she hadn't explored yet. The kitchen had been a delight with its French and WW1 finds, but she'd been disappointed it hadn't heralded more. Would she be any luckier here today?

Setting out a cloth and lining up her tools, it felt familiar, normal when the outside world seemed to be closing in. But ironically, it wasn't, was it? Familiar in her previous life. Not her married life. Henry had made all the promises in the world about her career and her ambitions but had reneged the moment they'd moved from London to Cairo. Promises of running her own department in the Cairo Museum —he had contacts—had never come to fruition. To appease her, he'd put her in charge of a home museum, within palace walls which was nothing but a collection of the family riches.

But this was hers alone. She settled into a rhythm fossicking through the dirt, pebbles, rocks and granules of sand. Time passed and she didn't notice. Her phone didn't ring, so Ish was okay.

The orange orb of a sun sat high in the sky, well above the trees. Ava adjusted her broad-brimmed hat to ensure it covered her neck from the glare of the rays and rolled down the long sleeves she wore. She drank greedily from her water bottle. A few droplets spilled onto a patch of dirt revealing a pattern. Wiping her chin, she poured a thin stream of water onto the spot. Touching it with her finger, it was hard, slightly raised and scaly. With her brush, she removed the top layer of dirt and dust, and a shape became evident.

Ava brushed her hands down her pants, jumped up and surveyed from height. A distinct curved shell? Sitting back on her heels, she brushed quicker, frantic to discover more. It was definitely a shell! Brushing gently but swiftly, her wrist cramped but she wouldn't stop. It was flat on top, not concave and around thirty centimetres in size. Pulling out her phone she captured shots from each angle. Brushing more towards the top, it appeared there might be more. Then she rushed to the rear. It was an animal, of that, she was sure. It had a prehistoric appearance. But surely not? It couldn't be.

This find had to be shared. Busting to tell someone, she ripped out her phone. With fumbling fingers, she rang Noah's number.

'Noah, I'm fine. Everything is okay. Oh, is he? That's great, I bet he's loved helping. But, Noah, I need to show you something, can you come down into the bush? There's a track, easy to find. Yep, now. It's important. Okay, see you soon. No, leave Duke with Alex if he's happy.'

For the moment, her fear disappeared and was replaced with unbridled excitement.

One day a black-haired beauty came to town
    Causing one man's heart to flutter when she was around
    Confusion, passion, desire and lust
    All make this man want to, once more, trust
    But can he open his heart and let her in
    Or choose to remain alone, even though she's under his skin.

Noah recited the poem he'd written last night after that moment with Ava. He drove the ute down over the green paddocks, leaving tyre tracks in the soft grass. Better to be quick even though Ava had assured him nothing was wrong. What could possibly be so important down here?

Pulling up in a small clearing, it was a short walk, following the path she said he'd find. Arriving, Ava had her back to him, kneeling with one knee in the dirt and carefully considering something.

'Ava? Are you okay?'

She clutched her hand to her chest in fright and leapt to her feet.

'Noah! Come and look at this.' Her hand gestured towards the spot where she knelt. He stood next to her and glanced at the dirt. Small mounds were off to the sides, heaped around what appeared to be a circle of sorts. Noah twisted his head to look at Ava and her expression was open, hopeful, waiting. 'Well?' Her hands rested on her hips.

Glancing down once more, he saw a pattern, sort of rectangle with rounded edges with smaller square shaped markings inside. A fish? An animal? Ava bounced on her toes. He gave up.

'I don't know!' He held his palms up.

'Urgh! It's a turtle shell, well I'm ninety-five percent sure it's a turtle shell. It's opalised like the other finds I've made. These are parts of the shell, see here.' She delineated those markings. 'The colour!'

'What? No way, I can see it now that you point it out! But wait, did you say other finds? You've found other stuff, things, that look like this?'

Her hand clutched his elbow. 'Yes. That's right.' Her tone lowered and she became more serious.

Noah turned back to the turtle. 'But it doesn't look like a normal, cute turtle, hey, it's not a dinosaur turtle, is it?' He didn't even know if that was a thing.

Frowning, she stood still for the first time since his arrival. 'Oh, I don't think so. Do you think so?'

He laughed then, deep from his belly. 'You're the archaeologist! I don't know.'

She joined in and her eyes sparkled with mirth, losing the seriousness of moments before. 'Nah, maybe, I don't know either. But I think we can agree it's old. A fossil for sure. The remains of an animal preserved in rock. As I understand it has turned to opal because it's been preserved in silica. I've been digging around here and there are lots of little objects that are beautifully coloured. I'm not sure what they are. But, I think, it could be a significant find. It's incredible. Obviously, turtles are sea creatures so what does that mean? Was this once ocean? Or did it become stranded here after a weather event? I don't know, or maybe a turtle that lives in ponds!'

Ava walked over to her bag on the ground and brought over a collection of other similarly coloured items. To him they simply looked like pretty rocks. 'You think these are fossils, as in were once a plant or an animal, a living thing?'

'Yep, definitely.' Her excitement was childlike.

He hadn't seen her like this before, she was always so serious and pensive and contained.

'Not entire creatures, these are parts of, or pieces of preserved fossils. Some of the shells and pinecones might be whole,' she said.

'Wow!'

'Yes, wow. And there's some connection to the house, I just haven't worked that bit out yet. There are pebbles, fossils throughout the house, those ones on the back deck, for example. Peter from the antique store said the previous owner made silver jewellery. I'm convinced one piece I found is jewellery with the remnants of silver that's worked away. He might have found these thinking they were opals and made them into jewellery.'

'The old place has quite the history, then.'

'Yes, it sure does.' Ava couldn't stop smiling.

'Honestly, this is incredible. Imagine how many people have traipsed over this land and never seen a thing. Never suspected something of such importance lurking just beneath the surface.'

Ava stared at him then, deep down into his soul so that he could feel her energy and warmth as if it was beams lighting him up from the inside. She contemplated him, but he wasn't sure what for.

'Thank you,' she finally said. 'Thank you for listening. For not making light of it, for not making fun of my excitement or dismissing what I've found as pointless or as belonging in the past. Or' —she pointed her gaze in the other direction, looking out over the hills and landscape— 'as something that a woman shouldn't be interested in or pursue. Preserving history is important to me. It always has been.'

He knew she wasn't simply referring to these finds. He'd reacted this way because it was important to her. It didn't mean much to him … unless it was important to her.

'From the moment I met you, it was obvious that restoring the house properly and with elegance and justice to the time period was the right thing to do, and therefore that's what you'd do. You care so deeply about everything: Duke, the dogs, the horses, local history and the relics you've found in the house.' Now he was veering wildly off course and this wasn't just about her passion for her job.

'What now?' he asked wanting to have his feet firmly back in safe territory. What had gotten into him?

'Okay.' Ava focused too, back into the present. 'I have some experienced archaeologists coming out to confer with me, but in the meantime, I need to protect this specimen. Can you help me do that?'

'You mean like a shelter or cover or something?'

'Yeah.'

'I have a marquee that I use if I'm working outside or for backyard barbeques, will that do?'

'Oh, yeah, that'd be awesome. Is it pretty big?'

'Yep, it'll cover this entire space with room to move.'

Noah retrieved it from the tray of the truck and they worked silently to construct the cover. Ava considered their handiwork. 'I don't want to leave. It's like having a newborn baby and not wanting to be parted.'

Placing a hand on her shoulder, he said, 'It'll be fine. It's your land for starters and no one comes out here. I've never seen this place before and I've pretty much seen every square inch of Bellethorpe.'

'I've trumped you, then.' They exchanged grins.

'Let's get back.'

'Has Duke been okay?'

'He's been a champ. Loved getting dusty and dirty with the boys.'

CHAPTER
Eighteen

BACK AT THE HOUSE, Noah spoke to his team, checked on their progress and returned to the deck.

'The kitchen looks amazing so far,' Ava commented, admiring the work.

'It's coming up nicely. Those Tassie oak timber doors and benchtops were a great idea. I probably wouldn't have chosen them myself, but they work.'

'Thanks. Glad you like them.' Ava's fingers itched to start recording her findings of the fossil and arranging her photographs.

'I have another idea.'

Placing her pens and papers down on the deck table, she said, 'Go on.'

'We haven't spoken any more about the sheds. Seeing you today, your excitement, all this stuff you're gathering and is covering your table. You need a workspace. Remember we talked about it before?' Noah walked to the edge of the deck where they had a clear view of the large, multiple-bay sheds that sat to the left of the house.

'Oh, yes! I'd forgotten.' Emotion bubbled under the fine layers of her skin. 'There's still so much to do in the house...' She tore her gaze away from him, looking longingly at the currently ugly galvanised iron sheds in a pale shade of green. Her own workspace! A dream come true.

'One of those bays could be to sort your, um, specimens, another could be a desk, you could set it up as an office with cabinets, shelves, whatever you need. We can make it comfortable with air-conditioning and heating, flooring too. Plenty of room for your boxes and equipment or, if you'd rather, it can remain a car parking bay. What do you think?'

'You'd do that for me?'

Her eyes flicked back, and Noah's face had blanched of colour. Ava laughed.

'I didn't mean for free! Of course, I'll pay you but I'm really touched you thought of it especially for me.'

'No, I didn't think that…of course, not.' He tugged at the collar of his polo.

'You did!' She touched his arm; her hand landing on his bicep, bulging and strong, and then quickly removed it.

'It's okay. I love your idea. Do I have a key for those roller doors?'

'Yep, for sure,' and Noah held up a key.

'Should we look? I have no idea what's in there.' Ava clasped her hands together to avoid hugging him in excitement and thanks. She skipped beside him as they walked to the sheds instead.

The building was tall, as high as the roof of the house. Perfect for tall equipment, ladders, high shelves. Only a few jostles and Noah had the first door open. The other two sprung open quickly allowing the daylight to flood the space.

Empty, except for shelving on three walls that were packed with boxes and what looked like garden equipment and other household paraphernalia. With the list of her to-do-jobs long, she hadn't made it out here yet.

Surprisingly, she'd expected something, anything, particularly for a property of this size. A rusted old car, perhaps? A tractor?

'Have a look at this.' Noah shouted.

Yes! She thrummed with the excitement of a possible discovery.

'What is it?'

'I think it's a toy fire engine.'

'Wow, yes you might be right.' The colour had almost disappeared, the rims bare where rubber tyres once sat and a tarnished bell lay on the ground next to it.

'How cute!'

Noah surveyed the area. 'This is going to be easy, given it's pretty much an empty shell; needs a good clean out, though.'

'Let's get started, I'll help.'

He scooted past her, his bare arms brushing hers. Ava let him pass and waited. Noah collected the heap of metal that was the old fire truck and hauled it outside, his muscles bulged in his arms and revealed in his dark green *Bellethorpe Builders* shirt. Through the thin cotton the knotted cords of his back were on display.

Oh boy, her body temperature catapulted. Maybe helping wasn't such a great idea? Ava Montgomery needed to be a very safe distance away from Noah Hawthorn. Either that or the rest of the day would be torture.

Noah sang out to Taylor, one of the juniors on his team to help and together they hauled out the contents of those shelves. The team of two men carried the stuff outside the shed and it was Ava's discretion whether it was tossed straight into the skip or kept.

While she professed to love history, the previous owner's years of tax returns went, along with a box of Tupperware lids, old treasured fluffy toys beyond repair and mouldy and irretrievable kid's toys. She rescued some Lego and Meccano. She smiled at the tattered box of Meccano pieces, remembering the phase Charlie went through obsessed with the building toy. Perhaps Ish would discover a love for it, like his uncle?

Taylor, wandered back to the kitchen after the job was done and Noah cleaned the space with a high-pressured hose.

Only one box remained. It was a heavy plastic tub and Ava couldn't shift it. Ripping off the lid, the box exploded with bolts of blue and green and silver. With wide eyes, she gasped and a shiver ran down her back.

An entire box of opals. More pieces of jewellery, intact this time. A band of thick silver nursed a square opal, not perfectly smooth, but as though it had been chosen for the unsymmetrical and less than perfect appearance. One swipe across it with her finger and the colours sparkled once more. Surely it wouldn't fit? Ava placed it onto her right-hand ring finger anyway. With the heat of the day and her slightly swollen fingers, it sat in place and didn't slip.

Maybe this one would be worth something and she could keep her ring? It was too late, anyway. As promised, Clive had told her of a place where she could sell her ring and she'd gotten rid of it. There couldn't be any comparison, her engagement ring had been worth *a lot*. There was no way this ring could match the value. Forget about it … she concentrated on her box of discovery.

Rummaging through the items, Ava extracted shells, and an entire range of objects that she surmised could be teeth, plants and other animal life.

Holy shit.

She slumped back on her bottom. The heat of the sun bit her neck, flies buzzed around her ears, a kangaroo bounced away and to her left, a kookaburra made its distinct call. Soft fur rubbed at her arm and Dolly puppy vied for her attention. She bundled the dog up, cuddled it close to her neck, and inhaled its scent. 'Look at this.' She put the puppy's face up close to her finds. 'Dolly, this place is special. And I need to keep us here, safe.' There hadn't been any further emails from her husband, thank goodness.

She stole a glance at Noah then, only to see more rippled muscles and looked away. 'It might just heal us all, Dolly. What do you think about that, huh, girl? Wouldn't that be something?' Dolly wriggled out of her grasp and she set the dog back down and it wandered away on its four adorable little stumps for legs and cute waddle.

A shadow fell across her. 'You've done it again, haven't you?'

'Done what?'

'You've found something else in this place, haven't you?'

'Yes.' Her face creased into a sudden smile.

'Want me to lift this box onto the deck for you?'

'Yes, please.' Her smile turned coquettish and shy.

'Are you going to spend tonight trawling through your box of treasures?'

'Probably. But I thought I might put on a barbeque for the boys first. Do you think they'd appreciate that as a thank you for their hard work today?'

'I think they'd love that and if you throw in a beer, they'd like it even more.'

'Hey, mate. What's up?' Noah answered the call on Bluetooth in his car on the first ring. Brady was a father in his support group; it must be important.

'Hey, Noah.' The male voice rang out loud through the car speakers, but he was alone travelling early to Brisbane. 'Elisha won't let me attend the kid's first day of school.' No pleasantries: it was often like this. These blokes weren't friends, they had common problems.

'It does fall on her day, but that's not the point, right? It's a special event and it shouldn't matter who the kids are with, right?'

Noah's breakfast churned in his belly. More conflict, but at least this time it wasn't his. His job now was to listen to Brady and help, if necessary.

'Agreed, mate. It's a neutral location.' Noah outlined the first day events he'd already miss: breakfast, shining shoes, plaits in the hair and first photo.

There was silence for a moment as Brady digested the information. 'Yeah, well, that other stuff is Elisha's field anyway, I still can't master plaits. But I want to see them at school.'

'Is she saying you can't see the kids at all?'

'Yep.'

Noah winced. But then with enormous clarity, the image of Ava popped into Noah's mind and her comment about the best interests of the child. Yeah, and he agreed. It was the best interests of Brady's kids that both parents were present on the first day of school. That was common sense, right? Would the social worker he was seeing today for these court ordered family report interviews concur?

Noah asked about the reasons his wife was refusing.

Brady groaned. 'She's pissed off at me, man because I've been late twice returning the kids during my visits and now, she won't agree to anything. You know how it is, and then she punishes me by holding time back.'

With Ava's salient words echoing, he tossed around different ideas with Brady. Noah suggested asking Elisha how best it would work for her. Brady arced up. He didn't want to negotiate. Noah reasoned with him—negotiate or not see the kids. Brady took some persuading but eventually agreed and to let him know how he went.

Noah thought Brady hung up mildly placated; he felt satisfied he'd helped.

He was halfway now on his trip and needed a break. Spotting a servo with café attached, he'd refuel, have a toilet break and grab a coffee.

With Ava on his mind, he texted her to advise that he wouldn't be working at her place today. Usually, he'd leave it at that. But he went further and told her why and pressed send before he could prevaricate.

She replied immediately, sending him best wishes. It buoyed him for the day ahead. With caffeine in his veins and the music blaring, he hoped it was enough. Trouble was it felt like he was roaring towards his fate and he was in the hands of the gods, and Noah wasn't a religious man.

CHAPTER
Nineteen

AVA HEARD the rumble of Noah's ute on the drive and her tummy did a funny flip-flop. Ever since he'd texted to say he was dropping in on his way back from Brisbane, she'd been a bundle of nerves. Luckily she'd had the team from the university here to distract her.

It was impossible to deny her growing attraction to him any longer. It had snuck up on her, slowly, and now every time she thought of him, an exquisite sensation skittered down her spine and out to her extremities and everywhere in between until her body buzzed. She walked lighter and often forgot what she was doing because her thoughts seemed to always drift to him. All the hours they'd spent together had transformed their relationship into something more than friendship. Noah was now a man she desperately looked forward to not only seeing, but also sharing her news with. She felt his absence keenly. Was it only because she didn't have any friends in Bellethorpe? Maybe, but Ava didn't think so.

And here he was. Dressed for a day in the city with clean, dark blue jeans and a black short-sleeved collared polo. The short stubble she'd grown to love remained but his hands and nails were clean and his shoes polished. Her heart sank a little, his appearance was a reminder of what he'd done today to keep alive his hope of having Emily return home.

Taking the steps two at a time, he stood in front of her. His gaze raked her face, his eyes tender and soft. Had he missed her, too? Was the attraction mutual? Her lips parted to ask him. But when his eyes lowered to her mouth and his tongue swiped across his own dry lips, the thrum of her body turned into heat.

He stepped closer and their lips met. His hot breath tantalised her and she was transfixed to the spot as if he was providing her with the air she needed to breathe. One hand was placed gently to her lower back and they connected, mouths parting, hungry, eager and desperate for each other. Her hands raked through his hair and their hips moved closer until she was snug between his legs. His lips trailed a line along her jaw and down her throat, across to her earlobe, his large capable hands cradling her face. Electric tingles pulsed through her … until the house shook from feet pounding up the back stairs.

Someone cleared their throat.

Noah jumped, the gulf between them suddenly great. Her lips remained parted when she turned and there were the two male archaeologists. One nudged the other with his elbow, a comical—you've been busted—grin spread across his features. Both were grubby, their long blue overalls with the insignia of the university on their breast, covered in dust.

She forced her mouth shut and rubbed her hands down the front of her pants.

'Sorry to interrupt, Ava. We're finished.'

Glancing at Noah, she noticed his frown.

'Noah, this is James and Matthew, the archaeologists from Brisbane. They arrived this morning and have been working all day. Guys, this is Noah.' The men shook hands. Ava filled the gaps of silence with her chatter. 'Noah is my builder; he's fixing this place up for me.'

'Oh, he does look very handy.' They both burst into laughter. At last, the corners of Noah's lips turned upwards into the tiniest of smiles.

'We'll go and clean up and then we can chat.'

'Okay, yes, I can't wait. Thank you.'

Noah busied himself unwrapping a large parcel at his feet. 'I found this today and thought you might like it.' He handed over a framed print of Nefertiti. The colouring was exaggerated with bold blues and golds more appropriate to the painted mask of Tutankhamun but it was beautiful. The Queen was depicted wearing her distinct head dress of a tall, straight-edged, flat blue crown. He'd remembered Nefertiti was one of her favourites! The one she drew her strength from. A warm glow flowed through her.

'It's gorgeous. Where did you find it?'

'I have no idea if it's authentic, but it was in an antique store next door to where the interviews were today, a place called New Farm. Very modern and fashionable suburb in Brisbane with lots of op shops and cute boutique stores. I thought you might like it in your new office space. It might inspire you.'

Tears blinded her eyes and her voice choked. 'I love it, it's perfect. Thank you.'

Noah used one finger to wipe away the moisture on her cheek before it reached her chin.

Before the moment was lost, Ava asked, 'How did you go today?'

Noah gazed at her, almost as if he couldn't concentrate enough to answer, his eyes darted to her mouth, then to her chest and back up. 'At times I thought it was going well. And then the social worker would ask, so, tell me Noah, if Emily is with you and you need to work, how are you going to manage childcare if she's not at school? Because if Emily lives in Brisbane, Lisa isn't working and can drop off and pick up each day and if not, she has her mother as additional support. Do you have anyone who can help you? And more about care routines and parenting styles...'

He looked down and away. 'It seems as if Emily's entire life is established in Brisbane. Lisa has her infrastructure and support network. I'm not sure I can battle successfully against that.' His voice was filled with pain.

'I would look after Emily anytime.'

'Thank you, I appreciate that. But I'm not sure that works for the official channels. Family is the preference, well, no I'm the preference but if not me or Lisa, grandparents are favoured. But my mum, while she's close, is old, you know, not really up to running around after an active six-year-old.'

Ava nodded, feeling glum for him.

'When is Duke seeing his father?'

The question was so out of the blue, Ava gawped for a moment before pulling herself together. 'I told you, he's overseas.'

'Yep, I understand, but doesn't he want to see him?'

'No, he doesn't.' Her words were firm and final, signalling the end of the conversation. They stared at each other as if holding a competition until Ava breathed a sigh of relief when James and Matthew came back.

'Noah, will you stay for dinner? James and Matthew are going to chat about the fossils. I get the feeling it's exciting.'

'I'd love to. Wine or beer?'

'Wine, please.'

Noah poured the drinks and she finalised dinner; it felt like a team effort. Everything they'd done recently seemed to draw them closer together.

Once settled at the table, Matthew clapped his hands together and then placed his hand to Paul's knee. Ava had worked out early in the day that they were a couple.

'Do you realise what's in your backyard?'

'No!' Ava put her drink down. 'That's exactly why I called in your expertise! My experience is in Egyptian and Sudanese artefacts at the British Museum.' Ava didn't feel the need to mention that the only dig sites she'd ventured onto were during her studies.

'Well, it was very wise you called for help. And we're grateful, sorry.' Paul nervous-giggled. 'The university is grateful you called on us.'

Ava threw up her hands. 'Just tell me!'

'We're so excited.' Their faces were ebullient 'Oh, yes, it's big, very big. Are you ready?'

'Yes!' She was just about popping out of her skin.

'It is a fossil of a horned turtle.'

Ava inched forward on her seat.

'They are extinct and from a family of land-dwelling animals that evolved during the time of the dinosaurs in Gondwana. They can be called meiolaniid and had horns in their heads, spikes on the back of their shell and a big club on their tail. This was like a set of armour to defend themselves against predators. It's old.'

'How old?'

'We don't know yet. We need our equipment and would have to do some testing before we can definitively advise. This is a reasonably intact fossil, but around it are opal specimens. They might be fragments of other turtle pieces but these are not complete and have become fossilised over time.'

'I've found many opalised fossils. Pine cones and shells are the most obvious but I'm guessing there could be teeth and plant life, as well.'

'I bet there is.' Matthew spoke now. 'We only focused on the turtle today but there would have to be other fossils. The site, it looks like it's previously been a dig site, is that you or someone else?'

'No, it is pretty much how I found it. I've dug around of course but been very careful to preserve the area and more recently I uncovered the turtle. But around the house, in the shed, there are loads of opals. I think the former owner assumed they were gems and didn't realise the significance of them being fossils. Again, I'm not sure, but he reportedly made silver jewellery and I've found a few pieces of that as well.'

And then she remembered. 'Oh, and here, this is one I found today.'

Out of nowhere James pulled on a head lamp and illuminated the ring on her hand. He held it to his face to examine it, turning her finger this way and that more closely.

'It's hard to tell, but I suspect each gem that appears to be an opal is actually a fossil.'

Ava sipped her wine and taking her lead, Noah refilled the glasses. He remained silent.

'Shit, this is huge.' Ava sat back in her chair.

'Sure is.'

'What does it mean exactly?' Noah finally asked.

'Let me give you a quick lesson,' James offered. 'These finds give us an insight into a different period of time; it's like a door to the past.

These aren't ordinary fossils; these are relics made of opal. They are of scientific interest and also very beautiful.'

'I don't understand. So, we have fossils and we have opals but we are talking about the same thing, right?'

Both men smiled at him. 'Yes, good question. Opals form in cavities within rocks. If the cavity is there because of a living thing, maybe a bone or plant, it's buried in the land before it turned to stone, then the opal can form a fossil replica of the object that was buried. A fossil is simply the remains of an ancient animal preserved in rock.'

'Or plant,' Ava intervened.

'Yes, or plant. Opalised fossils are similar, except they are preserved in silica. Most of the time fossils are preserved in minerals like agate, or limestone.'

'How does the silica get there?'

Ava revelled in the questions Noah asked. He was showing a real, intelligent interest.

'Another very good question. You sure you're not an archaeologist?' A pause for laughter. 'Usually from volcanoes. Opalisation can occur in two ways—firstly where the internal parts are not preserved and leaves an empty shell. Or secondly, the insides are preserved, leaving an entire specimen.'

'Do you have a whole turtle?'

'We haven't extracted it yet. Much detailed work required in that, it looks flat to me, what do you think, Matthew?'

'I'm hopeful, but most likely the way it's lying would indicate nothing inside is preserved. The shell might look different.'

No one asked her but Ava added, 'I don't think it's whole either.' And jumping up, she continued, 'and this is the tub I found today.' She pulled a few objects from the top after lifting off the lid.

James and Matthew sprang from their chairs and trawled through the container, exclaiming at each item they examined. 'These are incredibly beautiful. The colours! Noah, these will provide new information about our heritage and the evolution of our land. Matthew, are you aware of anywhere else that has these types of opalised fossils in Queensland? I know there are other states, but here?'

'Not sure.' He stood. 'But imagine if this is the first find. Here, and we are leading it. We need to call in the big guns at the university to formally register the find, secure some funding, establish a dig site, oh, and advise the press. This will go viral!'

James pulled out his phone.

'What are you doing?' Ava's tone had become high-pitched.

'Calling our contacts.'

Rougher than intended, Ava snatched his phone. Both men looked at her in surprise.

'Ava, this is bigger than us, this is huge, it is national. We need everyone involved and to tell the world!'

'No!'

'No!'

Noah simultaneously responded with an emphatic "no". She turned to him at the same time he faced her. Her eyes shot to her forehead while she spread her hands wide in confusion. He had the nerve to turn away, acting sheepish but her heart was already hammering in her chest. Holy shit, she hadn't thought this through.

Press?

International notoriety?

A dig site?

This was getting bigger by the minute and the safe haven she'd created, that she needed, wanted, was slipping away. Ish would be at risk. It was an impossible situation. And it was all her fault. Her desire to find out the truth of the find had led her here. And now she'd involved other people. Other people knew.

Back when she'd been building the courage to leave her life in Egypt, her reserve had become steely, ferocious in the way only a woman can become to save her child —the mother bear syndrome. Ava had risked everything to remove her son from an environment that was not in his best interests and to protect him and herself from a life that they had never agreed to be part of.

She would not jeopardise how far they'd come.

Like a suit of armour coming down, protecting her and turning her heart to stone, she needed to regain control. So often, these things were about control and she needed to be in charge.

Sitting up tall, she prepared herself. She'd done this before; she could do it again. 'This is my private land. Nothing happens here without my permission. There will be no contact with the press, nor outside parties about what we've found here. You've been invited here, and I appreciate your assistance. I'd like you to stay and preserve this site, find out what else is there, record the historical detail, but if you can't abide by my rules, then I'll have to ask you to leave.'

'Ava,' Matthew held up his hand in a placating gesture. 'We are employed by the university. They expect a report back, we are obligated to them. If we report what we've found, then they might provide much needed funding to run the site.'

'I can fund it.'

Ava saw Noah's legs start to jiggle but she ignored him.

'Oh, they'll love that!' James jested. Obviously, an in-house joke.

Matthew looked less sure.

'Oh, come on. I've been subject to a million confidentiality agreements in my career. You'll have to sign them if you want to continue. I guess, because the uni isn't funding it, you'll need their permission to continue this work?'

They nodded, also unsure, having not faced this unique situation before.

'This is weird.' James exclaimed. 'But wholly exciting nonetheless. I'd be happy to work on this project outside of the uni.'

'Matthew?' James questioned and tugged on his arm, urging him from the table. 'Excuse us, Ava, we have to talk about this before making any promises.' Matthew rolled his eyes but rose and the pair walked down the stairs and stood only a short distance away in the yard.

The words were muffled but their voices were raised and it sounded like a squabble about risk to their employment and the consequences. James argued they needed to think about this carefully and of their future. Ava kept her eyes glued to them and held her breath until they returned; Matthew gave her a nod as he arrived back at the table. Noah spoke up as they sat.

'Ava is right. This must be kept a secret.'

'What? Hang on ... what are you talking about?'

'This is too big to advertise. The risk is too great. If we do, the town will be trawling with tourists hoping to secure their own find and traffic will increase, the infrastructure will suffer and what is now a wonderful quiet hollow, will be overrun and unpleasant.'

'You're worried about tourists flocking to town?' Ava frowned.

'Yes. Bellethorpe can't be overrun. We don't need to attract more tourists or people rummaging around, interfering, wanting to build their big fancy shopping centres, or drive-ins or golf courses.'

Ava was incredulous. Of all the things she expected Noah Hawthorn to say, that wasn't it.

'You're anti-development?' asked Matthew.

'I promote the right sort of development for the town.'

'With finds like this, employment is generated, the tourist market benefits, as does the local community through visitors who contribute to the local economy by staying at the local hotels, eating food in the restaurants and—'

'I understand there are benefits, but they must be carefully considered. What you're suggesting also increases our traffic congestion so people can't find a parking spot in town out the front of their local shop. Then they have to queue for their coffee. Supplies run low. Litter increases. They're just the minor, local day-to-day affect. Then we're an attractive rural hub that's booming and suddenly out-of-towners want to build their fancy new resort to accommodate the additional visitors and the shops that goes with it and the new café. Suddenly we need additional housing for people to move here and then they don't stay. Over-development creates additional noise, pollution, disruption...'

Was he for real? It sounded as if Noah was wanting to preserve Bellethorpe as a pre-historic town never to improve itself. For it to remain forever stuck in the past. She had so admired his interest in the find and his questions, but this form of thinking was so backward, she was flabbergasted.

And where was his desire to acknowledge the historical significance of the find?

Maybe he wasn't so different to her husband, after all. The thought shocked her and made her doubt everything she'd believed about Noah Hawthorn. And that frightened her—a lot.

Regaining control, Ava stood. 'I need to think this through. I'm grateful for your time today and your help. Let's reconvene tomorrow. Come back in the morning and I'll let you know the plan. Until then, I trust you'll keep this to yourself. All of you.' She included Noah in her gaze. Then she dismissed them by walking away, shutting the sliding door and turning out the light.

CHAPTER

Twenty

NOAH RUBBED OTIS' head. The dog was loyal, never deviated in his emotions, both knew what to expect from the other. It was comforting, he realised. Unchanging. Static. And just the way he liked it.

From his point of view, it always seemed to be city versus country; us verse them; every situation boiled down to the same facts. Noah threw the ball and watched Otis run. Was it so wrong to crave a simple life? To live that life here in the country?

Lisa had thought she was different and that she could tame the country, make it fit her, make it work. And for a short while it had. She'd loved the novelty of the lifestyle, the sunrises and sunsets, the fresh air, slower pace.

Tracing back through his memories he tried to recall when exactly she'd become unhappy. Or had she always been miserable and he hadn't noticed? He didn't think so. It was a gradual thing. Lisa didn't have the passion Ava possessed. Noah thought her enthusiasm unusual. Lisa wanted to be a mum and had been happy to give away the grind of nine-to-five. But it was different, he justified. Lisa didn't have a career; when they'd met, she had a job as a secretary in an architectural firm that she neither loved nor hated. It was a job that paid good wages and had worthwhile perks. It was, as they'd discussed, a transportable job; one she could do anywhere, and she'd easily picked up other work here in Bellethorpe in the chamber of commerce.

He knew she'd become unsettled though. Often their arguments denigrated into the lack of life in Bellethorpe: there was nothing to do, nowhere to go and nowhere to hide from the prying eyes of locals. To her, it had begun to feel like a fishbowl.

For the first time since Lisa had left him, he felt a flicker of empathy for her. He thought creating a new family, their family would satisfy her but perhaps being far away from home, the comforts of where you'd been raised and your extended family was simply too hard? Noah didn't want to give her too much credit though. Could she perhaps not have had this epiphany prior to their having a child together and her dragging that child away so that he never saw her? His bitterness settled in the base of his stomach once more.

The city and country didn't mix.

Ava was different. A focused, intelligent woman with ideas. His chest deflated as he released a breath. He threw the ball again, and watched Otis fly across the ground. Ava had kept a quiet life since her arrival, barely meeting townspeople and making few ripples. But now, now with the possibility of this new venture, well, it might be huge. Or it could be nothing. Was the location of a rare old turtle fossil that important? He understood it was to people in that field, he'd gleaned that clearly last night. Sort of like him restoring an old historic build-ing, he guessed. The three archaeologists were beside themselves with excitement. Thankfully, Ava had put the kybosh on revealing the fossil to the world. He didn't understand why, but he was grateful. This wasn't the city and they didn't operate like their town folk. This was Bellethorpe and sometimes, he felt like he was the only one protecting its interests. Why did everyone think it had to develop? Progress? Get bigger and better resources? Attract more people? Honestly, he found the whole concept befuddling. And annoying.

But as he'd tried to sleep last night, another thought occurred to him. Would this fossil bind Ava to Bellethorpe? Make it become her home and the place she wanted to be? Would it be enough to make her stay? The prospect caused ripples of excitement but likewise, the disadvantageous attraction it might become, also made him nervous.

Otis brought the ball back and Noah rubbed the dog's neck. 'Let's go visit Mum, hey?' It had been on his mind for a while. He needed to visit his mother anyway, hadn't check in for too long. But since his family law saga had begun, he'd developed a burning desire to ask his mother how she'd coped with a husband, like Lisa, who initially accepted the country and then rejected it. Perhaps these answers would help him see more clearly.

'These things aren't easy.' Noah's mother spoke slowly, thoughtfully as she drank her black tea, no milk, no sugar. They sat on her back deck, Otis picking up where he left off with his ball game. But yeah, Noah was kind of looking for more.

'You've always been so accepting of the situation, of Dad leaving. You never spoke poorly of him. Why? How could you think what he did was okay?'

His mother shook her head. 'No parent should denigrate the other to their child. But of course, I was hurt, devastated. This was my home; our home and he chose another life over the one we'd made together.'

Yes, Noah could relate to that sentiment.

Noah's father had left when Noah was five-years-old and he'd severed contact. Maybe things were different back then. Easier? The mother's responsibility was the child and there was no question as to who raised the children. Father's roles were different. So, perhaps not easier, but the society's view of parenting had considerably broadened since then.

That didn't make him feel one iota better.

His father had been a city bloke who'd come to the country seeking adventure, found love instead, and stayed on. But not for long. Bellethorpe had never become his home.

How ironic that his situation was identical. Was it destiny?

Noah brushed away those woo-woo thoughts.

'But eventually I realised, it wasn't me. It wasn't my fault,' his mother continued. 'If he was unhappy living here in Bellethorpe, I was never going to be able to fix that.'

'If he'd asked you to move to the city, would you have?'

'Probably,' she said and took a sip of tea. 'I would have done anything to make our marriage work. Keep our family together. But he knew the country life was my choice, what I loved and he didn't ask that of me. I think Lisa was the same. She understood your passion for Bellethorpe and didn't want to make you choose.'

He'd not contemplated that before. So, Lisa was the one making the sacrifice? Not wanting to upend him and his life? Leaving so he could be free to continue his life on the land?

Imagine if his mother had followed his father. Imagine him a city kid? That made him feel sort of sick. His mother was born and bred country; she was probably the only other person he knew who loved this life as much as him. So, to give that away for love. Noah was no longer convinced love was strong enough to combat all the ills in the world. And he knew without thinking too hard that he would have been very unhappy in the big city. And any such future would have been destined to fail.

'How is Lisa?'

That was an interesting question. Most people asked about him, or Emily or the status of his family law battle, not after the welfare of his ex-wife.

'I don't know. Seems to be doing well if you consider she's made a new life for herself in Brisbane, has a new partner, new house and is trying to destroy mine.'

'Oh, Noah. You can't let this situation eat you alive. You must overcome it, make the best of it. I believe in you. You are a kind-hearted, sensible man. And a wonderful father. Now is the time to demonstrate to your daughter what a great man you are.'

As had become her morning habit, Ava walked around the house, looked out each window, checked the surroundings in each direction, and then again. Only when she was satisfied that there was no immediate threat, did she unlock and open each of their screens. Next, she pulled the curtains across to allow the sunshine to fill the rooms with beautiful brightness. Any attempt to lighten her mood was a good idea. She was edgy, unable to keep still, a skittishness that had her pacing back and forth and twisting the opal silver ring on her finger. She hadn't felt this way since they'd fled, since they'd arrived in Bellethorpe and into the unknown.

Perhaps Henry had thought the email address was wrong because she hadn't replied? Had he thought he'd found her only to be disappointed? She didn't know but there hadn't been any further messages and it was easy to think they were okay, for the moment.

But she remained agitated.

At the back sliding glass doors, she stood and surveyed the lower paddocks. Nothing seemed different and yet her entire world was out of whack and tilted on an axis. Ava had a very real awareness of being alone, once more. A creeping sense of community had been developing and slowly embracing her, like an old fluffy blanket. Now, that certainty and comfort had been ripped away and frenetic energy rippled through her.

There was nothing to see.

Flicking on the television, she made a cup of tea in their new kitchen, only half-listening to the morning bulletin. The first sip of scalding tea and the world returned to some sort of rights. Until Jamila's name rang out loud and clear and she turned to flashing footage of her friend outside the Old Bailey in London, people surrounding her, wrapped in winter coats, heads bowed. The powerful and rich Egyptian she recognised as Jamila's husband, Mohammed, stomped up the concrete flight of stairs, a scowl obvious on his face. He'd flown to court on his private jet with his entourage to defend his case and inform the court of the elaborate lifestyle he provided his wife. She never wanted for anything was the catchcry.

Ava wasn't aware of sitting until she landed on the couch with a thump, the hot tea spilling into her lap.

Yes, it was true, neither she nor Jamila had ever wanted for material possessions. Expensive jewellery, handmade conversative linen clothes, perfumes, anything a woman might desire they were lavished with. But it was the fundamental human rights that had been lacking. Jamila had thought her charismatic tycoon husband was divorced and marrying her, his third wife. However, it became apparent very quickly that her new husband had never divorced his previous wives and was choosing to remain married to each of them, and more startlingly, he was allowed to do so.

For Ava, it had been the pressure to convert to their faith. The basic segregation of men and women, the lack of personal freedoms like movement, who she spoke to, the clothes she wore and what she did. Slowly and subtly each aspect of her life was stripped from her as she was monitored, controlled and reported upon. Quite ironically she'd been like an exhibit in a museum display. While Jamila was blindsided by polygamy, Ava had married an Egyptian living in England and living a British lifestyle. Never, ever had she expected that their supposedly temporary move to her husband's home country would result in her becoming a prisoner in her own home, a prisoner of her own life. And that her son would be raised with the values and beliefs of her husband's family and culture.

Her gaze remained fixed on the screen as bile burned in her throat and nausea threatened. Crowds jeered outside the courthouse as Mohammed emerged. Tea sprayed from her mouth as the cameras panned to the man beside him. Henry. His face serious, hands out deflecting the crowd, flinching at comments flung at them, their personal security protecting them.

The reporter's voice droned on and Ava raced for her laptop. Adrenalin spiking, she logged in to her emails. Would there be a message?

As she read she clutched her stomach as nausea swirled. Her eyes zeroed in on another email, an unread letter from Henry...

Ava,

You have not replied to my last letter. I was hoping to hear from you and receive some news of your welfare, of how Ismail is. Is he well? Where are you?

We need to discuss matters. Please reply.

Hamid

. . .

Reaching for her phone, she started to punch in Jamila's number, stopped, started again and then threw the phone onto the lounge. 'Urgh!' Ava retrieved the phone, started typing a text message, but again, deleted the words and gave up. She slammed the laptop lid shut only to open it again and search the court case and its progress before devouring every article. The words blurred on the screen but Ava didn't move until the familiar thump sounded up the back stairs. Daisy dog didn't raise an eyebrow. During the wee hours of last night, she had formulated her plan and the news coverage only reinforced her view that the turtle fossil had to be kept secret. She could not risk a leak of this news and its connection to her.

Over a cup of tea that didn't turn cold this time, she confirmed her plan to James and Matthew. 'I'm so grateful for your help and your expertise and I'd like you to stay and help me. If you can please report back to the uni and seek their permission for your secondment to this project, if you want to that is, and tell them this is a private project funded by me, they have no control, but I'll offer them first rights on any professional papers that I write and deliver. Any papers you write and deliver will also be your own but they cannot be published until after my findings. If this is what we think it is, it will be a long-term dig, to ensure we've captured everything that might be found. So, I think you'll agree, there is a lot for the university to benefit from. Most importantly, what we are doing here must remain confidential until I say it isn't, except for the bare minimum of information to provide to the university. We'll work together as a team but you will be answerable to me. I do, of course, fully respect that you have the knowledge and I don't, so it is a team effort. I will fund whatever you need.'

Ava twirled the opal ring.

The two men sat back, deliberated for all of one second and agreed. 'We'll talk to our people this morning and get the approval we need,' James said. He glanced at Matthew. 'We don't understand your insistence on privacy though, Ava. Most who make a discovery of this magnitude would be reporting on their incredible skill and luck and wanting the world to know. Why the secrecy?'

Ava shook her head. 'This is about the integrity of the find and the site and working out what we're dealing with and establishing what we need to do and getting it done. Eventually, our findings will not be kept a secret because they'll need to be known, analysed, researched and recorded, but they'll be made public when I'm ready. And not before.'

'Look, you seem pretty trustworthy, and we really want to be involved in this dig, so we'll agree, but yeah, that's unusual,' Matthew said.

'Thank you. Let's get to work.'

CHAPTER
Twenty~One

'KNOCK, KNOCK?' The voice was male, but it wasn't Noah.

Ava froze. Whoever had come up the back stairs had arrived silently. There had been no sound of steps, no movement as there usually was, not even a squeak from Daisy or the puppies. Daisy never cared who stomped up the back stairs but if the puppies were around, they'd yelp and wriggle around with excitement at the prospect of a visitor.

Damn that open gate!

Last time she'd checked, Noah was knee-deep in dirt and dust working in the shed. Relations between them had been decidedly frosty. But despite this, he'd continued with the shed as priority. And now knowing that he was adamantly opposed to the dig, she was surprised he continued at all.

Ava's hands shook as she scrubbed the grime off them in the kitchen sink. Through the window, she glimpsed a man. He removed a cap from his head and wiped his brow. He had a creased face with deep crevices in the hollows around his eyes and extenuated lines across his brow. His silver-grey hair was worn long, his clothes wrinkled and he slumped, like he needed a good day's rest. Regardless of how innocent he looked, her heart still dropped to her stomach. Wiping her hands on a dish towel, she walked out hesitantly. 'Hello. How can I help you?'

'Hiya, I'm Geoff Hunter from *The Bellethorpe Times*. I understand you've found something on your property. Can you tell me about it?' Despite the directness of his words, he twisted the cap he held in his fingers. It was obvious he knew he was invading her privacy and he was uncomfortable about that.

She would take advantage of that vulnerability, particularly as he was a journalist. Argh! She swallowed her scream as she realised with abject horror that somehow, someone, had revealed her secret. A hot ball of fury grew in her chest. Could she honestly not trust anyone! Who was it?

'I'm not sure what you're talking about?'

Geoff's eyebrows arched. He turned his head behind him, scouring the path he'd just taken. 'This is Kinross Road, right? And you're the archaeologist new to town?'

Responses were ricocheting around her mind. Lie? Be honest? Not respond? What should she do? 'Um, yes. I'm pretty sure you know this is Kinross Road. Who sent you?'

'No one. I'm the editor of the local paper and I'm sourcing a story. I've heard that you've discovered something on your property and folks are keen to learn more. Locals love local news. Particularly, if it's big.'

Ava stood up taller, placed her hands to her hips doing her best to be intimidating. 'Geoff, I'm so sorry you've wasted your time. What do you call it in the industry? A red herring? This sounds like someone has given you a dud steer. Nothing here, nope, zippo, except loads of dust and dirt from the renovations. Do your folk want to hear about the restoration? I'm paring the house back to its original state with the help of a local builder.'

'They are probably very interested in that and grateful, too. We love our old and unique buildings and homes being cared for, but I'm told it's more than that.'

Geoff Hunter's general dishevelment had her thinking he was too busy on the hustings chasing stories to worry about his appearance. Plus, she suspected if she pushed hard enough, he'd back off.

Suddenly, down in the bushes, a loud bang echoed. Something big and heavy connecting with the compacted earth. Out of the corner of her eye, she glanced at Geoff. Damn, he'd heard it too. She'd feign ignorance. But her spirit of subterfuge sank a little observing the yard. James' utility vehicle was parked haphazardly; the open tray containing large boxes in the rear, tools laying around, and dirt tracks ran through her paddocks, off into various directions. Even a lay person would know something was going on here.

Becoming addled, she wasn't sure what to do. But private property meant no access, right? She had the say…

'Hey, Geoff, thought I saw you arrive. What's news?' One look at Noah's face and he knew something was up.

'Hey, Noah, all good, mate. You doing this reno?'

'Yeah, big job, I'm stoked.' For once, she was pleased with him being a man of few words.

'I'm following up a lead about a discovery, no word on what but that's what I'm here to find out.'

'A discovery, huh? Gosh, word gets around. But, Ava, where do we start? The sheds behind me' — he gestured to the building— 'were empty, but there was an old fire engine that I'll restore. It's in pretty good nick. Some of the furniture left behind in the house is antique, silky oak and Tasmanian oak timbers, fully restored that'll come up a treat.'

Ava laughed. It was more of a nervous titter, but oh, Noah was a genius! For a moment, she couldn't contribute as she gathered her thoughts.

'Noah!' She slapped her thigh in an exaggerated fashion. 'He isn't interested in the furniture! It's the French coins, postcards and old newspapers that we found in the kitchen and under the floorboards that has rumour circulating. And I'm sure Geoff wants to hear about my preliminary investigations into the returned soldier who used to reside here.'

That piqued Geoff's interest. Noah gave her a thumbs up and slunk away, his job done.

'Oh, look, okay, I wasn't going to say anything yet, but I guess I can give you a quick look. For the moment, these items are in safe keeping and I have plans for them. You can't print this because I haven't discussed it with Harriet yet, but I'm thinking of revitalising the history centre and trying to locate as much memorabilia as possible. The history is here in Bellethorpe; I've found it, there must be more. For such a little place, there is a lot of history and we need to showcase it. I hope to write a dossier on each returned soldier that settled in Bellethorpe. That's a big task because as I understand there's so little known about them. I'm starting with my fellow, of course.'

Geoff wrote hurriedly in his little spiral bound notebook. Did journalists still use those? And his notes were copious despite her saying it was not for publication. She didn't really care about that, if *The Times* and the rest of Bellethorpe was off her tail about the real finds out here; she was happy.

And none of what she said was a lie. Before she'd found the turtle, researching the history of the town and its returned solider scheme, along with improving the history centre, had been an idea. Make the centre a destination, a place on the map. But now she was distracted and hadn't pursued the idea any further.

But in the circumstances, she was decidedly happy with herself for this diversion. Well, she'd have to thank Noah later. He'd saved the day. Geoff's attention was completely focused now on the coins and postcards she'd laid out before him. She wasn't letting him touch the papers, but he got the idea. He snapped photographs with an old Canon camera that he'd likely had for decades.

The low hum of a vehicle engine echoed on the breeze up the hill towards them. Ava stood in front of Geoff blocking his view. 'Geoff, ah,' then she frantically piled up the coins and put them away, wrapped up the cards. 'That's all I've got time for now. If you have any questions, give me a ring.' She pushed him in the back, through the long narrow corridor of the house and out the front door. His long fringe fell into his eyes and he clutched his camera and notebook to his chest.

'Oh, okay, thank you. I'll be in touch.'

'Bye now!' She sung out in a too cheery sing-song voice and stood waving until he was halfway down the long drive. Safely far enough away.

Matthew and James were up for smoko and were boiling the kettle. 'Did you tell someone about the fossil?' Now she replicated her hands-on-hip stance matched with her mother voice for when Ish had done something wrong: firm and fierce.

'What? No. We haven't seen or spoken to anyone! We agreed!' Both appeared quite affronted.

'Not a soul?'

'No one.' She believed them. Argh! It had to be Noah. Storming from the deck Ava strode the few paces to the sheds. Inside remained dark despite the windows being open and cleaned and the roller doors propped up. She squinted, her eyes adjusting slowly.

'Noah, did you tell someone about the fossils?'

He was banging around and didn't hear her.

'Who did you tell?'

His eyes narrowed and then they opened wide. 'Oh, shit. I'm so sorry. I told Alex because he needed to know with doing the bathrooms and stuff, he'd be running the team out here and had to know about the additional people on the property and what they were doing. Hang on.'

He whipped out his mobile phone and spoke to Alex. Her heart was lodging further into her chest with each word.

'Sorry, Ava. I guess I didn't make it clear that it wasn't public knowledge. He told his girlfriend, but then she mentioned it to someone in the coffee queue and then the grapevine that is Bellethorpe no doubt took over.'

Bugger. Bugger. Bugger.

'But this grapevine, it doesn't know the detail, right? You didn't tell Alex it was a rare and extinct turtle fossil that is a major archaeological find?'

'No, I didn't give him any detail. Simply said that you'd found something old and you had a couple of fellas in to help you sort it. And to be honest, he didn't care for much more information. It's not going to be most people's cup of tea.'

Her smile was rueful. 'Okay, so you can go back to him, and tell him that it's coins and cards and French stuff from the war just like I've told Geoff. That's what we'll run with. I'm guessing that you can also, say, go to the pub tonight and reveal this too, and that'll get the word around town pretty quick. So, it's not a disaster. Even though I did tell you not to mention it!'

She turned and stormed back to the house.

CHAPTER

Twenty~Two

'NOW, this is a rare thing. Something occurring in this town that I'm not aware of. A first, for sure.' The voice was familiar. Two female feet encased in rather lovely blue sandals appeared beside her.

Ava's hand stilled over the back leg of the turtle fossil still in the ground but slowly taking shape and forming a distinct animal form. It was slow and meticulous work, and she savoured every minute she'd spent with Matthew and James while they worked. The fossil was so perfectly preserved that the exact features of the short and stumpy foot and where the claws would have once been, was obvious. Extraordinary. And what Ava loved the most was that time slipped away, was forgotten and her troubles non-existent when she was here, on site, lost in the world of Herbie as she'd affectionately dubbed the turtle.

However, focusing on it to the exclusion of everything else had consequences and things slipped, and visitors turned up unnoticed.

The shoes she could see were not suited for the dig site, nor traipsing around the paddocks. The lower calves were bare, the woman must be wearing a skirt.

Matthew and James stalled also, aware that no one should be on site, or in fact aware of its existence. They looked at their visitor, their eyes returning to Ava's, grim expressions on display.

Ava stood slowly, gathering herself and turned. Flashing eyes and big, too white teeth.

The mayor. Ava felt a certain sense of satisfaction. On their first meeting she'd known this wasn't a woman to rile with and it seemed that she was correct.

'Ava,' Jacqueline Kennedy addressed her first.

'Mayor, I'm sure I left my gate locked.'

'No one in Bellethorpe locks their gates and if they do it only causes suspicion and thereby invites people to investigate.'

Was she for real? Privacy didn't exist here?

Ava ignored that comment for the moment. 'It can't be the case, surely, that you're aware of every single event in town?' Ava wasn't sure mocking her was the right approach, but they were already on shaky ground, could it be any worse? That million-dollar politician smile dazzled in Ava's direction.

'Oh, yes, trust me, I'm aware of everything. Except this. So, tell me, what is going on here?'

Ava thought quickly. She'd run with the established line—French finds. 'Well, Geoff was here earlier and he's going to report on my finds. There are some French relics of coins and postcards and old Bellethorpe papers.' Ava rattled off a similar story. Watching Jacqueline's reaction, Ava knew she wasn't buying it.

'That's fabulous. The town will appreciate any assistance you can offer with recording its past and those of the soldiers who gave their lives in the war and chose to reside in Bellethorpe afterwards. I knew you'd have a project to offer the town. I'm sure once you start talking to people, they'll also have similar objects at home not realising their historical significance. The town will love that, thank you, Ava.'

A loaded pause. Matthew and James shuffled their feet sending small dirt particles into the air.

Jacqueline was a shrewd operator and was waiting for Ava to continue. If the house and surrounds had looked awry, then how could she possibly explain the tarpaulins, the gazebo shading them and their prized fossil from the relentless midday sun and the other shelters housing their valuable tools and chairs and a place to sit in the cool while they rested in between shifts. Dirt was piled around them, small and large mounds, rocks, pebbles and tailings everywhere.

How cluey was the mayor?

Surprising Ava, Jacqueline went down a different route. 'I'm aware Ava that you and your family lived in Bellethorpe previously. I'm informed that your family were valuable members of the township and enjoyed living here. We're delighted that you've chosen to call it home again after all these years. I have a wonderful sense of people. I know you're going to be a valuable member of our community and love living here. I also sense that there's more to you than you're revealing, and that is okay, too. Everyone has a story, everyone comes from some-where, everyone has a past. But I've learned in this job and from running this town, that you can't outrun your history. I hope that in time you can trust us. We look after each other here. There are no recriminations, only welcome.'

Ava swallowed at the heartfelt words and the sting of their message. The air stilled between them, the heat of the day suddenly feeling overtly oppressive. Ava was mute. Words of denial formed on her tongue, slipping around, ready to be released, but something held her back. Ava thought she had a good sense of people too, but since she'd been irretrievably and devastatingly wrong about her husband, she hadn't trusted her inner voice. Regardless, Jacqueline was a force to be reckoned with and Ava sensed it was futile disagreeing with her even though every essence of her wanted to claim she was wrong.

Only one thing to do.

'Jacqueline, what I said about the relics and adding to and contributing to the history centre is true. I will do that. I want to record that history for the town. But here, we have found something so extraordinary and incredible...' She fumbled, glanced at Matthew and James who offered curt nods of encouragement. 'I don't want to tell you about it. If I do, I need you to keep it a secret until we know more, until we decide what to do next, until we know what we're dealing with.'

Her persona softened instantly and Ava knew she'd made the right choice. Having Jacqueline on your team and as your ally was a much more sensible option than lying to her.

She came close and patted Ava on the arm. 'Thank you for trusting me. But before I make any promises, I need to know what your amazing discovery is.'

Okay, not the answer she wanted, but one step at a time. Instead of telling Jacqueline, they showed her. Matthew and James introduced themselves and stood over the fossil. Jacqueline pulled off her multi-coloured scarf and placed it around her head to protect her face from the sun. Ava squirmed. The sight of the head covering made memories flash back to her with speed and she'd rather forget about having to wear the cultural head scarf whenever she'd left their home in Egypt. It wasn't that she opposed it for those who adhered to the faith, her resistance was against lack of choice and free will. Of being forced or facing the consequences. She shivered and focused back on the ground where the two men were showing Jacqueline Herbie.

'This is incredible.' Did she wipe away a tear?

'You cannot keep this a secret—'

'No, no, Jacqueline—'

They spoke over each other.

Jacqueline grasped Ava's arm. 'Ava, this turtle could revitalise the town, our economy, increase our tourism beyond wineries and short weekends away, make us a destination.'

Ava shook her head which only made Jacqueline grip tighter. 'The agenda of every small town is to survive. We need attractions to keep us alive. Yes, we're a farming community, yes, we have the best wineries in this region, and a handful of other attractions people will only visit when they are already here. Jobs are getting harder to maintain every year. People are moving away in droves, only the sturdy remain.'

Jacqueline dropped her hand now and held it aloft, moving it as she talked. 'This could be a museum, a site where amateurs fossick, people learn about bones and extinct animals and whatever else there is. A spot of historical and cultural and educational significance. You cannot keep this to yourself.'

'You misunderstand me, Jacqueline. Nothing this important to history, to science, to archaeology could ever be, should never be kept quiet. It is for sharing and learning. I will do that. But not yet...'

Already Jacqueline moved around as if sizing up the site for future development; she picked up items, shifted others, admired rocks, examined the gazebo.

'Stop! This is not for you to decide. This is private property. I would never, ever keep this to myself but I will decide when it is revealed to the world and until then it needs to be kept safe and protected.'

Jacqueline's glare was deadly. 'You have two weeks and then I'll take matters into my own hands.'

'Jacqueline, you are the mayor but you run this town with a council and you need to inform and advise your council and take a vote before any decisions can be made.' There was venom in Noah's voice as he appeared out of nowhere.

Sheesh. Another person on the dig site. If Ava couldn't keep people out now and no one knew about it, how could she protect it when people were aware. An image of security guards manning her gate flashed into her mind, and it wasn't unwelcome. That is how she felt. Violated and exposed. No one appreciated her dilemma; she needed to keep her identity a secret. The day was steaming, but Ava sweated buckets.

Noah approached the small group. 'Jacqueline,' he nodded in greeting. 'I saw you arrive. But I'm afraid I agree with Ava. Her approach is the better one. Let her continue her research, keep the press away and things quiet for the time being—'

He was going to continue but Jacqueline cut him off. 'My agenda is always for the greater good of the town, c'mon, Noah, we're on the same team. But resisting anything new, any project that might attract people to the town should not be your automatic response. Do you honestly want Bellethorpe to stay like this forever? It is hardly reaching its potential. This is huge. Could be transformative for the town...'

Ava stood back and the pair bantered; clearly this was an old argument. She crossed her arms on her chest, listening to them sparring, very interested in Noah's opposition, wishing she believed that he was truly on her side and didn't have ulterior motives.

'If this place becomes what you suggest, a tourist attraction, if we monetarise this find, profit from it, yes more people will come for the weekend, might mean we build additional accommodation and some unfortunate person might set up an extra café with some fancy city food, but we need long-term growth and infrastructure to keep this town alive. Industry, farming, a bustling family community, not a quick buck. Any attraction you speak of might attract a few city people on the prospect but they never stay. We need long-term residents to make this town prosper.'

'I admire your position in the face of opposition, Noah, even though it's exhausting. But you're right, that is why we have a council of like-minded folk who decide together what's in the best interests of the town.' Jacqueline turned to her then. 'Yes, Ava this is your property, but I simply cannot sit back and allow this not to benefit our town and I'm very confident that my fellow members will agree. Nothing needs to happen today, but it will happen, be sure of that.'

CHAPTER
Twenty~Three

'AVA, sorry, I didn't mean to intrude. I came down to see you for a reason,' Noah said. They were back at the house now, Jacqueline had left, her car was just visible on the far winding road. Another vehicle zipped across the paddocks and Ava watched it disappear. It was Matthew and James returning to Clive's place where they'd set up home for the duration of their stay. Clive had been very generous in offering them use of his house. As the car slipped out of sight, she gave him her full attention once more.

'The lads are onto the bathrooms but won't get the two rooms completed today, so the water's off as they've pulled everything out to start fresh installation tomorrow.'

'Oh, wow. Is that ahead of schedule? Or am I losing track?'

Noah thought it was a bit of both. Since her days had been filled with more than simple house renovations, Ava's focus on the house had lessened. 'Well, that's the other thing. We need to finalise the fittings. I know we've talked about it but it's crunch time. So, you and Duke are welcome to come to my place and shower and I'll put on some dinner, and on the way, we can stop at the hardware store to pick up those last few fixtures.'

'Okay, um, yeah, sure. Duke, can you grab whatever you need and then feed Daisy and the pups and make sure they're comfortable.' After collecting her clothing and toiletries, Ava went around the house and secured each window and door. Noah controlled his eye roll.

It was a fifteen-minute drive to the homemaker centre, a big, large warehouse chain store on the outskirts of the main drag of town.

'This is such a modern store,' Ava commented as they trawled the long aisles filled with goods. Duke dragged along a few steps behind them and Ava kept glancing back to check on him.

'It's new, been open a few months now. The owners are from out of town. A local would never set up this venture. That's half the problem, city folk have the resources and the ambition but not the ticker to persevere over the long haul, when one day blends into another and life in the country becomes ordinary, they head back to the city to chase fun and entertainment.'

'But Noah, where would we buy the bathroom fittings but for this store? It's an advantage, isn't it, for you, me, and everyone else in Bellethorpe that the business be a success.'

He stiffened, the muscles of his jaw balling. 'We've always had to travel over to the next big town for supplies. Nothing changed there. And we will again when this place folds. You don't understand, Ava. This place will be wonderful for a while, but they never last. These are the third owners this site has had with its numerous incantations. Different names, different owners and the same goods for sale. I give it three months.'

'But Noah, business is booming. It's late and the aisles are packed. You're being unfair. And you're shopping here.'

Ava ran her fingers along the edge of a gold-rimmed claw-foot bath on display. 'You've already chosen your baths.' He didn't want them wasting time. 'And the two waiting to be installed look remarkably similar to these.'

'They are beautiful. I cannot wait to have a bath in this.' Noah tried not to reflect upon Ava naked in the bath. Luckily, she moved away. 'What else is on the list?'

'We've got the matching gold towel rails and toilet roll holder and cleaning set. That will look fantastic together. Lights and vanity are done, tick. I've never been a fan of dark mahogany timber, but I think it's going to come up a treat next to the white porcelain of the bath and the gold trims. The tapware, you've chosen these, yes?' Noah held up rather simple but elegant faucet and matching hot and cold waters taps.

'Yes, do you like them?'

'I do, but these ones are half the price.' He held up an alternative but Ava didn't consider it.

'Tiles?' she asked.

'Yes. You want the traditional small, coloured triangle with the slightly larger white or off-white tile, don't you? They'll have stacks of those.'

Ava considered the tiles and went with a gorgeous, deep russet small red tile and larger rectangular ones in cream for the walls. 'Do you like these, Duke?'

He grunted in reply.

'Okay, I think we're done. I'm so excited for these rooms!'

Noah tried not to grimace as the items were rung up and the figure was mind boggling. Out of character, Ava chatted in a garrulous manner with the shopkeeper. Noah couldn't even recall their names.

'Ava, see that corner shop?' Noah stood outside, pointing. 'The one that is shut and boarded up. It's been like that for months since the owners returned to the city.' He pointed across the street. 'See the Chinese take-out, it used to be one of the most vibrant businesses, until it wasn't and hasn't been open for about six months.'

'Yeah, but there's another Chinese restaurant, competition will drive out business, too.'

He ignored the comment and kept pointing out examples. 'We haven't had a video store for twelve months and the local corner shop for last minute essentials after the grocer is closed, shut recently, about one month ago.' He placed their purchases in the tray of his ute and secured them down. 'It is an endless procession of opening and closing businesses'

'Noah! Video stores died out ages ago. They've closed in Brisbane too. That is not a country thing. But the rest, well, isn't that part of the essence of small towns and also isn't it an unfortunate offshoot of the pandemic, many businesses lost trade and couldn't survive.'

'That didn't happen here, we look after our own. These businesses closed because of poor planning, poor insight and some wishful thinking that a dream life in the country would hold the answers to their problems and it didn't. That's the one thing I don't understand. The people living in those cul-de-sac suburban streets with the white picket fences and their square-foot patch of backyard grass are dreaming of the wide-open spaces here. They leave the city for a reason. But don't realise living here is a commitment, it's hard work and if you can hack it, it will pay off.'

'You're so harsh, Noah. There's attrition in any place that people live. My family was born here, and we left but not because we didn't like it. In the end it was a business decision for the welfare of my family and my father chose the teaching position in another town.'

'Yep, another good example, the last teacher at the local primary school was forced to perform her country stint, did the time, made connections, friends, became part of the community and then up and left the moment her contract ran out.'

She had to see, didn't she? On the short trip to his place, Noah provided another four examples. 'The worst are the folk that come out here with an outlandish pipe dream—turning their land into an elusive estate, or bed and breakfast style accommodation or even thinking they'll start a vineyard or apple orchard.' He was aware his words were sour, and it saddened him to admit he was bitter at what was happening in his town.

'Here we are.' His house was a simple shack. It couldn't compare to the house Ava was creating; Kinross Road was three times the size and double in grandeur. This was a cottage of three bedrooms, small living area and kitchen. It was cosy in winter with a fireplace that warmed the entire interior, with the stone-brick walls absorbing the heat and low ceiling capturing the warmth. In his opinion, those features also provided enormous character. But it was the view…

'Oh wow! This is incredible.'

The view that always enraptured people. His simple little home backed onto fields of glorious verdant grass, always kept too long and ran away into the nearby hills, as far as someone could see. He didn't know where his land started and the bush beyond took over.

They'd missed the sunset, but it had left the sky a violet hue, purples turning pink and orange. In the warmer months, the deck was where he spent most of his time. It was open with no railing, narrow but wide enough for chairs and a table and Lisa's left behind potted plants that had not only survived but thrived.

'Noah, it's gorgeous. You must love sitting out here.'

His phone rang, the ringtone loud. He glanced at the screen. 'I have to take this. The bathroom is down the hall and on the left. Fresh towels in the hall cupboard. Won't be long.' With his neck craned holding his phone onto his shoulder, he quickly poured a glass of wine and handed it to Ava before disappearing.

'Hey Tom, what's up?' he answered as he headed inside. Through the windows at the rear, he watched Ava return to the deck after showing Duke the shower; she sat and sipped her wine. Otis kept dropping the ball at her feet until she got the drift and threw it for him.

'Oh, no.' Noah paced as he absorbed what Tom was saying. 'Okay, thanks for letting me know, keep in touch, yeah.' He opened the back screen door and let it flick back as he entered the deck.

'Is everything okay?'

'Not really. That was Tom, the leader of the father support group. Brady, another guy who's had some trouble with his wife and kids, tried to overdose. It got too much and he couldn't take it anymore.' Noah hung his head, his eyes downcast.

'Oh, do you need to go? Are you close to this guy? I didn't know you were part of a support group.'

'He's in hospital being treated. Only family allowed, so there's nothing I can do for the moment. I spoke to him a few days ago because his wife was being difficult and we talked through options.' Noah's voice cracked.

'I'm sorry.'

'The group has been invaluable to me since Lisa left with Emily. I didn't know what to do, who to talk to and they were there to support me.'

'Will he be okay?'

'No one is sure yet.'

He thought his situation with Emily was dire. But how bad would it get for him to act like that? If custody of Emily was ultimately awarded to Lisa, would he want to end his own life? What good would that do because then Emily wouldn't have a father? But would life be worth living without her? Thinking about it made his heart heavy.

'Is your group only fathers?' Ava sipped her wine, the mood now sombre.

'Fathers have only attended the meetings I've been too. I guess mothers are welcome, but the men seem to need the support.'

Ava's cheeks had turned pink. 'How is your case going? Any news?'

Noah shook his head. 'The report interviews have concluded. Luckily, I only had to travel to Brisbane once. The social worker is writing their report apparently. I'm trying not to think about it. Everything hangs on the result. My lawyer says that the judge will follow the recommendation because that person is the expert on knowing what's best. So, I wait. In the interim, I'm seeing Emily as often as I can.'

Noah was glad Ava didn't make the usual platitudes that everything would be okay. It was far from the truth. His lawyer had warned him, he had to brace himself for the worst, the cards were stacked against him. He hoped every day for a good result. Surely, the court would see what a great dad he was and how much he loved Emily?

'I'll grab the meat from the fridge. I hope you're okay with another barbeque. My mother dropped around some potato salad, so we'll have that with our sausages and steak. Back in a tic.'

Ava stood next to him at the grill when he returned. 'You never mention your parents. Are they still local?'

His stomach clenched and he concentrated on cooking the meat. 'Yeah, mum is local. Getting on now. She's lived in Bellethorpe all her life. Done it tough but stuck it out. She does a bit of cleaning work and I help where I can. Lives back over yonder, not far.' Noah didn't lift his eyes, he didn't want to see sympathy or any other expression on Ava's face.

'And your dad?'

'Left when I was five.'

Ava's glass was empty and he reached for the bottle to refill it. 'This is wine from Blake's vineyard, his prize-winning Verdelho. He's put years into it and now it's making waves in the industry. Delicious, too.' Their hands brushed and heat blazed along his arm, radiating to his torso.

'Blake is new to town, he told me. Made a joke about having to live here for twenty years before being accepted. I think that sounds about right.'

'No, honestly, it's a joke. Often cited in the country.'

'You like Blake. Why, he's from the city?'

'He's making a real go of it. He has long-term plans and is committed to the local community. He's become a part of us, is a coach of the local footy team, is making the estate something special and now he's had Adele join him and they make a great team.'

'But he might leave, too?'

Noah gazed at her then, stared a moment too long. Was she jesting? Making fun of him?

'I'm just reciting the facts, Ava.'

'I guess you're waiting for me to become one of those statistics, too? Gosh, I didn't realise your level of animosity to newcomers. You must really resent me. First, I take your property and then you must think that I'm here for a good time, not a long time?'

He didn't reply. Yes, he had thought those things, deep down he probably still did, but things between them had changed. They'd kissed. He was attracted to her and it seemed, no matter what he did, he couldn't stop those feelings. God damn if he hadn't fallen for a city chick. Bloody hell, of all the things.

But he wasn't an idiot. Things had cooled between them, become a little formal. Add in his uncertainty, his doubts with his practical head reluctant to entertain taking a risk on desire and attraction. He got the sense Ava felt the same.

'What about your father, was he from here? Where did he go?'

'My father came to Bellethorpe for a twelve-month working contract on one of the cattle properties. It's quite common now, wasn't so much back then. The young fellas graduating high school apply to be a stock hand on properties usually out west and experience life on the land.'

'Sounds like a great program.'

Yeah, maybe.

'During those twelve months he met my mother, they fell in love and he stayed on. Flittered around between jobs, nothing ever really suited him. He didn't like the hard yakka of cattle work or farming after a while. Had a few office jobs, milk run, retail. Nothing ever stuck. I was too young to remember much, of course. I couldn't articulate it back then because of my age, but I understood he was unsettled. Even a kid could sense that.'

'So, he left. Went to the city, I presume?'

'Yep.'

'Did you see him growing up?'

'No.'

'He didn't visit you? Why not?'

'He never wanted to.'

He busied himself with the barbeque. Noah had successfully compartmentalised that pain a long time ago. His mother had always been his only parent. No family law biffs when he was a kid. His dad left and they never heard from him again. Did his father know he had rights? Things were very different back then, maybe he thought there weren't any options or he didn't have the right to see him? It was something he pondered often. The alternative was too hurtful.

'Not everyone you love leaves you for the city. Your mother stayed.' Her statement came out of nowhere. He felt the weight of the words and focused on turning the sausages.

'Facts say otherwise. My mother was born and bred in the country. My father wasn't. My wife wasn't. I should have known better. Instead, I simply repeated the mistake of my mother.'

'You can't help who you fall in love with.'

But you could; you had too.

The door slammed shut after Duke came out on the deck. She ruffled his wet hair. 'Now the shower is free, I'll jump in quickly before you serve up.'

Ava's scent lingered in the night-time air and it was all Noah could smell.

CHAPTER
Twenty~Four

ISH LANDED on Ava's bed with a thump, his knee slamming into her stomach. 'Mumma, it's carnival day! Wake up!'

For days he had been begging her to attend; his friend, Sam, was going to the Bellethorpe annual summer fair with his family and Ish wanted to go too. He might even make more friends he'd hinted several times. That was the clincher, of course, she'd do anything for that kid, and he was fast becoming aware of that fact. Making the decision easier, and as an added bonus, her friend, Bec, had a son of a similar age and they'd be there too. From what she'd heard, Ava was sure most of the town would be.

'I can't wait for the rides,' he said loudly into her ear. He jiggled about and encouraged Daisy onto the bed.

'Daisy, off!' She rolled over and moved Ish to the side.

Of course, she'd agreed. Ava wanted him to have fun and love their new home, their country life, but now that the day had arrived, she churned inside because the timing was ironic. The turtle fossil was the most exciting moment of her career to date and the more she learned of its history from Matthew and James, the more excited she became. The potential of more finds on her land was possible and that was extraordinary.

But that also made fear claw at Ava's belly. She'd fought off one journalist, how long could she keep her secret? Of the many secrets it felt like she had closed away inside of her? Inadvertently she may have brought danger of detection upon her and Ish and for that, she would never forgive herself.

'C'mon, Mumma, get dressed. We don't want to miss out!' Ish bounced on the bed.

'Okay! Can you please feed Marmalade and Honey, throw the scraps to the chickens and feed the puppies!'

Her son's groan was loud and clear, but the weight lifted off the bed and her bedroom door slammed. She jumped up, raced to the back glass door and watched Ish as he ran towards the horses, them nudging his hand with their long noses and him responding with pats and food.

Next, her eyes scanned the horizon. To the unsuspecting, there was nothing to see at the far edge of her land. But only a few hundred metres inside was an entire other world. In the quiet moments, she dreamed of the academic papers she'd write, the reports, maybe a book, and of the future this historic find might deliver them. A future of paid work. They were okay for the moment, thanks to her selling her ring, and she still had the opal jewellery up her metaphorical sleeve. They'd be okay. But perhaps this find was the answer to her job problem. Her mind stretched in further directions.

Jamila. There was no word and Ava hoped that didn't mean bad news. Shivers danced up her spine thinking about it. There'd also been no further emails from Henry, either. Had she managed to scrape through this time?

Ava needed a new plan and she didn't have one. Her only solution was to bunker down and get on with the job of keeping their location a secret. But the town of Bellethorpe with its summer festival and general busybodies were preventing her from keeping a low profile. It seemed each day their precarious position became more fragile.

Today, they were okay; she'd focus on that.

———

Ava tilted her head towards the bright, orange sun sitting high in the royal blue sky, closed her eyes and enjoyed the sparkles shimmering behind her eyelids. The warmth radiated through her skin and down, deep, inside her soul. Unlike the locals who bemoaned the heat and humidity of the summers, she hadn't tired of the high temperatures, yet.

Ish's hand slipped from hers and her eyes opened.

His face wore an expression of wonder: eyes open and bright, mouth in a perfect 'O', feet ready to move. The weather was glorious; a perfect day for the Bellethorpe Summer Festival. Held in the local showgrounds, central to the main street, it was the last hurrah before children returned to school and families said farewell to the last of the long, lazy days of the holidays, of swimming, sleep-ins, and too much food; before the New Year really began.

Groups of young people raced past. It seemed the entire townsfolk were out wearing their broadest smiles. Ava plastered on her grin, hoping she fitted in perfectly. Inside, her nerves were frayed, like the end of a tassel being stretched in too many directions. The distraction would serve her well. It was supposed to be a day of fun and relaxation. A day the whole community turned out to support one another, celebrate achievements, be merry.

Ava had heard talk of the annual Bastille Day Festival that was held on the national French day at the same location, except deep in the depths of winter. Something to look forward to in what she imaged was a cold and bleak time of year.

It seemed the town of Bellethorpe liked it celebrations.

Today there was no red, white and blue, instead there were endless stalls under white marquees, animal pens and food vans. Band music emanated from a central stage. Excited screams spilled from the rides, people talked animatedly and she found herself swept up in the fun.

'Sam!' Ish shrieked and sprinted towards his friend. The boys hugged and the sight swelled her heart. Next to him stood another little boy.

'Mumma, Sam's Mum is going to take us on the Ferris wheel, please?' he pleaded. 'And this is Jack, he's our friend too and he's going to hang out with us today.' Inside she screamed, no, but outwardly she checked with Sam's mother who was happy to supervise. Jack was Bec's son. She hoped she saw her old friend today.

Ish galloped away, his small backpack taking up most of his tiny frame. Every instinct within her was to reach out, grasp him back to her, hold him close. It took all her might to resist. She swallowed down the lump in her throat, and suddenly, Ava was alone. Except for Daisy dog and with enormous relief she petted the dog's nose and rubbed her back, grateful for the company.

Reaching for a tissue in her dress pocket to wipe away the moisture at the corners of her eyes, she took out the lip gloss she'd need to reapply later, two tissues and another scrap of paper that was screwed tightly into a ball. Unwrapping it revealed lines of writing and a scratched, blacked out mess.

Pain, hurt, feeling sick

The next line was scribbled out so furiously with black pen she couldn't read it. Words were inserted above and below but they were indecipherable. *Absurd. Agreement. Train wreck.* Ava had a flashback to another piece of paper with the same handwriting. The tax invoices Noah had issued from Bellethorpe Builders who didn't have a fancy electronic accounting system so he'd handwritten the fee notes. The loopy 'r' and 'f' and 'g' were the same. Where did this come from? Stretching her memory back to last night, she remembered emptying her pockets onto the bathroom basin at Noah's before her shower. Had she accidentally swiped it up with her things? And was this poetry written by Noah? This heart-wrenchingly, sad poem?

As if conjuring him up, he appeared, over near the fairy floss stall where he spoke head bowed, to another man. Their expressions were earnest, nods with some hand gesticulations until three small children, including Emily, bounced over holding up bright-pink fairy floss on a stick. The two men broke into grins and chatted animatedly with them. Daisy recognised Otis and tugged Ava towards the group.

'Ava!' Emily exclaimed and hugged her around the hips.

'I'm so glad you could be here for the festival.'

'Yep, me too. I couldn't miss it. Dad picked me up early this morning and I had a sleep in the car so I'd be as bright as a button.'

Ava glanced at Noah who acknowledged her with a tight smile.

Small grey pouches of skin gathered under his eyes. Poor Noah looked like he could do with a sleep, too.

The children were gesturing to the other man and demanding they pat the animals in the petting zoo, so he waved and headed off.

Noah moved in closer, the dogs circling them, Daisy always the slower of the two. 'That was Tom, the guy I spoke to last night. Apparently, Brady is going to be okay. He'll be laid up for a few days yet, but he'll pull through.'

'I'm glad.'

'Where's Duke?'

'He ran off with his friends, Sam and Jack. They are going on the Ferris wheel.'

'It's so unusual to see you without him. It's good, he'll have a great time.'

Ava wasn't sure how to interpret the comment. She was an overprotective mother? Overbearing? A little frisson of something passed through her tummy.

'Hey, Lincoln.' Noah greeted another man.

'Ava, this is Lincoln Reid, local lawyer. He's acting in my family law matter.' The men exchanged a handshake and Lincoln reached into his breast pocket and extracted a card that he gave to her. Interesting way to do small talk.

'Any news?' Noah leaned in.

'Nothing yet. Won't be long now, I'm sure. These family reports take a while to prepare as they are usually very detailed and lengthy to justify the recommendation made. I'll advise you as soon as we hear.'

Ava glanced at the card. Would she need a lawyer's services into the future? How was she ever going to be free if she didn't divorce her husband? And how do you divorce someone if you married overseas? Questions for another day as Lincoln raised his white and grey fedora hat in farewell and departed. She placed the card in her skirt pocket.

Noah seemed momentarily lost in thought until a loud excited scream from a ride to their left made them both jump.

'I'm volunteering on the father support group stall for a while. Come past and say hi, later.' He grasped her elbow to avoid being jostled in the crowd. Their eyes met and held, unspoken words passing between them before he dropped his hand and kissed her on the cheek.

Watching him walk away, the spot still warm from the touch of his lips, tingled.

Over the tops of heads and balloons bobbing in the air, Ava spotted the top of the giant wheel. She might as well head over there. Daisy walked obediently beside her, only stopping to smell a morsel of food dropped by a child. After her inspection, Daisy dragged her forwards, keen to be moving, her nose twitching. Pausing at a chicken wire fence, her tail wagged eagerly. Ava spied Adele and Blake and a bunch of their alpaca inside the coop surrounded by children who fed them, their excited giggles travelling over to her on the breeze. If Daisy could have fit through the fence, she'd have been in amongst them too, no fear of the strange mucus-snorting animals. Ava waved to them and walked away. The enticing smell of coffee encouraged Ava to the coffee van; she'd buy Noah a thank you for the many take-aways he'd delivered to the house. In the line, people she was sure she'd never met, waved, and muttered congratulations. Strange; they must have her confused with someone else. She recognised Trevor Fletcher from the hardware store being dragged along by a very cute little girl in plaits.

'Oh, sorry,' A woman wearing a long, purple apron emblazoned with colourful flower petals, bumped into her as she passed.

'Howdy, stranger. How are you settling in out there on Kinross Road?' asked Mac Turner who she hadn't seen since the day she'd met Noah.

'Oh, yeah, great, thank you. The house is coming along.'

'No doubt, it will be fantastic, particularly with Noah Hawthorn at the helm. If you want to capitalise on the renovations and sell up when it's finished, I'm your man.'

Luckily by then, Ava had reached the front of the coffee line and had to leave Mac and place her order. Honestly, sell up after she'd renovated? Where would she live? But what if she was found... ... would she sell then? She dashed those thoughts away and heard Mac giving someone else his spiel while she waited. Walking a little further on with the coffees in her hand, she spied Caleb and Bridie and their French pastry stall.

'Yum!' she exclaimed as she approached.

Bridie came out of the stall and embraced her. 'I'm sorry we haven't caught up since last time we saw each other. How is everything? I hear you did end up choosing Noah as the builder. So glad I could help and reassure you. Where's your gorgeous little boy?' Bridie scanned the surrounds.

Ava laughed. 'Oh, he's off with a friend going on the rides. The kids love them, don't they?'

'Sure do. He'll probably run into Sybella out there somewhere. But don't worry, they're perfectly safe. It's a community around here, we look out for each other.'

Someone patted her back from behind. 'Such exciting news, so happy for you.'

Bridie gazed at her with raised eyebrows. Ava shrugged.

'These look delicious, Caleb. Can I have one of each please? I'll save one for Duke and deliver a treat with Noah's coffee.' She watched as Caleb made his selection and her mouth watered at the strawberry tart, chocolate éclair and lemon meringue with its toasted caramel top. Bridie grinned in her direction, the gaze seemingly loaded with the words she wasn't saying.

Hands full of goodies now, she needed to find Noah to lighten her load. It was Otis they saw first as they passed the animal petting zoo, the kebab shop with its divine frying onions scent and then on past the Laughing Clowns game where a bunch of kids were lined up hopeful of winning a prize. Then there was an aquarium and second-hand book stall and antique bric-a-brac. She'd check that one out later. Finally spotting Noah, he was once again deep in conversation with a man who appeared distressed.

'Coffee and cake,' she whispered and left the goodies on a table to his left hopeful he'd get a chance to take a break and enjoy. Departing the marquee with its long, narrow table of brochures, Ava picked one up and read the attention-grabbing headline.

Fathers, you have rights too! Are you in the middle of a family law dispute? There are two parents in every divorce, you are just as important as the mother. Don't let a heavily biased system rip you off. Join our group to ensure your rights are protected.

What sort of group was this? A half-dozen men stood around chatting, their arms gesticulated with force, faces were screwed up with emotion and the entire space was filled with hot testosterone. Not her sort of stall. She dropped the flyer back on the table as if it burnt her fingers.

Noah was generally calm, but there'd been those few occasions she'd seen him worked up. Usually when talking about his daughter and about the development of the town. Those subjects caused his feathers to ruffle. But she'd never heard him yell or lose control. A loud commotion erupted behind her and she glanced back and flinched. One man pointed a finger at another while others rushed forwards to calm him. Goose bumps erupted along her arms and legs, cooling her skin. Her husband had never spoken to her like that, but she'd been in the presence of family members who'd had no qualms about shouting into their wives faces and making them recoil in fear until they submitted. Ava had always wondered how long it might be until Henry did the same. Jamila's husband, on the rare occasions they'd been alone, had spoken to her in terms she hadn't appreciated but he'd fallen short of shouting; but the words themselves were enough to instil dread.

Ava scooted out of there. Out of the corner of her eye, she spotted the Ferris wheel and headed towards it. There was a pink carriage at the top and tiny hands reached out through the cage and were waving at someone, metres below. Now she had to watch where she was walking as she navigated through tables and chairs set up for patrons to have a rest and enjoy their food. Peter from *Café Antiquities* sat at one table alone. With half a coffee remaining, she'd sit with him for a moment and then find Ish.

'Peter, hello.' Would he remember her?

'Oh, hello, love.' His gaze was distant. She saw the moment he placed her. 'Having fun?'

'Um, yes, I think so. Might I sit for a minute? Would you like to share my French chocolate éclair?'

'No, thank you, dear, but only because I've just finished one of Caleb's delicious strawberry tarts. Wonderful! And now I'm finishing my tea.'

They enjoyed a few minutes of quiet chat before Sheila joined them.

'Ava! I've just heard! How wonderful for you. I didn't realise what you'd found out there in that big, old house and its land that spreads for miles. Exciting. You didn't mention it, did you? I would have remembered?'

Sheila spoke quickly and Ava struggled to keep up. When she'd finished, she fussed over Peter wiping his chin with a serviette, pouring him more tea from a flask and plonking herself down in a chair. Then she turned to her expectantly.

'Um, I'm not sure what you're talking about. A journalist from the local paper came around yesterday and I told him about some French relics I've found at the house that I'll eventually donate to the History Centre. Is that what you mean? But how could you have possibly found out so soon? Surely it isn't in today's edition?'

Sheila gave her a quizzical look, reached into her duffel bag and retrieved *The Bellethorpe Times*, threw it down onto the plastic table where it landed front page up. The headlines screamed at her and the food she'd just eaten raced back up her throat, stinging and tasting of bile. She covered her mouth.

Major historical fossil find on property in Bellethorpe

A quick scan of the first three sentences confirmed her worst fears. It mentioned an extinct old horned turtle found in the bushes of a property owned by her, it revealed her name! Albeit her maiden name, not her married name. Her eyes danced over the rest of the words, blurring as she sped-read. Folding open the spread, the piece covered two pages, today's top and best news. Random photographs had been included that she didn't recognise. An archived turtle shot that she was pretty sure wasn't like what they'd found and some grassy fields, dig sites. She squinted. Was that her property? Fear didn't claw at her belly now, it suffocated her. Did the photo give away her location? It didn't appear so, but she didn't quite trust her vision that was now blurry and she rapidly blinked and rubbed at her eyes to clear them.

Sheila spoke. 'You're very lucky. Often our local stories get picked up by the national newspapers. This'll be across the country in no time. Our little town will be famous!'

She looked up. Daisy barked. Across the field walking towards her were three men in dark suits, wearing shaded sunglasses, white string ties, and leather shoes. They wore thick wristwatches and matching black hats with white bands. Had her husband sent his henchmen? Were they coming for her?

Jumping up, she grabbed the paper, her bag and Daisy's lead and walked in the opposite direction.

Behind her Sheila shouted her name, asked what was wrong. She needed to find Ish. Head down she weaved her way in between the chairs and tables, knocking over furniture in her haste.

'Hey!' someone scolded but she didn't pause. Where the hell was the Ferris wheel? She passed the dodgem cars and an old timber roller coaster and moved past a dress up stall.

Finally at the base of the large, round wheel she screamed his name. People stopped, stared and clutched children by the shoulders to move them away from the crazy lady. She didn't care, wouldn't stop until she found her son.

Shoving her way through the line, he wasn't there. At the entry to the ride, she scanned the cages for disembarking passengers; he wasn't there either. She demanded the ride assistant circle each cage so she could scour the occupants. He wasn't anywhere.

Running back out, she rushed through the crowds, saying his name repeatedly.

A hand touched her shoulder. 'Ava, what's wrong?'

She shrugged off the hand but turned to face Noah. 'I can't find Ish. Have you seen him?'

'Ish? Do you mean Duke?'

She nodded, frantically, wildly.

'Why are you calling him that?'

'Because that's his name,' she screamed into his face and Noah retreated. 'That's his real name,' she said it softly this time, the words coming out as a sob.

'Okay. Okay, he can't be far. I'll search with you.'

Then she saw Samuel and Jack. Dropping Daisy's lead, she ran. Arriving at the boys, she gripped Jack on each arm and swivelled him to face her. The child recoiled, and Sam stepped back out of reach. 'Where is … Duke? Where is he?'

'Ava,' Bec touched her arm, drawing both boys into her body for protection. 'What's wrong? We thought Duke had returned to you. After the Ferris wheel the boys had a turn on the cars and then he ran off. I assumed he'd gone to find you.'

Bec? No! No one could keep her son safe except her.

Ish was here alone. She needed to keep searching but her legs collapsed beneath her and she fell to the ground. Noah supported her by the arms and dragged her onto a haybale. The straw scratched her bare legs through the summer dress she wore.

She heard Noah speaking but the words were muffled. Something was shoved under her nose, astringent, foul-smelling and the world around her became clearer. Bridie clutched one arm. 'Ava, honey. It'll be okay, he must be here. Everyone will look, everyone will help. You stay here, I'll stay with you. Caleb and Noah will get people to help.'

Ava willed her body to move, her feet to run, to assist, but like a lead weight, she stayed seated. The trio of men in suits approached and she grabbed Bridie's arm, her knuckles turning white. Bridie followed her gaze, but the men walked straight past them.

'Who are they?' she whispered.

'Them? They're the Blues Brothers. A musical act appearing this afternoon, you know from the eighties?'

The air left Ava's lungs and her body sagged. Then there was Caleb yelling, they'd found him, they'd found him. Something clicked, and Ava was up, running, Bridie in her wake. Outside the showgrounds, she crossed a road, passed a creek. She saw him. Uncontrollable sobs released, her lungs heaved with the effort but she ran and did not stop. Flinging her arms around him, she crushed him. The boy cried, wet tears landing on her, rolling down her front. She wouldn't let go, ever let go, never wanted to. But as her heart rate slowed, she pulled him out in front of her, examined him. She ran her hands up and down his arms and legs, across his chest.

'Are you okay?' she asked at last. He only nodded and then she noticed something in his hands, a bundle he was protecting.

'A puppy,' her voice croaked. 'What's a puppy doing here?' Daisy appeared, nuzzled the bundle too and then howled, a loud, agonising wail that pierced her ear. Ish held the puppy, it was limp and lifeless.

'No, Ish, no,' she said which caused him to cry harder.

'It's my fault. I put Jasper in my rucksack. I wanted to show Sam and Jack how cute he is. And then —' he hiccupped in succession— 'and then, I forgot about him, and we went on a couple of rides and when I remembered, I pulled him out and he wasn't breathing.' He held the furry bundle up against his cheek, rubbing the fur.

'I brought him over here, thinking he needed a drink, a play and he'd be okay. Will he be okay?'

Together they bent over, embraced each other and sobbed.

CHAPTER
Twenty~Five

DRIVING HOME WAS A BLUR. Wiping away her own tears, she focused on the road while Ish nursed the lifeless puppy, petting Daisy beside him who was also inconsolable. Since finding a sad and lonely Daisy under their eaves, she'd been nothing but a loyal and caring dog; a companion who'd helped both mother and son settle into life at Bellethorpe. Ava had let her down.

Vet, Zac Coleman, met them at the gate; a kindred spirit had rung ahead to give him the heads up.

Ish dashed from the vehicle the moment she stalled the engine. 'I'm sorry,' he said to Zac, holding up Jasper. 'I didn't mean to hurt him. Can you do anything?' The words pierced Ava like a sharp-edged blade right through her chest.

Zac confirmed what they already knew and talked calmly to Ish about what had happened and what he needed to do now, how it was important to make Jasper comfortable and bury him somewhere safe. Then Zac talked of taking proper care of the other puppies and the attention they required. Ish listened, his lips trembling.

Noah arrived moments later and spoke quietly to Zac.

'Do you want Zac to take Jasper and, um, dispose of him or would you prefer to bury him here? I can help?' His hand resting on her shoulder felt like a heavy weight.

'We'll do it, keep him here.'

Noah nodded and informed Zac. 'Let's do it now, I'll help you while there's still some daylight.' Noah retrieved a shovel, probably one of his tools left behind, and she gathered the children. Ish carried Jasper cradled now in an old cloth, his eyes forever shut, and Emily carried two puppies and Ava the other two. Daisy followed.

Ish chose a tree close to the house so that they could visit him often and perhaps place a special flower at its base. Daisy sat obediently; the puppies wriggled. Once in the ground and covered, Noah asked Ish if he'd like to say anything and Ish whispered, 'sorry', and sobbed some more.

Noah kneeled at Ish's height and held him in a grip by the shoulders. 'You made a mistake. You didn't mean to hurt Jasper, everyone understands that. You understand now that you can't take puppies like that in your bag, don't you? I know you won't do it again. You're going to take extra care of Daisy and her pups now. Your Mumma forgives you' — Noah placed a hand on Daisy's back— 'and I know Daisy forgives you, too.'

Ish glanced at the dog who licked the moisture from his red and tear-stained cheeks. It was the forgiveness he needed.

'I'm sorry you lost your puppy, Duke. It was a silly mistake. Daisy and the other puppies are still very lucky to have you,' Emily piped up.

After burying the dog, they wandered back to the house and Noah casually slung his arm across Ava's shoulders; it felt right. His body not a weight but a comfort.

'Can you stay?' she asked, her voice a whisper. Not waiting for his answer, she moved away to switch on the lights in the living area and the outside deck and kitchen. Ava wandered down the long hall and did the same to each bedroom on adjoining sides. The house was lit up with not a shadow invading even a corner crevice.

Noah helped himself to a bottle of wine and poured two generous glasses. The kids disappeared and Ava plonked herself at the outside table and shoved the newspaper across, the article spread open for his attention.

'Noah, I'm scared.'

Lights illuminated her long drive and Ava flew to the edge of the deck. Transfixed watching the car approach, she gripped the railing watching the lights dip with the undulations in the surface, until eventually she saw Bridie's hand waving out of the passenger seat and her body slumped. She wanted to scream, low and long and hard. The up and down of her emotions was exhausting.

Fear and anxiety had her in its grip.

Bridie called out as the vehicle arrived and she and Caleb sprang out of their car. 'We're not going to stay, love, just delivering dinner and treats and a drop of wine. I think you need it after the fright you've had.'

Despite her resolve, Ava cried. Hot, large tears rolled down her cheeks. She wiped them away furiously, annoyed and angry at herself. Head bowed, she remained at the edge of the deck, attempting to regain her composure. Bridie served dishes, set the table and delivered food to the children before placing a hand to her shoulder. 'You're in good hands. I'll ring you tomorrow.'

The aroma emanating from the food made her mouth water. At least she could still feel; if she were numb, things might be irretrievably worse. Noah grasped her hand and lead her towards the table. There was even one solitary, single candle, its tangerine flame flickering. He served her and she nibbled a morsel that took too long to chew and got stuck in her throat. Faced with food, the last thing she wanted to do was eat. It sat in front of her, the curls of steam wafting upwards.

'Yeah, the article, well, it sucks. How did that happen? And what do we do? I guess you can deny the story, but eventually people will learn that it's true and then they'll accuse you of deceiving them, and the folks around here, they're great, but don't like being lied to.'

'Oh.' Something else occurred to Ava. 'I need to thank everyone. The folk at the fair dropped everything, stopped their good time to help look for Duke. How do I repay them?'

'You don't need to. It's what we do around here.'

Inwardly, Ava groaned. Along with many other things, she was tired of hearing that phrase, but she refrained from voicing that opinion.

'The only thing they expect is that you'll jump in and help them next time. That's the extent of it.'

'Okay, I'll take your word for that.'

'Good. Well, as I said, they appreciate honesty. I thought it best to keep your discovery on the quiet, too, but now, it's too late. Maybe tell the locals, then they might lose interest. But as for Jacqueline's hare-brained idea, that's a different story.'

'Noah, it's so much more than that. This,' she waved her hand across the paper, 'is a disaster. It's really bad and I'm scared.'

'Of what?'

Ava's face had blanched white. A deep sense of dread gripped him around the middle, holding his torso too tight, squeezing. Ava's wide-eyed innocence was like a smokescreen where the smoulder was slowly descending revealing something else, something sinister and his gut twisted with apprehension.

Ava took a large gulp of her wine. She swallowed and Noah imagined the dry, cool liquid lining her throat and giving her courage as the alcohol coursed through her body.

'Did I ever tell you I developed my love of history from my father? He was a history teacher and would often take me to the museum on the weekends. One time there was a special Egyptian exhibit with mummies and artefacts and original items on loan from the Cairo Museum. That was it. The pivotal moment my life changed. I was hooked and from that day I wanted to become the person that discovered these amazing artefacts and learned about these ancient civilisations. I wanted to know everything. It was that day I vowed to become an archaeologist.'

Okay, this was going somewhere he didn't expect. Ava's gaze went to the far reaches of the deck. He could tell she was reliving that special day. A hot breeze blew and she rubbed her bare arms.

'After I finished my studies in Tasmania, I moved to London hell-bent on making my way to Egypt, realising my dream. My bags were packed before I'd even graduated. If I had to wait to get to Egypt, London was the steppingstone. The lure of the bright city lights, the furious pace of the place, being in a city that never slept. It attracted me with so much excitement. I needed money and a job and I took whatever I could at first, always thinking that one day I'd be on a dig site. But then I found the perfect position at the British Museum. I shared a house with a group of people, one of them became a good friend, and I ingratiated myself into the antipodean lifestyle in London. I absolutely loved my time there.'

Noah guzzled his own wine and took a few mouthfuls of the steaming hot lasagne to avoid the look of wonder in Ava's eyes; at what was, a life in one of the largest, busiest cities in the world. And nothing like here.

She nibbled on the tiniest portion of food at the end of her fork. 'I worked in the Sudanese and Egyptian department with relics and antiquities. I dreamed of specialising in Egyptology, but that was a big jump with no experience, so at the time a dig site in Egypt felt impossible. In retrospect I should have made it happen. Instead, I got complacent and enjoyed London too much. I thought the museum was a wonderful compromise. Each day I surrounded myself with precious items and whilst they might have already been discovered, there was still so much to learn. I was often in charge of new displays of objects that required cataloguing and to record its history. On other days I was in the inner sanctum of the back rooms with incredible machines to perform X-rays and scientific research into what might be inside a discovered mummy. So, there was still the thrill of discovery in many ways.'

Now she had a glassy, far-away look in her eye, of a time past.

'I'd been working for about twelve months and was at a function at Claridge's. It's an expensive and wealthy venue, exclusive for those that can afford its luxury. The owners were a wealthy Egyptian family who were significant benefactors of the museum and donated large sums of money. And at this one event, I met Henry. A son of the wealthy family of benefactors. Henry was Egyptian but living in London, living an English lifestyle. To me, he was English. We fell in love, and within the next twelve months we were married. It was a whirlwind, wonderful romance. The year we dated was the best time of my life. We saw and did so many things, it was incredible, a dream. I wish I'd realised that at the time, perhaps it was a dream, perhaps it wasn't real.'

'We had a large and lavish wedding at Claridge's; a wedding girls dream of—beautiful and extravagant flowers, a designer wedding dress, specialty food and wines, the best musicians and my parents and brother flew in from Australia. They were the only people I knew at my own wedding. His family paid for it and controlled the guest list. It was an A-list of important people, but none of that mattered to me. I was marrying the man I loved.'

That dreamy looks on her face was killing him. It was whimsical and distant, and made him feel like nothing else that ever happened in her life would live up to those memories. He focused his gaze on his drink, slipped his fingers up and down the moist stem of the glass.

'We settled into life in London, and I continued to work and enjoy myself. Our move to Cairo was gradual but in retrospect very quick. He said his family needed him at home, his father was unwell, his mother was asking for him and soon, it became quite urgent that we visit. At first, I thought it was a visit. And of course, this was the country I'd always dreamed of visiting, so I was excited. But once we arrived, my entire world changed. *He* changed. It became about his family; they started making the decisions. Another relative was chosen to manage the business affairs in London, Henry was no longer required there. It was clear his family wanted him—us—to remain in Egypt. But then it was no longer a choice, it no longer felt temporary, and we were suddenly staying.'

'Henry placated me, told me I could finally do the dig work I'd always dreamed of. Then when that didn't happen, I was told I could work in the Cairo Museum, at the coalface of discovery and exhibits of the largest collection of Egyptian antiquities in the world. That changed too, and I was told I could oversee another, smaller museum. In fact, that was the family collection and it wasn't a museum at all. By then I was pregnant with Ish, and work became impossible. I gave birth to a son who was revered because he would grow into an important man of the family. By contrast, I became invisible. There were so many rules: I was forced to wear traditional dress and in public, I was forced to cover myself for modesty. I was not allowed to wear makeup. I was not permitted to talk to people outside of the family without my husband's permission.'

'Each new day the rules seemed to grow until I was unable, as an independent free-thinking woman, to make any decisions for myself. I probably could have, would have endured that for the sake of my marriage, but I couldn't allow my son to grow up in a culture where his life as a toddler was considered more important than mine as an adult woman. That he was allowed to be educated, whilst his female cousins and any other woman in the family was relegated to indoors and forbidden reading material or to educate themselves. That our lives were controlled, but his was not. And that would have only worsened as he grew older. I could not, will not ever permit him to be that sort of man. The sort of man that my husband became in his home country. I became a vessel for having children and I knew eventually my enthusiasm for life would be whittled away until it had disappeared and I, as a woman, had disappeared too.'

'And there was constant pressure for me to convert to their religion. And worse, there was polygamy. Whilst not a common custom anymore, it was still prevalent. Henry resisted, but I dreaded, thought, in time, that would have been inevitable, too and something he would have been unable to refuse if his father commanded it.' Ava shivered and he watched the line of bumps raise along her arms and the hairs stand up.

Noah grasped her closest hand. A sign of solidarity and support. It sounded truly horrible and untenable for any woman to live like that. He was aware of these controlling places, saw and read the news but had never heard it from a first-hand account.

Giggles drifted outside through the crack in the sliding door. The glow of the television lit up the living area inside where Emily and Duke sat watching cartoons, innocent, and child-like. She must have caught his glare and turned her head to stare.

'His real name is Ismail. It wasn't my first choice but satisfied his family being culturally and religiously appropriate. Duke is his middle name and we thought when we moved here it would be easier for people to pronounce but it was tricky because I never remembered to call him by that name and he didn't answer to it, either.'

'What's, um, is your real name Ava Montgomery?'

'Yes, but it's my maiden name not my married name.'

Okay. Made sense. But he had to ask. 'He, Henry wasn't abusive to you, was he? Didn't hurt you?'

'Oh, he hurt me alright, but he wasn't physically violent. He betrayed my trust and turned into a man I didn't recognise, who didn't stand up for me and my rights as his wife and the mother of our child. Made me complicit in a relationship I had never agreed to. Treated me as if I didn't exist once we were in his homeland. And, for a short time, I allowed it to happen. I was in such shock, I wasn't sure I quite understood what was going on. You know how things appear so obvious, but you think they cannot be what you imagine, it can't possibly be true?'

No, he didn't think he did, but, okay, maybe he did. One day, his wife loved him and their life in the country, and the next she didn't. He didn't change, his wife did. But he guessed, that is exactly what Ava described; her husband changed and she was placed into a compromising position. But his example was different, wasn't it?

'But how did you leave? That must have been difficult?'

'Yes. If not for Jamila, my mother-in-law. I honestly think I'd still be stuck there, desperate to flee. She was much worse off than me but Jamila came from a similar Arab family. She, too, was given reassurances, promises that were never kept. She was powerless. All women in this family are powerless. Jamila became aware of how her husband was treating his older daughters, children from previous marriages. This was the turning point for her. They were young woman desperate to get out, to live a more liberated and free life. And they tried. Two of them escaped, literally ran for their lives in elaborate plots to leave the country. They were caught and punished. Jamila didn't like how they were treated afterwards. Couldn't tolerate such behaviour. If her husband was capable of that … doesn't bear thinking about.' Ava bowed her head as if the memories were too painful. 'She feared for the safety of those women and her own children. She has a son and a daughter.'

'She hatched her own plan to get out and begged me to run, too.' She looked at him then. 'Do you understand, Noah, how bad it was that we were prepared to risk our lives to flee?' Noah listened to the story transfixed, and only offered a murmur of support. 'She helped me. Without her, I was helpless.'

'And your husband let you go?'

'Oh, no, he would never. He didn't know until we were gone.'

CHAPTER

Twenty~Six

WITH A SHARP, shooting pang to his chest, Noah realised. How could he have been so stupid?

Jumping up too fast, the glass slipped from his hand and smashed to the deck and shattered with jagged shards scattering across the flooring.

Ava scrambled for the dustpan and brush and cleaned up the mess. He moved to the railing at the edge of the deck, caught the dusk breeze. It cooled his rising temper. He gulped in great breaths until it felt like it snagged in his throat. Then he paced.

'Noah?' Ava queried, coming to stand behind him. Her presence was too close now, cloying. He strode to the other end of the spacious deck, turned and faced her.

'Just so I have this right and am not reaching the wrong conclusions I assume his father, your husband, knows where you are and has agreed to let you live here in Australia with Ish?' His voice was soft, each word accentuating his pain.

'Noah, we fled in the darkness of night, scurrying along underground alleyways, quiet as mice, and never looked back, not once.'

His hands balled into fists. 'Okay, so Henry doesn't know you're here and didn't give you permission to take your child?'

'What are you talking about? After what I've just told you, what sort of question is that? I ran for our lives, for our safety, to keep my son safe.'

He doubled over, lent on the back of the nearest chair for support. 'You can't do that, Ava. Ish has two parents and one of those parents does not get the right to decide where that child lives and when the other parent is allowed to see them. He has rights as a father.'

Ava stalked backwards now, sensing the mood in the conversation shift.

'He's my son and he needs to be with me...'

'Damn it, Ava, you've stolen him!' He turned away, embarrassed at his outburst.

'I need to protect him because his father won't! A parent cannot leave their child to be harmed, raised in a toxic and unsuitable environment.'

Noah's ears were ringing. He knew at a deeper level there were always two sides to a story, but this, how could she?

His head throbbed as he recalled that scene with Lisa. The one where she'd begged him to move to the city, start fresh, start over and he'd thought she was joking. Where he'd ignored her. Didn't ask any questions. Had Lisa felt the same as Ava? Obviously, not fear but that depth of desperation, that deep level of unhappiness that made her feel like she had no choice? She must have, because eventually, she fled, too.

Regardless, both women had taken their child and run.

Were there justifications to such an act? To deprive a father of his child? It was easy to blame Lisa, the person who'd done the running. It couldn't be him, could it? He'd stayed the distance.

'My wife took our daughter, disappeared with her while I was at work. Then she started dictating terms about Emily's future. I have rights, Ava, I'm her father.' His voice caught on a sob. 'I deserve to be with my daughter just as much as my wife does. Your husband needs to be with your son just as much as you.'

'In this instance, you're wrong. My situation is different and your view is clouded by your own circumstances. My child was in danger. I had to act, I had to protect him. And myself.'

A searing pain burned in his chest. 'But it's not, is it? This is the universal story, the father is not as important, the father does not matter, the father is the second parent. It seems to always be about the mother.'

'Don't you do this, Noah. You're wrong. This is not an argument about mothers and fathers. This is about the safety of my son.' Her legs buckled under her.

'It makes sense now. The secrecy, the different names, the seclusion and isolating yourself away. You were harbouring your son so that your husband never found you. Hiding.'

Noah watched as Ava unfurled, grew in strength and confidence once more. Her shoulders pushed back and she stood and strode towards him, her face only inches away. This was a woman he'd never seen cower in fear, was confident and strong, intelligent. And yet she had acted the same as his wife. She had stolen her own child.

'If my husband finds us, he'll take Ish and I will never see him again. He will be indoctrinated into the family and that male-dominated patriarchy and I will never, ever be allowed access. Is that what I should submit to?'

She spoke calmly but her body was rigid, her pupils dark and foreboding and he was impaled by her challenging glare. The tension built with frightening intensity before stretching into silence.

His stance softened, the fight leaving him. 'Okay. Your circumstances might be different. But there is still a boy who needs his father. A father that I'm sure wants to know his son is safe and well. If you fled for the right reasons, then you need to do the right thing now and tell your husband that your son is safe. Do it, Ava, otherwise I fear I will.'

Hours later, her mobile telephone rang and numb, unthinking, Ava answered it. On the other end a voice said they were from a national paper, there was a big story breaking in Bellethorpe and was she the finder of the relic? They wanted the exclusive and could be there within the hour. Ava dropped the phone without responding.

Moments later, it rang again, and again, repeatedly. Ava powered off the device and threw the phone across the room. She didn't care where it landed, never wanted to answer it again. If journalists had her details, it was only a matter of time before they turned up, demanding to know more and determined to run a story with or without her permission and any factual basis. Right now, they were probably filming and photographing her home and property from the air. Snapping photos of her and Ish if they dared leave, or even stand at their own window.

Ava had witnessed what they'd done to Jamila. Reporters had camped out the front of her doorstep for days waiting for the perfect shot. Ava understood what they were capable of. Had seen it splayed across her own television screen multiple times recently. No doubt, these reporters were driving from the city now and would arrive, soon.

Her name attached to the fossil was probably viral on the internet already. No one needed to wait for the morning edition of the paper anymore, there was access twenty-four-seven to world-breaking news. And if this information was somewhere on the web, Henry or someone associated with him, would see it. He would find out. Might already know.

Should she flee? Run and establish themselves someone new? It would be easy. Australia was a big continent. It wouldn't be hard to disappear again.

Yes, she could do it. Ava rushed to collect their belongings, filling her arms until they were overloaded. She ran into her bedroom, dumped the pile on her bed and reached for their bags. The largest case toppled from the top of wardrobe and a corner wheel landed on her toe.

'Argh, damn it! She dropped to the ground and clutched her pinkie toe. The stuff she'd piled on the bed slipped off and landed on her. Then she sobbed.

Sleep was impossible that night. Instead, she paced; walked a track into her floorboards. Exhausted, occasionally she curled up in the armchair, the entire house illuminated except for Ish's room where he was safely tucked into bed, unaware of the danger, still mending his broken heart over the puppy.

She wouldn't flee. One look at the house she'd renovated and she knew she couldn't leave. Their life, however small, had become something here. She was enjoying it; no, she was happy here. Ish was making friends and had the space to be a little boy and was growing and developing in leaps and bounds now caring for their own hobby farm with its menagerie of animals and their vegetable patch.

Would Noah betray her?

Her heart ached remembering his searing look of disappointment, of disdain. She was gutted that he thought of her as a recalcitrant parent, the sort of parent she was sure they lambasted in their father support group.

But he didn't understand. And if he couldn't, there was no hope for them. She would never ever again submit to the demands of a man that were not in sync with her own beliefs. Better they work this out now, she guessed. Her hopes of a relationship shattered, splintering like broken glass. She was sure the pain would lessen, eventually.

She took his threat seriously, though, but it was probably the least of her worries. By the time Noah had located Henry, he'd know where she was. Probably had surveillance chasing her tail right now and she was about to be snared in a trap.

She dozed eventually but woke with a start. She'd heard a noise, a heavy thump like someone was on her deck. Flinging herself upwards quickly, she kinked her neck, and her legs didn't work properly. She peered around the kitchen blinds. Nothing. The rooster was crowing, heralding a new day. A sound she'd grown to love. A sliver of golden light lined the horizon, the sun on its way. The grassy knolls wore a light layer of mist before the heat of the day set in. All around her was a picture of serenity and calm. Glorious beauty when inside her chest her heart hammered so hard, she must surely be having a heart attack. She craned her neck against the glass panelling but couldn't see anything unusual. Tiptoeing in socked feet, she veered around the kitchen doorframe, her eyes reaching one corner of her beloved back deck, where she'd grown to enjoy sitting in the morning and evenings. Now it felt tainted, with unfettered access to her house and her safety.

There was a blur of black and movement. A figure moved across her yard, past the trampoline and towards the rear fence. Clive: his distinctive hat and gait. She released a sigh and loosened her grip on the door handle at the sight of him retreating.

Then she saw it. At the top of the staircase sat a large square cardboard box. It looked innocuous. She waited a moment, and another. Creeping without a sound, she pulled open the screen door, checked left and right and proceeded onto the deck. Peered over the edge, into the fields, checked the long drive. Watched the disappearing figure of Clive now returned to his own property, the horses neighing nearby, hoping it was breakfast time.

Ava felt a presence to her right and spun to see Daisy pad out. Ava suppressed her scream. Wherever Daisy was, the puppies were sure to follow. Ava surveyed the box and there was no address label or sender details. Turning it over revealed nothing.

Clive must have delivered the box. Why? If it was left at his place by accident, how did he know it was for her? A knot the size of a rock sat on her chest, the pressure making it difficult to breath.

If Clive delivered the box, it had to be okay, didn't it? But why did he do it in secret? Needing answers, she ripped open the sticky tape holding the folds together. Inside, the items were bubble wrapped for protection. This piqued her interest. Lifting out the smallest item, she unwrapped it, carefully and slowly as if it might be precious. Colour dazzled through the hazy plastic revealing bright blues and golds, splashes of red.

'Oh my…' Ava looked up, to her left and right. It couldn't be. It was so beautiful. And there was only one person who knew how much she would love this scarab amulet: her husband.

Small in size, the dung beetle in deep blue sat in the middle and shapes like wings spread out on each side and were multi-coloured and encased in gold-trim leading to a figure point at the top where an orange-red jewel sat like a crown. The scarab symbolised birth, life, death and resurrection.

It had to be from Henry. He had, once, listened to her, knew about her love for this particular piece of Egyptian history and the many versions in which it was emulated.

Clutching the ornament, she examined the other bulky item in the bottom of the box. It was larger, and of an odd shape. Tape held the corners of the package in place and she used her fingernail to peel away each layer to reveal a remote-control car. A present for Ish.

A wave of realisation hit her. Noah was right. She had done the wrong thing. Yes, she did what she thought was right to keep her son safe and to avoid him being raised in a strict, masculine environment against her beliefs. But it was still wrong.

She knew what she needed to do now and calm descended upon her. It was time to make amends, to make things right for their future. She was no longer prepared to be scared, to run, flinch at each noise she heard. To hide. They both deserved to be safe and live without fear. Now, she needed to act, control this situation she'd created. Henry deserved to know where his son was and that he was safe, whatever the consequences.

CHAPTER
Twenty~Seven

NOAH DROVE through the night fuelled by anger and energy drinks. That had kept him awake during the darkest hours. That and compiling his newest poem.

Precious daughter growing strong
Only ever wanting the day to stay long
The sun rises on a new day
His desperation is for her to stay
But by the time the moon shines high in the sky
She'll be gone, it's always hard to say goodbye

The car windows had fogged with the dip in temperature and he used the sleeve of his shirt to clear the view. He'd been sitting in the car outside Lisa's house for an hour now waiting to make his move.

One thing had become clear to him. Noah Hawthorn needed to take matters back into his own hands; take back control. Just like the fellas at the support group always urged. If Ava could take her son and get away with it; if Lisa could do it, he could too. If it was all about the right reasons, he had them, too. He'd come to claim what was right-fully his and restore the natural order of things.

He'd worked out the details. It might mean living in a new country town, not his beloved Bellethorpe, but it would be worth it. A fresh start for both of them. As long as he remained in the country, with its fresh air and rolling green hills, he figured he'd be all right.

He'd waited long enough. Noah flung open the car door.

Henry,

Ismail and I are safe and well in Australia. We are settled in a small town in Queensland. I am sorry that I fled without telling you and taking Ish. There's a lot to discuss, can we chat?

Ava

Despite the time difference, Henry's reply was instant.

Ava,

Thank you for making contact. I know where you are. I'm coming to visit. Will be there soon.

Hamid

Whoa! What? Coming now? Was he already en route? He did know where she was. Instant travel was easy for him, of course. The family had their own collection of private jets. Would he come alone? With an entourage? With security? Each thought escalated her growing fear.

Would Henry come with his brother, Ahmed? Ahmed was the youngest, the most indulged, the least skilled but most ambitious. The most dangerous. There was one secret Ava held that she wouldn't disclose, to anyone. That one night...thinking about it and sheer black terror swept through her. It was late and she'd stayed up in the library reading when Ahmed had come home from a night out drinking. Ava was returning to her room when they encountered each other in the long, narrow and darkened hallways. Ava had never liked him but had never feared him before. Fuelled with alcohol, he'd been belligerent about his rights as a son, his role in the family and that he should be able to share his brother's spoils. Despite her best efforts, Ava hadn't been able to get away. He'd cornered her, held her in place and lifted her nightgown before running his fingers over her body, across her breasts, and laughing at her fear so that his spittle landed on her cheek. His eyes were wild as he undid his belt buckle...Instinct had kicked in and Ava had kneed him in the groin and luckily, he'd hunched easily due to his inebriation and she'd escaped.

Imprisoned already by then in the palace surroundings by Henry, everything had worsened. Ahmed's embarrassing defeat had angered him, and he sought retribution. After that, nowhere was safe.

It was impossible to tell Henry. Ava had tried; the family was loyal, they pandered to the youngest member of the household, guided him, never accepted his faults.

Icy shards of fear settled in her spine. Had she made a grave mistake?

———

Noah greeted Sienna in the office of Lincoln Reid, unamused that he now knew the receptionist by name. It was not a place he wanted to frequent. Dare he dream that after today, this might be the end?

Sienna offered him a coffee that he accepted; anything to calm his nerves. It tasted vile and he downed the espresso in one sip. The caffeine travelled through his veins quickly and worked its magic. Except now his foot tapped.

'Noah, come on through.' Lincoln held his door open and observed him. 'Is everything all right? Are you okay?'

No, it wasn't. He'd been an absolute idiot. But the three-hour return trip from Brisbane to Bellethorpe had sobered him. Should he tell his lawyer what he'd done?

No. He'd done nothing wrong. In the end he'd climbed a trellis, peered into his daughter's bedroom like a common beggar and at the sight of her—safe, comfortable and warm in the most beautifully decorated little girl's bedroom—he'd scarpered out of there quick-smart and spent the morning hours berating himself for being a right royal jackass. Embarrassed, that's what he was. Of his behaviour. Of his lack of self-control. He'd lost his mind, but he'd found it now.

Man, he'd be pouring out a poem later, that'd be sure. And it wouldn't be pretty.

Lincoln pushed on, unaware of any of this.

'Okay, the family report has been delivered to the court and the parties each have a copy.' Taking a seat, the lawyer avoided further pleasantries and Noah was thankful for that. 'I've read it thoroughly but rather than send it to you, I thought we'd talk it through and then you can take your time making a decision.'

'A decision? About what? I thought that was the whole point of this expensive report process? Doesn't the social worker make the decision?'

'The report writer makes a recommendation and bases that recom-mendation on the content of the report, and that, of course, is the infor-mation she has gleaned from the interviews with each of you and any other investigations she conducted. It is for the court to endorse the recommendation or make another ruling on who Emily lives with and how often she spends time with the other parent.'

Okay, more legal mumbo jumbo, but whatever. Lincoln rattled on for a bit longer. 'Lincoln, just tell me. What is her recommendation?'

A heavy pause. 'She recommends that Emily remain living with her mother in Brisbane.'

A knife pierced his chest and sent shooting pains to his extremities. 'When do I see her?'

'Alternate weekends and each holiday excepting a rotation of special days like Easter and Christmas, her birthday.'

'So, despite Lisa moving my daughter away from the only home she's ever known without my permission, she is allowed to keep her and I'm to only see her on weekends and holidays?' He couldn't help another outburst. Surprisingly, his voice was steady.

'Noah, Emily is not an object. Lisa does not get to keep her.'

Okay, yes, Lincoln was right. 'Sorry, wrong turn of phrase but you know what I mean.'

'This was a tough situation, and the report writer acknowledges that. You'll see it when you read the full report. These are unfortunate circumstances and a decision had to be made for the future and none of the options were ideal.'

Tough for him only, it seemed.

Lincoln spelled out the specifics of the time allocated to Noah. He was to drive to collect her each visit. The report writer didn't think Lisa was up to sharing the transportation. Lisa was fragile? Holidays ... special events ... phone time every second night...

It was the worst-case scenario.

'What do we do now? Is this recommendation written up and becomes law?'

'No. You have options; this is not the rule absolute. You can accept this recommendation and avoid attending court again by entering into consent parenting orders as per this report. Or you can seek alternative orders. Something like seeking Lisa be partly responsible for visits or you return Emily to school on a Monday morning in Brisbane and not Sunday evening. Minor tweaks. Or you challenge the recommendation and run the matter to hearing. It would be one day and there would be three witnesses: you, Lisa and the report writer. We would argue that Emily lives with you.'

Noah held up his hand. 'And my prospects of success in obtaining that order?'

'Less than fifty/fifty. It's difficult to get a court to rule opposite to the evidence of a highly skilled and experienced counsellor.'

And then Lincoln told him the cost of running his case to that one-day hearing.

His eyes watered and Noah hung his head. His limbs were heavy and hard to move. He needed sleep. Every ounce of energy drained from his body. His fight ebbed away like a slow-trickling stream.

With Ava's big job still in motion, he could find the money and fight for his daughter.

'Take the report, read it carefully and absorb what the social worker is saying. Understand why she made the decision. Remember, Noah this is about Emily not you as father and not Lisa as the mother. If you can keep that in the forefront of your mind, it'll make more sense.'

Noah shoved the report into his back pocket where it stuck out and rubbed against his lower back, like an annoying spasming muscle that couldn't be eased no matter how much it was rubbed or medication applied.

CHAPTER
Twenty-Eight

TWENTY-FOUR HOURS LATER, the first helicopter landed, then the second. The low-lying grass was flattened and everything else in the wake of the high-speed blades sent flying.

Men in black clothing with aviator-type sunglasses and fancy belts with equipment, exited first. A quartet of them scattered in each direction. One performed a dramatic forward roll as he alighted the aircraft and found himself in long grass. Ava rolled her eyes as Ish exclaimed, 'Wow!'

It was like a scene from an action movie, except she wasn't a damsel in distress that needed saving. Damsel be damned.

The all-clear must have been given by Henry's security men, Ava refused to call him Hamid, and he exited the second chopper. A fifth man accompanied Henry but stayed back at a distance and her husband approached the house alone. At no sign of Ahmed, Ava exhaled all the air she held in her lungs.

Ish raced across the short slope from the house. She had her arm out to prevent him, but it was left hanging.

'Papa! Papa!'

Ava stayed on the deck. In the distance, she spied movement down near the dig site. Of course, the commotion would confuse Matthew and James. What would they think? She should have warned them. Thank goodness the builders weren't here today, how on earth would she explain? But then, it came to her, swiftly: the truth. From now on, it would be the cold and hard, ugly truth.

Standing like a preacher in her pulpit, surveying her kingdom from the sanctity of her deck, Ava watched Henry bend low and scoop up their son, crush him to his chest and twirl him on the spot. Her body tensed with fear. She hadn't thought this through. Did Henry step forward? He was facing the chopper now. Was he going to make a run for it? Steal Ish back right in front of her? Her hands gripped the railing undecided whether she should dash across the yard and lunge for her son. She hadn't come this far to lose him.

But then, as if in slow motion, the spinning stopped and Henry lowered Ish to the ground and handed him something.

Her son's hands sagged with the weight of the package as they walked together towards the house.

'Mumma! Papa bought me Lego!' he yelled across the space, the words travelling on the wind now that the noise of the engines and blades had ceased. The valley otherwise echoed silent. Only Ava could hear the accelerated beating of her heart.

Willing her face to comply, Ava plastered on a smile that stretched her cheeks too wide. Henry trailed Ish onto the deck, making no qualm of looking around him, sizing up their home.

'Quaint,' he said and she was transported, that accent, those smooth and honey-deep tones, the lilt of the vowels. It had always been a mix of his homeland and upper-class British. It was out of place here in Bellethorpe along with his exotic, dark, good looks. It felt like a slap to her face.

It was the strangest sensation, knowing someone so well; the intimacies they had shared, the dreams, lives melded together and yet, not knowing them at all. Before her stood a stranger.

'Ava.' He approached and kissed her on the cheek.

He is not the enemy.

'Henry.' Her smile was tight.

'Mumma, can I build the Lego, please!'

'Yes, of course. You build it, and Mummy and Daddy will chat. There's lots to catch up on.'

Ish had only just slid the glass door shut when he started.

'How could you do this, Ava? To us, to our family? We could have made it work.' His words were perfectly pronounced but his jaw was set hard, his chin locked into position, his face determined.

Clenching and unclenching her fists, buying time, she willed herself to stay calm, talk without conviction and remain focused. She was not going to cower in fear. The moment had come to tell him how she felt. She owed him that. Hadn't done it before she fled and she should have. A life without fear.

And she would be honest, but she would not reveal the very worst of it, the real and very live threat to her safety at the hands of his own brother.

'Only for you and your family. I married you and our life was in Britain, not Egypt. How could *you* do this to us? Change the plan, the future without thinking of how it would affect me and our son?'

'It wasn't what I had planned either. But family is everything and my family needs me at home. My father remains unwell so I continue to run the family business in Cairo. I must obey. So should you as my wife. You should do as I say and not disrespect history and convention and tradition.' As he spoke, his words rushed and his ire grew.

'Do you want to stay and live in Cairo, be with your family and run the business?'

'Yes.'

His tone softened then; the scorching heat left his words. It unnerved her. Was this a trick? 'Surely you must have known it was a possibility when we married? You should have told me, warned me. It would have made a difference.'

'We were in love. I loved you. I thought we could make anything work as long as we were together.' His words sounded sincere.

'It's not fair to me. I will not live like that. I worked hard to become an archaeologist, I'm not prepared to throw it away, to be a servant to you and my own son—'

'Damnit, Ava! You could still work, I told you—'

She didn't let him finish, held up her flat palm. That was a gesture she was confident he did not receive at home, where he was in charge, where his word was gospel. 'That's a token and not even an enticing one. Would you permit me to work in the Cairo Museum?'

'That's not possible.'

'Urgh, I shouldn't need your permission. And of course, that's the answer then, I rest my case. I will not live subservient to you and to my own son. I will not raise him to be superior, to treat women the way your family treats them. Your mother, the other wives, they might choose that life. I will not be controlled. I do not choose to live like that.'

He hung his head. In sorrow? Sadness? Time passed and the silence continued. Clenching her jaw tight, she refused to be the one to fill the gap.

'I understand.' Long pause. 'I was shocked and saddened when you left.'

What?

'At first, I wanted to chase you, hunt you down, make you pay. I really did. This woman I loved had taken my only son, my heir, and rejected the opulent life I'd offered her. I was embarrassed, furious. My family was angry, and of course, you did it in cohorts with Jamila and that only made the situation worse. Without my intervention, my father would have had no hesitation in finding you, taking you prisoner against your will and returning you to the homeland.'

She knew it, but hearing the words out loud, the reality of what she'd been running from, caused a shiver to race up her spine.

Henry turned and faced outwards then, towards her land and the sky deepening to a royal blue and now scattered with marshmallow clouds. A gentle breeze blew away the flies. It was idyllic.

'It is beautiful here, very Australian. This is where you grew up, yes?'

She nodded; words were difficult to form. He had just been telling her that his father would have held her captive against her will and now he addressed the scenery? Her nerves rattled and her body tensed even more.

'Do you love it here?'

'Yes, I do.'

'Is this where you wish to remain with Ismail?'

'Yes.'

He looked at her hard and long, his gaze so intense her insides squirmed but she refused to turn away. Did he see her resolve? Did he sense her determination?

'Ish has grown into quite the country boy. He has raised a litter of puppies, is responsible for feeding the chickens and collecting their eggs and is assisting the neighbour feed and water his horses. He spends a lot of time outside in nature.'

Henry smiled, whimsical, his eyes distant. 'And tell me about this fossil.'

'You ... you, know about that?'

'Of course. I know everything, Ava. I know about the dogs and chickens and horses and this house and your life here. How much you paid for it, how you sealed the contract. Everything.'

'Have you known where we've been all along?' Her voice dropped to a whisper.

'Not immediately, but soon thereafter.'

Deep down, she'd known that too, but he hadn't come.

'The fossil?' he repeated.

'I assume you know all about it, then?'

'I want to hear from you. It sounds important, significant to your work.'

'It's historically significant. It's a rare and extinct turtle and most likely there are other opalised fossils nearby, there usually are but nothing else has been located yet.'

'The gems are pretty, huh?'

'Yes.' Of course, he knew about them, too.

'Valuable?'

'Most likely. But these are not necessarily items that value can be ascribed.'

Pacing towards her, he grasped her hands in his. The gesture was quick and hurried and caught her by surprise. 'You will not return with me? Are you sure?'

She ripped her hands out of his grip and stepped back, creating space. 'No.' She swallowed. 'Will you force us?'

He laughed. But it wasn't contagious. 'No. I will not. I could, you understand. But it is because I love you that I will not. One of the many reasons I fell in love with you was because of your determination, intelligence and your feisty grip on life. As you understand now, women are not like that at home. You were a breath of fresh air, an enigma. But I should have known better, you are right. Some things cannot be altered. I do not wish you to be unhappy or resent me or the life you'd be living. Of course, I wish you'd change your mind. But things have changed, too, in your absence.'

Her stomach clenched for another blow. He spoke with his gaze focused on the distance, the rear fence where Marmalade and Honey raced along the boundary, their manes flying. 'You will always be my first wife, but I have taken another since you've left and she is pregnant with a son. The future is secure and the family are happy.'

Not unexpected but still a blow. But what did it matter? She'd been replaced and so had their son. It made things easier really, she should be pleased. The news steeled her heart, clamped it shut and turned it to ice. Yes, she'd loved this man, but she no longer did. He was a great love and her son's father. Only.

'If I had asked your permission to leave, would you have let me?' she asked quietly.

The weight of the words hung in the air, loaded and heavy.

Henry hesitated, opened his lips to respond, closed them. 'That would have been hard. My family would not have liked it. If you had not run, you'd most likely still be there.' The steely glint in his eye unnerved her.

Simply nodding, what else could she do, she asked, 'Okay, what now?'

He wasn't quite finished with his platitudes. 'I understand you are a strong woman and want to be in charge of your own life. You are not suited to being part of my family. I am sorry.'

Her body sagged.

'I will grant you a divorce. I will make the arrangements, quietly and swiftly, and our son will remain living here with you. I could never take him away, even though he has an important role in the family, of course... I will visit when it suits and continue to focus on my life and the family dynasty. I will grant you an allowance—'

'No, Henry, that's not necessary. I'm fine. We'll be fine.'

'Very well, I will give you a donation for your work here with the fossil.'

Again, she shook her head, words of denial forming.

'It's for the research.'

'Papa, Papa! Come and see!' Ish yelled from inside. Henry sought her permission to enter and he went inside the house and sat on the floor where a racing track and garage had been constructed. Ish showed him how the cars spun along the track and jumped into the air at one point. They laughed together. Henry bent his head low, their foreheads touching. She couldn't hear the words spoken, but Ish gazed up at him, his eyes watering, his nod, barely discernible. Henry kissed him on the head and rose.

But Ava needed more. This wasn't enough.

'Henry?' As soon as he stepped out onto the deck. He paused mid-stride.

'I need to go, there's a meeting I must return for.'

'Please, I need your reassurance that we are safe here. Your family won't hurt us, you'll let us live in peace. No surprises?'

'You have my word.' A curt nod to her and he started to move away. 'Oh, and one more thing. This is for you. A parting gift.' He placed a small package into her hands before skipping down the stairs. Clive stood at the fence, his horses near, him petting one on the neck. The commotion would have had him intrigued; Ava was sure. Instead of Henry striding back towards the helicopters, he headed towards the fence where Clive received him with a wave. The men chatted for a few minutes, hands gesticulating in speech. Henry patted Clive on the arm and departed.

CHAPTER
Twenty~Nine

'THE FATHER GETS SCREWED over again. Noah, you must fight this. You have to stand up for your rights and fight for your daughter.'

The members of the father's support group spoke over each other, expressing their rage at the recommendation of the report writer in Noah's family law matter.

Usually, he found solidarity and support in the group; a place of comfort and of a united front, sometimes the only place he felt heard. They could discuss and agree on action and sustain each other through the painful times. Today he was hollow. He listened to their outrage, and part of him agreed with their sentiments, but none of the comments registered, the rallying did not buoy him like it usually did. It was like they were talking about someone else, not him, not his life.

For the first time since this disaster had started, he thought about moving. Not stealing Emily in the dark of night and finding a new home this time, but him relocating to the big city. A place he hated and didn't want to visit, let alone live. But if Emily was the most important factor in this scenario, a fact made clear by the social worker, then surely, he could, should, make the sacrifice to spend equal time with his daughter. If he was prepared to move, there was an alternative recommendation that he and Lisa share equal time with Emily. Live with their mother and father on a week about rotation. The implementation of this shared care arrangement had been hard fought by advocacy of this very group and the win celebrated.

But the reality of his precious Emily being transferred like cargo to a different bedroom each week didn't fill him with any joy. What sort of life was that? He couldn't even imagine it. It simply didn't seem right. He kept those views to himself.

Then he flipped his thinking. He'd stay in Bellethorpe and give it twelve months of commuting and see how everyone coped, including him with the long periods of transport. You never knew how a situation would play out until you'd tried it, right? Yes, it wasn't ideal. But if he thought of it as temporary, it might be manageable.

And then his thoughts flip-flopped again, and he was outraged once more: at himself, his situation and life in general. At the unfairness of it all. And that view was being rammed down his throat repeatedly by his father friends. However, he was slowly learning that he could cry foul, but the proclamations didn't change anything. Didn't deliver his daughter back to him or make the recommendation more palatable.

So, he could wallow in his own misery or accept his fate.

'We will support you, Noah, through the entire process. We can assist with the costs, do a fundraiser, make some noise, advocate on your behalf.'

Only a short time ago, it would have been the advice he'd have given, too.

'Thank you for your support. I'm grateful and appreciate it. But I'm not going to fight anymore, I'm tired and can't contemplate an ongoing battle.'

There were nods of recognition, some disappointment, partial understanding but many vehement shakes of heads in disagreement.

'You can't give up, man.'

'I'm not. I'm stopping the fight. There's a difference and perhaps we need to learn that, too. I'm no longer prepared to fight with my ex-wife about custody of our daughter. I'm no longer prepared to fund lawyers and the court system. I'm choosing my daughter. I'm choosing her happiness and if the experts are telling me she needs to be with her mother for the moment, I'll agree. It is not healthy for anyone to be involved in this conflict.'

His monologue was met with silence.

What he'd not told anyone was Emily's wishes. When asked directly by the social worker who she wanted to live with, her answer had been her mother. The words on the report blurred as his tears had fallen onto the page. What an idiot. He'd never once asked his daughter where she'd prefer to be. She was only six-years-old, after all. Was it possible for her to make such apt decisions at that age? The experienced child therapist thought so. Said it was not the determining factor, but if the child, even one so young was black and white in her answer, it needed to be listened to, didn't it?

Man, it hurt. But it was the only thing he'd been thinking about since; hours spent rationalising it. Perhaps girls needed their mothers? Or perhaps young children needed their mothers? He'd read about bonding. But he understood in his rational moments, that her answer didn't mean she didn't love him or want to spend time with him. The response didn't lead to any of those answers and the report writer had kindly pointed that out. But she went further, said, it was a delicate age where children rely upon their mothers providing those basic needs.

And that is true. In his hours of reflection, he'd remembered that Lisa had been the stay-at-home parent while he went out to work. Mother and daughter had spent endless hours together. If Emily needed food, she asked her mother. If she'd grazed her knee, she wanted comfort and a Band Aid from her mother. Any basic need was provided by Lisa.

If Emily wanted to be tussled upside down and squeal in delight, she came to him. If she wanted to be chased and tackled, Dad was her man. Any game, fun or silliness, he was the preferred parent.

He'd never thought about it like that before, but it made sense. They had different roles to play. He could, of course, provide the basic needs too, and as she aged, those basic needs would be different.

'Something's happening out at Kinross Road.' Bobby piped up after checking the alerts on his phone.

Noah's ears pricked, zeroing back into the present. 'What, what do you mean?' Had journalists finally found Ava?

'Um, I don't know exactly, there's reports of helicopters and men in surveillance gear.'

Noah stood; the words had stolen the oxygen from the air around him and suddenly he couldn't breathe. Was Ava, okay? Rushing out, the door slammed after him.

Outside, the street was busy. Cars not touched by dirt roads were parked at odd angles, people milled beside them scrolling screens and talking on mobile phones in rapid voices. While Bellethorpe was not a large town, a population of five thousand or so, it was always obvious when out-of-towners had arrived. These people were not local.

His ute was parked outside the community hall at the end of Main Street. Approaching his car, a man jumped in front of him and shoved a Dictaphone into his face. Noah swiped for it and narrowly missed as the man moved it out of reach.

'Timothy Flynn from *The Australian*, can you guide me towards this newly-found fossil?'

Otis growled at the man's heels.

'Get out of my way.'

'Are the reports true? Has someone found an extinct and valuable fossil? We understand you've been working at the house? Can you at least tell me what you know?'

Noah shoved the man hard in his chest, sent him roiling backwards, bumping into his car and wobbling on his feet. The reporter didn't take the hint and Noah bunched his fist and stretched his arm back, ready to strike.

Timothy held his hands up in front of his face. It wasn't fear in the man's face, it was annoyance but that flick into a small semblance of panic was enough for Noah to hold his arm steady. What was he doing? A split second more and he'd have decked the guy. Noah uncurled the fist and lowered it. Not a great example for his daughter.

Ignoring the reporter despite his renewed shouts for information, Noah hopped into the car and gunned the engine, unintentionally squealing the tyres as he took off too fast.

The town was abuzz. Queues for coffee were out of the café premises, the bakery had standing room only and there wasn't a spare picnic table at the park. He slammed his fist on the steering wheel and drove too fast to Ava's place.

She probably didn't want to see him, but he needed to know she was okay.

On Kinross Road, he ignored the trawling reporters, these ones with high tech cameras towering on shoulders with long lens pointed towards the house. Despite the long driveway, he had no doubt they could spot the detail on the outdoor gabling and the ornaments on the front verandah. Pests.

He didn't spot any helicopters. Noah silenced the radio; nope, no distinct hovering of blades in the sky above, either. Had the reports of aircraft been wrong?

His thoughts tumbled around his head. Yes, it seemed as if the media had been alerted to the story. But his mind went elsewhere at the news of trouble. Had Ava's husband found her? Yes, he'd made threats but he would never have followed through with them. Noah wanted Ava to act and he hoped with those threats she might. And that had never meant he wanted her or the boy harmed.

He blew out a breath as he approached the gate and deviated off to a side road. He'd go another way, up Clive's drive. Moments later Noah pulled up too quick, yanked on the handbrake until it clicked, took a deep breath and released Otis from the cab. Noah jumped Clive's fence and ran towards Ava's house until he reached the back stairs.

Then Ava was there. Her hair loose, tumbling around her shoulders, messy, knotted, her cheeks stained with tears, her eyes clouded. He traversed the short gap between them.

'What do you want?'

CHAPTER
Thirty

'STOP! Otis, that's my new Lego!' Ish shrieked from inside the house.

The dog shot out the door, its teeth clenched around a red brick. Noah commanded the dog to stop and drop the piece and then collected it and returned it to Ish.

'My dad bought me this new Lego kit. See, it's a racing track and look how fast the cars go!'

Ava watched where she remained on the deck before mobilising and moving towards the kitchen.

The kitchen was complete now. At least she could thank Noah for that. The chalky-coloured marble benchtops flicked with splashes of black, complimented the Tassie oak cabinet doors with panelling to replicate the veejay walls. With golden knobs and new appliances, the entire room shone. One of her favourite things was the deep-set large and rectangular sink. A true country sink in her view. The room was warm though, inviting, with contrasting colours from her Egyptian knick-knacks. And the room was always filled with light; the spacious windows facing the deck and rear of the property provided endless sun, and in the evenings, a vista of the never-ending sky filled with diamond stars.

Flicking on the kettle she felt Noah's presence in the kitchen behind her.

'Happy?' she asked and reached for the new cups she'd recently purchased. These were vintage fine china in the most gorgeous muted yellow and gold trim with a patchwork design that reminded her of the mosaic tiled floor in their home in Egypt. Seemed fitting.

Noah didn't say he wanted tea but she made it anyway. His eyebrow arched at the dainty cup and saucer she served him.

Were they going to pretend hurtful words hadn't been spoken? That he'd threatened her? If they couldn't be together because she'd acted in ways that were reprehensible to him, then why was he here?

She took a sip of the hot tea. The gold handle caught the glint of the sun and sparkled furiously. Bizarrely it provided the fortification she needed.

'Thank you for the kitchen. I love it. It's just as I dreamed.'

'You designed it. And I agree it looks rustic and authentic and really suits the house.'

With the bathrooms also complete, the house was finally feeling like a home, something she had created for her and Ish. It would be beautiful. The living area still needed furnishings and personalised touches but they were getting there. In such a short time, they'd achieved a lot.

'Maybe you should go? There's nothing to say, is there? You cannot understand my position and why I did what I did. You should focus on your own family.'

Noah paused mid-sip.

'I was worried. There were rumours that something was going on out here. I wanted to check you were okay. Duke said his father had given him the Lego. I assume the talk about helicopters is true then. Did he visit?'

She wandered outside, the deck was like Switzerland, neutral territory where any matter of things could be discussed. 'Yes, he was here. Exactly as you wanted.'

Noah had the grace to wince.

'How did he know where you were?'

She sat now, gazing out over the view of her home. 'You were completely out of line threatening to reveal our whereabouts.' She threw a glance in his direction then, briefly, but turned back. 'That was not your place, was never your information to divulge. However, you were right. His father should know that his son was safe and where he was living. Every parent deserves to know that about their child. I was wrong in withholding that information, but I've already justified my reasons.' Noah went to speak but she shushed him. 'Anyway, I made contact and Henry immediately replied saying he knew where we were and that he was on his way.'

'He knew?'

'Yep. He said he'd always known. I give him credit for not ambushing us. He waited until I made contact, I appreciate that. It was good of him.'

'So, he arrives, seriously in a helicopter with security staff?'

A frisson of annoyance at his surprise spread through her. Hadn't she told him enough of the family she'd come from and of the very real risks she faced? No point dwelling on the facts as she knew the truth. 'Yes. Two helicopters in fact. The first scoured the place to ensure his safety and he alighted from the second, but those details are irrelevant. We talked and sorted things out.'

Noah's face expressed incredulity. 'In one conversation, you've sorted everything out?'

'Well, yes, verbally, obviously there are still issues to address, matters to organise. He's agreed to our living here, and for Ish to stay with me. He'll visit when he chooses and stay involved but, his interests have changed somewhat since I left.'

Noah walked to the back edge of the deck. Ava imagined he was thinking about his own marital dispute. Instead, he asked, 'What other interests?'

'He's taken another wife and she's expecting a child.' Ava let those words sink in.

'Shit.'

'Exactly.' Noah went quiet again. 'Have you had news?' It was only decent of her to ask but he didn't deserve her kindness.

He kept his back turned away, his voice distant. 'You take your child across the world and your husband isn't fighting you for custody? And he just rocks up in his fancy helicopter to say that's okay?'

'You're being facetious, you know it's not that simple.'

'Have you ever asked Duke who he wants to live with?'

The question surprised her. She hadn't but was confident of his reply. 'I don't need to. My husband was largely an absent father. I cared for Ish, it was my job.'

'Yeah, I understand now. I didn't before. I understand about the dynamics of these things, of the basic biological needs of children.'

A surge of irritation bubbled under the surface of her skin. Biology? 'It's futile to compare your situation to mine. They are vastly different. It is best for Ish to be with me.'

'Yes, it's in his best interests.' The words were elongated and she couldn't determine if he was being sarcastic.

'What's happened, Noah?'

He told her.

'I'm sorry. You must be devastated.'

Noah slumped into the nearest chair, looking like a defeated soul. 'I am. Regardless of what is best, I'm shattered that I have to snatch time with my daughter. That we can't live together here in the country. I did the best I could to be a good dad and husband. I'm disappointed my marriage failed, but I guess with hindsight brings clarity and I know I could have done things differently, but it's too late. So, my life looks a little different to what I'd hoped. Ava, it's so easy to be angry. Because anger puts the blame on someone else. When there's only me to blame. So maybe I was angry, but now I'm simply sad and that's the worst feeling of all.'

A sob settled in her chest, stuck there. She was pleased Noah was sad and not angry. She felt for him, but...

'If Emily was to live with you in Bellethorpe, how would you manage? You work long hours. How would Emily get to and from school? After school sport training? What about holidays? You have no support here. Your mother can't help. Of course, you could hire some-one, a babysitter or put her into the local care service.' She paused, took a deep breath. 'I understand, I truly do, that you want your daughter here, with you, but that is what makes parenting tough. Doing it alone with no support isn't easy. You need to earn an income. How do you do that and parent full-time? It doesn't work. At the moment Lisa can devote one hundred percent of her time to Emily, drop her to and from school, make her afternoon tea, spend time with her. In Bellethorpe, Emily would be spending time with you in the gaps. You'd be spread too thin … that is the practical reality. No one is diminishing your role. You're a wonderful father and she loves you dearly.'

'I could make it work. It is different in the country, there's always someone to help out. But that's not the point anyway.'

But he didn't say how and didn't sound convincing. 'Just because your parents separated, and Lisa chose to return to the city, none of that means you aren't worthy, Noah. That you aren't a wonderful parent, that you cannot have your own family. You can. This isn't about city versus country girls, nor the city versus country. Not all women are like your wife. Not all men are like your father. It wasn't your fault that you couldn't make Lisa happy here in the country. It wasn't your mum's fault your father was unhappy. You can move forward, focus on being a great dad, even if it's not one hundred percent of the time.'

'How do you make it work?'

'I work around Ish. I've set my life up that way. That's a sacrifice too, you understand. I love my work but to do that full-time is not possible firstly, from here, and not if I'm the sole responsible parent for my son. It's not a sacrifice because I'm happy to do it.'

'But more importantly, Noah, what about the future for Emily? If she chooses to live here one day, what are her prospects? Where will she work? What will she do? What if she's worked hard to qualify with certain skills but can't find employment in Bellethorpe? She'd be forced to live elsewhere. Or what if she has a family but can't secure childcare, or what if she simply wants to borrow a book for her child from a fully stocked, operational library that is open every day of the week? Preventing development might just drive your daughter away. Don't you want a town where people are happy and don't have to grumble about driving two hours for hardware?'

His nod was half-hearted. He wasn't ready to hear it but now was the time to make him.

'How do you do it, Ava? How can you not work? I don't understand.' His words weren't accusatory but pleading, desperate for knowledge, for it to make sense to him, to make sense of his own situation.

Nonetheless, it was exasperating.

Ava shook her head. Perhaps he deserved to know. 'Jamila was affluent in her own right. Plus, she had access to money, lots of cash. To be honest I didn't ask too many questions. It was better not to know. But she helped me escape. She gifted me freedom, enough to run, enough to survive temporarily. I was lucky to have a friend like her. And not that it's any of your business but I had some expensive jewellery and I sold it to make ends meet.'

It reminded Ava that she needed to check on Jamila, particularly now that she'd been found and wasn't in hiding anymore. She could speak to her friend more freely.

'Noah, I like my work. I want to work. It's always been my intention to work and I will return to it. It's a dream, really, a lifeline. With the location of the fossil, I mean. I have plans, Noah, for the site, for work, for the future.'

'Plans to turn Bellethorpe into a thriving metropolis?'

'Is it only because two of the people you loved most in the world didn't choose the country, that you reject any form of development? Is that it? Because otherwise I don't understand.' Then she had another thought. 'If there had been more on offer here, more opportunities, perhaps they would have stayed? I'm not sure, of course, but it's possible.'

His face became a patchwork of emotion he worked hard to conceal. 'The country is the country, you either like it or you don't.'

'Oh, c'mon, Noah! I'm a city girl. Do you expect me to leave too?'

CHAPTER
Thirty-One

AVA CONTINUED TALKING, not realising he hadn't responded.

'There is nothing wrong with having a great local restaurant, good coffee, a cinema, a shopping complex. Those are part of our modern world and aren't the remit of only heavily populated towns. You have the monopoly on green rolling pastures, flies, an abundance of animals, bushes, fresh air, magic skies, and room, loads of room. No matter what is constructed in Bellethorpe it will always be special because it has those things that the city can never offer. That is the beauty of this place.' She spread her arms wide to indicate. 'Paradise.'

'And you know what else?' She kept going. 'Modern life creates different families. Boring old nuclear families are so passe! These days we have single-parent families, extended families, childless couples, stepfamilies and children living with grandparents and other carers. And what about same-sex parents, too. Anything goes!'

His lips curled towards a smile but just as quickly he dropped it. He'd been living in fear for some time now. It was exhausting worrying about the future with his daughter and of the town. But there was more. This new woman to town, she'd complicated things, reopened old wounds so that they festered, caused hurts to resurface, his failings become so obvious, his fear about everything become heightened. She'd been honest with him; it was time to put it on the line and take a risk. He'd faced the worst already; he could handle more. 'You will leave, won't you?' The words caused the air to still.

Turning swiftly in the chair where she sat, she faced him then, the tables turned, her face expressing shock and surprise. The same emotions he was sure she'd seen on his face during this discussion.

'Why would you think that?'

'You've said it yourself a few times. There are comforts you want that belong in the city, not here in Bellethorpe. Now that you don't have to hide in the country, you can live anywhere.' Noah didn't breathe through the sentence. But now he kept going. 'You are an archaeologist. Your work is bigger than this place, more than any fossil you might find in your backyard, your life is bigger than here. Doesn't matter how much money you channel into this house, it's still a Queenslander on acres in the country with the smell of cow dung in the air. Your signal will remain patchy and you'll never get Uber eats.'

'Lucky I'm not a fan of food delivery, then.' Pause. The gaze stretching between them was long and vast. 'What are you afraid of, Noah?'

'Falling in love with you and you leaving.'

Desire, longing, waves of something fizzed in the air between them. Ava rose to stand in front of him. 'I never ever wanted to fall in love again. My experience of love was being controlled by someone else, to love them so unconditionally that I lost myself. To have to negotiate how I live my life. And more, for me to love them and then they change. We aren't so different, you and I, Noah. I understand your pain about Lisa. Unfortunately, people change. My husband changed; he betrayed my trust. I never thought I could trust another man, want to trust another man, that I could believe in them. Then in the little old backwater of Bellethorpe, along came highly principled single dad, Noah Hawthorn. Noah who loves his daughter and life on the land passionately; a man who has firm ideas who runs a successful building business and is good with his hands.' She smiled, paused then, uncertain. She wanted an affirmation from him. He reached for her hand and held it.

'But one thing I've learned, is that you are a man of your word. You do as you say. You can be trusted. You are an honest, honourable and sincere man and you make me feel safe. But likewise, you are vehemently opposed to something important to me, and no matter how much we might care for each other, I will never again give up my dreams, my goals, my work. My husband said all the right things but he failed to keep his promises. My career was indispensable. What I've found on this land is important, to me, to history, to science and to civilisation. It needs to be properly treated and researched, and if that brings development to Bellethorpe, which I hope it does, then so be it.'

Both of them heard the helicopter at the same time and raced into the yard, their hands stretched across foreheads, blocking the late afternoon sun. 'Phew!' she exclaimed the moment she saw the large, red '7' emblazoned on the side. 'It's not Henry back! Only journalists.'

'You need to stop this circus.' His face scrunched into a scowl.

'It's only a circus because it's uncontrolled. I need to control it.' Grasping both of his hands, she pulled him close. 'Noah, I've fallen in love with you, and I think we can have something special together. But I will not give up my dreams for you. I will not be made to feel bad over what I did. Over the steps I took to protect my son. I will not give up this circus as you call it. I will not. My intention is to make it a formal dig site to enable the research to continue. But then I have grand plans. These finds will benefit research, but they'll also benefit this town. I will build a museum and visitor centre on my land and encourage people to learn about these fossils and where they came from, what they mean and maybe I'll offer some sort of experience so people can try and find their own fossil or a gem. It will attract visitors and employ locals. But those are grand plans, for me personally, I will write about this research, prepare academic papers and perhaps write a book. I may not have discovered the pyramids of Cairo but this is pretty darn good.'

They stared at each other. 'Can you love me as I am?'

'My biggest fear has already happened and I couldn't stop it. I lost my daughter.'

Ava's eyes bulged.

'Okay, okay, I know, but it feels like I did. I would still prefer she live with me. But you're right. I will not fight anymore. I will agree to those parenting orders and I will maximise my time with Emily and I will see her as often as I can and be the best father I can be. I accept she needs her mother and I accept that Ish needs you and the best place for him is here, with you.' He cleared his throat, looked away hastily and shuffled his feet.

'If allowing development to occur in Bellethorpe means that this community I love will thrive and prosper and my daughter might one day live here' —a pensive pause— 'and if it means you will stay, then okay.'

'Okay? What did you say? Say it again.'

'I do accept you as you are, Ava. The fiercely intelligent, focused, determined woman who is committed to your son and your work and to a life in Bellethorpe. I love you the way you are. I will not ask you to change. I am a man of my word. But I'm nervous as hell that now I've admitted it, things will change and I'll lose you, too.' He reached for her, pulled her close until their bodies aligned, and squeezed his eyes shut. It was the first thing today that felt natural and real and didn't suffocate him with fear or reprisal.

'Noah, I'm nervous, too. We can be nervous together and find our way. Let's just be honest with each other, sincere and genuine, hold each other's interests close.'

He moved close and whispered in her ear. 'I've been wanting to hold you close for so long. To kiss you again. Each time I'm near, it's been incredibly difficult to control myself.'

'Please, don't control yourself any longer.' Her lips parted into a cheeky grin.

His mouth found hers, and she tasted exquisite. Gentle pressure in the beginning, slow and thoughtful, sensual, their mouths against each other and desire built quickly. The kiss sent his entire body into a spiral of ecstasy, his hunger for her insatiable. His lips wanted to explore the soft folds of her skin and he trailed feather-light touches along her jaw, collar bone, teased up and down her throat. Her chest heaved against his, he heard her exhalation and inhalation of breath, the smell of her hair … until Ava nestled her head into his shoulder and stayed there, it was almost as erotic as their shared kisses.

'I would love to invite you to stay but that's probably a jump too far at this early stage. You know, with Ish.'

He agreed even if his body did not. 'Of course, I get it, and I have an early start tomorrow. I'm back to Brisbane. It's my last court appearance to hand up these consent orders and snatch a few hours with Emily.' Her smile dazzled in his direction. He would never tire of it, of her. 'Even though I'd love to stay.' Leaning close to her ear, he whispered again. 'You will be in my dreams when I drift off to sleep tonight.'

CHAPTER
Thirty-Two

ISH HAD BECOME adept at his chores around the property and Ava no longer had to remind him. Today he tore off, Daisy in his wake. Daisy the devoted dog who followed Ish everywhere and had forgiven him for his misdemeanour.

Daisy perched at the door to the chicken coop, ready to pounce and chase a hen, while Ish threw their grain. Against Ava's better judgement, they'd kept the remaining four puppies. They had plenty of room and after the incident with Jasper, Ava couldn't bear to part with them, neither could Ish. It was silly, they did not need five dogs. Such was country life.

Ava spotted Clive near the fence and she accompanied Ish to feed the horses.

'Howdy, neighbours!' Clive sang out at their approach. 'There's been quite the song and dance around here after leak of your find, hasn't there? All those reporters and television crews in town made a menace of themselves. I was lined up at the hardware store and a journalist hit me up for information!'

Ava offered a tight smile but didn't engage in pleasantries. 'Clive, how do you know my husband?' His eyes darted left and right, his hand reached for Honey's mane and his feet shifted position. 'I saw him approach you the other day.'

'I'm sorry, Ava.'

Sorry, for what? Her stomach swirled and dropped. 'What for, Clive?' She willed her voice to remain steady.

'Hey, Duke, can you please go and brush Honey and Marmalade. There's a few sweet carrots and apples inside as well, they'll love them.'

'Sure, Clive, but my name is Ismail!' He ran off.

'You know his real name is Ismail, don't you?' Ava was running on gut instinct now.

'Yes. Very soon after you moved in, I was contacted by someone in your family...'

'My husband's family,' she corrected.

'Yes, your husband's family, asking questions, probing for information about you. It sounded odd and I brushed them off, saying I didn't know you and knew nothing about your circumstances. I promise, Ava, I did. But obviously, your husband has means and he's rather persuasive.'

'Oh, yes, he is.'

'He found out that I worked at the university and offered a sizeable donation to my anthropology department and later, to the archaeology department on the condition I report back about you. I refused, of course. A complete invasion of privacy.'

That provided her some comfort.

'He was quite manipulative and any refusal by me was met with a withdrawal of his generous offer. I was placed into an untenable position. The university really wanted that money and weren't aware I was being blackmailed. So, I either had to provide the information or I would lose my position at the uni, or so they threatened anyway. Honestly, Ava, I thought about telling you, about retiring early to get me out of the pickle. I disagreed vehemently. But then I realised, someone would be spying on you if it wasn't me and, in the end, I thought it'd be better if it was me who had some principles and my intentions were at least worthy.'

'So, this whole looking after the horses, loaning them to us, was a ruse?'

'No, it wasn't. That was genuine. I needed your assistance and I've appreciated it. In the end, it did however, provide another purpose.'

Gosh, this was a real kick in the guts and she said so. 'I thought we were friends.'

'We are, well I hope we are and can come through this. I mean, I don't know much about your husband but he has provided some serious financial support to the uni. It has benefited enormously and our programs have been extended and broadened because of his kind donations.'

Well, at least that was something. She hoped the archaeology department would use it wisely.

'It's family wealth. But tell me exactly what you divulged?'

Clive winced and she was glad. It was all so sordid. 'At first, I was very dubious, but honestly, it seemed that your welfare was his paramount consideration. He wanted to know that you and the boy were okay. That you were safe here.'

Oh, the irony. She was frantic about their safety too, but for other reasons. She quizzed him further.

'So, yeah, it was details that you lived here, what you were doing. I told him that you rode the horses, got some chickens, had the puppies. Were renovating. He was very interested in the fossil.'

'He was?'

'Yes. And of course, so was the university.'

'What? What do you mean?' Ava tried to think back to the course of events. Clive had conveniently come across her and the fossil. She'd sought his counsel and he had assisted her with her enquiries with the academic staff.

'Are Matthew and James in on this?'

'No! No, they know nothing about your husband or your past, well not from me anyway and there was a strict "not to discuss clause" with the staff at the uni. Your husband insisted on it, lest word get out that he was stalking you.'

'Okay, so—'

'What it meant is that the uni was extraordinarily keen to be involved and continue receiving the funding of this generous benefactor. So, there was never going to be a problem with release of their staff to help you on this project.'

Ava's mind spun. In some twisted way, this could work to her advantage. Seasonal academic? Research academic? Permanent funding by the uni for the dig? Or simply their assistance in publishing her research, supporting it, advertising it. Because, deep down, like other aspects of her life, she really wanted to maintain control of her project.

'I can't believe this was all going on and I had no idea.'

'I know and again, I'm sorry. The good news is that now I don't have to be the go-between anymore. You've made contact, he's visited and I'm told that you'll be communicating directly now.'

'And this, Clive?' She held up the topaz engagement ring. 'You helped me sell this and then Henry gifts it back to me?' She paused for effect. It had been Henry's parting gift. 'I assume you told him about me selling it?'

'Oh, wow. Only as part of information dissemination. I didn't know he bought it back. He never told me what he did with the information. I assumed it was always about keeping you safe.'

Ava nodded. Ish returned, ending their conversation. Then her mobile phone rang. It was Jamila, returning her call.

'Thanks, Clive. No hard feelings, you're a great neighbour and were put in a tough spot. I understand how forceful my ex-husband can be.' She waved off and answered her phone. Ish jumped on the trampoline.

Jamila was pleased for her. Pleased they could talk openly on a public line and express their true feelings. It didn't mean of course, that Ava's father-in-law didn't bug the line from Jamila's end but she was prepared to take the risk.

Jamila was also optimistic about her own circumstances. The hearing was over, judgement pending. Her lawyers were confident of a positive outcome. That would mean security; her long term stay in London with her children and a property settlement to set her up for the future. It was now a waiting game. She wasn't going to downplay her ongoing vigilance, however. Each day she acted as if they were being watched and she remained on the lookout for suspect activity. What a way to live. Her heart ached for her friend, but she was also grateful she no longer had to live that way.

Ava pressed end on the call and her step was lighter. It was the first time they had spoken where their conversation wasn't shrouded in secrecy and nerves and fear.

She sat in contemplation for a moment, reflecting on the telephone call. Then, her fingers scrolled her phone, checking social media sites, something she had avoided for months for fear of being traced. So much had happened, or she grimaced, not much at all as people she'd once known were still attending the same restaurants, visiting the same movie theatres, taking candid happy snaps at the beach, at the shops, at parties.

Next, she checked her mobile banking app and dropped the phone. It clanged to the ground with a thump. Picking it up, she checked for cracks in the screen and wiped the glass with her shirt to remove smudges. Had she got that wrong? Blinking over the numbers in her bank account again, she blew air into her cheeks, stood up, sat down.

The man she'd once loved was not a monster, even though he had let her down in the most painful of ways. But he was attempting to make amends, was perhaps turning into someone she could rely upon, believe in. Glancing down at the phone screen again, she couldn't believe it. There had been a significant deposit into her bank account. An addendum to the deposit said: *donation to fund research into the fossil found by Ava Montgomery, archaeologist.*

This money would allow her to fulfil her dreams of a culture centre, right here in the lower paddocks. Her mind whizzed but then a car horn sounded and she heard voices. 'Yoo, hoo!' singing out.

Ish rushed out of his bedroom. 'They're here, Mumma!' His friend, Jack was coming to play. Ava pocketed her phone and beamed as her friend, Bec arrived on her back deck—perhaps she should simply seal shut her front door—or just get used to country ways? 'Bec, hi. Hi Jack! Time for a cuppa?' This time she would welcome a chat with Bec and enjoy catching up on old times.

Hours later, Ava savoured the peace and quiet. The solitude as she sat in her new workspace. Bec had suggested she take the boys out for ice-cream and to the new, local water park. It was the first time Ish had been out of her sight since the Summer Festival and she didn't quaver at his whereabouts and his safety this time.

Now she had a few precious hours to develop her plans, to finally, think about and get excited about the future. First, she scribbled down her ideas for the history centre and the work she could do to improve their knowledge of the local past and find and collate dossiers on the returned serviceman.

Above her, the rows and rows of shelving provided space for her belongings, her equipment and tools as well as the odd finds, some quirky things. Now, she reached for the postcards and fossilised opals. They might discover some incredible plant, nature and animal fossils, she hoped so, but nothing, surely, could be as beautiful as these gems. The colours always shone and sparkled in the dappled light. While there were high-power fluorescent bright lights for her special and finely detailed work, Noah had also had the foresight to instal skylights that covered the span of the ceiling space and illuminated the area during the day. She loved the effect of being protected from the sun but feeling the outdoors at the same time. He was clever that man.

It was also a warm space, a shed she was drawn to with a large and spacious functional desk, bigger than a usual office and an area with a colourful woven rug and armchair for reading or contemplation. The walls remained corrugated iron and the floor concrete and completed its rustic work design.

She would see through her vision for the history centre if the town approved her idea. It was her way of giving back to Bellethorpe, to honour these previous residents, to acknowledge how the town had welcomed her and never made her feel like an outsider, just like she imagined they did all those years ago.

Before anything, she'd share her ideas with Noah and gauge whether it was too outlandish, too modern and innovative and once they'd discussed it, she'd take it to the town council. She imagined the mayor, Jacqueline Kennedy swallowing up this idea, whole.

Reaching for another notebook, Ava opened a fresh page. This was her dig site pad. No suitable or appropriate name had come to her yet, but first priority was the site. Making it a fully functional, working site to make it easy to excavate and preserve whatever they found. Once established, it would be an ongoing live site until they were confident nothing else was hidden amongst the dirt.

On a clean and blank page, she sketched a rough idea of what her future museum might look like. Nothing fancy or too modern, a real, working building with a platform to view the dig site and watch the experts and a specially constructed area where guests could try their luck at searching through mounds of tailings to discover their own gem or fossil.

She was dreaming of a café and gift shop when she heard shouts behind her and banging on the shed door. Her heart accelerated in fright.

'Ava!' It was Matthew. She shot out of her chair and raced outside.

Matthew stood there waving his hat. 'You've got to come and see this!' His smile was as wide as the Cheshire cat. Grabbing her third notebook, this one a detailed and in-depth record of their finds, she threw on her cap and they raced back down the hill.

Epilogue

TWELVE MONTHS *later*

'It is with enormous pleasure that I unveil the monument to the returned servicemen who made their lives here in our region after the Great War and also, to officially open the newly refurbished history centre.'

The entire population of the town gathered on the expanse of green lawn and clapped as Jacqueline Kennedy cut the ribbon and the red linen cloth fell to reveal the names inscribed on a plague affixed to a granite boulder. The form of monument had been hotly debated, as only Bellethorpe folk could do, and this final design had won; the prominent rock symbolising the terrain that dotted the area and the bronze plague naming the men identified so far, with room left to add more as they were discovered.

The tribute stood outside the entrance to the history centre, same location, same church building that had been extended. By Noah, of course. By agreement, the complex had kept the similar façade and historic feel, but inside, there were dozens more exhibits of relics found, not only by Ava, but by the community. Rather than being piled one atop the other ad hoc, they sat in a neat order, lining glass shelves and inside cabinets for those more precious. Next to her carefully preserved coins, postcards and old newspapers were other donations. After putting out the call, the locals delivered, often what they thought was rubbish, and Ava had tirelessly sorted through the items, most of the prized possessions being a gateway to learning about their settlers. The dossiers in the back room were growing; her soldier now had a history:

Edward George Adams

Occupation: Blacksmith

Born: 19 July 1899

Enlisted: 16 June 1917 (aged 18 years)

Rank: Private

Regiment: Light horse regiment

Later married with two children, George and Alice

Discharged: 29 September 1919

Arrival at settlement: exact date unknown, late 1919

Died: 16 August 1969 (aged 70 years)

There were lots of gaps in the information, particularly about his son, George who lived at the property after his father's death. The information in the archives was scant. Ava had collected morsels of information: George seemed to be a bit lost, didn't work and locals at the time interchangeably thought he was a no-hoper or an eccentric. Either way, he kept to himself. There were rumours he might have been unwell. What is apparent, is that his father had skilled him up as a blacky, and he seemed to apply those skills to jewellery making. The only conclusion that Ava could draw was that he was responsible for finding the opals and assuming they were simple gems and keeping them to prepare jewellery. Since, Ava had found more opals. For the moment, she was keeping those to form part of her museum.

George Adams was the first of many men whose lives were finally being recorded.

'And where is she? We must of course, thank Ava Montgomery for her tireless efforts in enhancing and further establishing this centre and for the intricate and detailed record keeping she is undertaking to ensure that the men who served their country and called Bellethorpe home, are never forgotten.'

Ava acknowledged the thanks and Noah kissed her on the cheek. She quietened the group. 'We must also thank Peter Shoebridge who has been invaluable in both remembering facts and people and for his meticulous research skills.' Louder applause rang out for long-term resident, Peter and he ducked his head in embarrassment. Beside him stood his wife, Sheila, who couldn't contain her grin. These days she'd happily lost her help in the antique store, and Peter worked most days in the history centre, out the back, scrolling through history books and sometimes the computer, when he could be convinced of the fancy fandangle thing, adding to and completing the collection. His long-term memory served him well and on task, he was efficient researching a fact or two. Sheila had been nothing but grateful, but it was Ava who was thankful for the help.

It had been Peter's idea to commemorate the men by naming new streets in their honour. And some parks, too. There would now be an Adams Road, Poole Street, McMahon Avenue. With as many as up to seven hundred returned soldiers, that was a lot of new streets. Noah scowled at the thought!

Cameras flashed around them, and this time, Ava didn't mind. Geoff from *The Bellethorpe Times* was on the job, running the news story. He was still waiting for his new recruit. The last cadet had reneged and now he for waited for another employee. The addition would double the size of his team. The gossip was that owner and founder of the paper, Wyatt Hummingbird was tiring of the production and was handing the reigns over to his son, Angus, who was an owner of a local cattle farm. Ava wasn't sure where the future of the local rag lay.

Her parents, Jane and Damien jumped into a shot, beaming smiles at being here to celebrate with her. Now she was free, she looked forward to seeing her parents more.

Matthew and James sidled up next to them, both enjoying a cup of tea and a scone, heavily ladened with jam and cream. Noah gestured that he'd get them something to eat too, and he wandered over to the refreshment table. Like only country folk can do, the official opening was a celebration with food.

The duo had become a firm feature around Bellethorpe and their couple status, slowly accepted. Most people didn't care that they were gay, they welcomed the pair with open arms. Both remained employed by the university on secondment to her project.

'Are you guys going to be okay while I'm away?'

James snorted and Matthew laughed but ended up coughing having only just taken a large bite of scone. Her comment had exactly the effect she desired. These two were the brains of this project; their skills were phenomenal and she'd be lost without them.

'I think we'll manage,' they said as they recovered. Ava spent many days on the dig site, covered in layers of dust and dirt and trawling through only centimetres of area. And she'd contributed to the mounting number of significant finds. But it was the dynamic duo who had more recently discovered the jaw of a crocodile and sizeable fish fossils. With more discoveries, came necessary documenting and reporting and she'd commenced writing academic papers. It was also true that the co-ordination and construction of the museum complex and the work on the history centre had chewed up large chunks of her time.

'Oh, remind me again when you leave?' Bridie popped up at their side.

'In under two weeks! I'm so excited! And thank you so much for looking after the animals. Ish will miss them desperately and is happy to know they're in good hands.'

'My pleasure.' She leaned in conspiratorially. 'Avoid the scones, Evelyn made them and they're as hard as rocks. Caleb will fix you up with a treat if you run past the restaurant,' and she kissed her on the cheek and was gone in a puff of strawberry-scented perfume.

Noah arrived at just that moment with a plate laden with scones that didn't appear appealing anymore. Emily and Ish raced past and stole two.

'Have you finished your paper?' Matthew asked.

'Yes, almost. Will you both read it when I'm finished?'

They agreed. 'I'm presenting at the conference in London upon arrival and meeting with others in the field over those next few days. Then catching up with old work colleagues from the museum, as well.'

Ava stole a bite of Noah's scone and after chewing said, 'Noah will be playing tourist with the kids. Emily is excited to visit where princesses and princes live and to ride on the famous red buses. Ish sort of remembers London, so he's playing it a bit cool.'

James and Matthew were called away and talked to townsfolk eager to learn more about when the site and museum would be open for business. Ava spotted Adele and Blake chatting with Clive and she waved. Clive was a more permanent neighbour now, having retired to Bellethorpe full time. He volunteered on the site some days. Ava hoped that arrangement might continue when the centre was open. Clive was a wealth of knowledge.

Noah's building tasks, firstly finishing her place and then working on the history centre had prevented him from making any real headway on her development. They hoped it might open its doors within the next twelve months.

Plus, he'd been busy as the newly elected President of the Parent Support Group, formerly known as the father's support group. They welcomed both mothers and fathers struggling with separation and, in Ava's view, provided a much more balanced and supportive environment. He was often on call, fielding distressed parents and offering advice. He had also taken on the voluntary role of development co-ordinator for the town council, an unelected position that allowed him to view and research development proposals. Ava was proud of him. It was better to be involved and have a say than to condemn any effort to improve the town. He'd taken to the role with gusto and sought her opinion often, and he listened, and so far, had made balanced recommendations. Ultimately, it wasn't his call, but he did the legwork before the elected council made their decisions. He was slowly accepting that certain development could have a positive impact on the town.

Ava understood he'd taken on these new roles to keep busy. In an ironic twist of fate, and best of all for Noah, Lisa's new husband, Darryl, an engineer, had been offered a too-good-to-refuse contract in Saudi Arabia, a place Lisa wasn't prepared to take Emily. Six months into their parenting agreement, she asked Noah for Emily to live with him rather than take her overseas. Overjoyed would be an understatement at this turn of events.

They'd both held off, clutching to their independence and living separately, until Emily returned. Until then, it had been easy for Noah to stay over without difficulty. When Emily arrived, it wasn't so easy. Since then, they'd all bunked in together at Kinross Road, as a family.

'I'm so happy to have you by my side every day. So happy that you moved into the house that you longed for and dreamed about.'

He kissed her before responding. 'It was my ideal family home and now I'm living there with Emily. She has a new brother and another female in her life. It isn't a dream, is it?'

The kids raced past once more, a trail of followers in their wake. Otis and Daisy not far behind, followed by the now not so little pups. More confident and older Emily had assisted Ish settle in and make more friends. The pair had become inseparable.

Just like she and Noah had been by each other's side. A united force and together they had witnessed how each child had missed the parent that wasn't with them. Noah understood better now. And that is why Noah was accompanying her to her archaeologist conference and they were bringing both children. Henry was going to fly in and spend some time with Ish and Lisa was going to the do the same with Emily. The trip from Saudi to London was much shorter than a return to Australia.

Henry had made a few trips out in the past year. The town was considering building a helicopter pad just for his flying visits.

'When the kids are with their mum and dad, we'll get some time alone. What on earth will we do with ourselves in a fancy room at Claridge's?'

She leaned into him, her lips touching his. 'Oh, I hear the room service is exceptional and there is a very good movie selection and endless alcohol available. I don't think we'll even need to leave the room.'

'That is exactly what I'd hoped for!'

Their mouths connected, lingered, savouring each other.

'If this is a dream, it's the best dream I've ever had and I hope I never wake up.'

She rested her arms around his shoulders, the crowd, the noise, everything muted. 'Thank you, Noah. Thank you for being you and doing as you say and believing in me and being someone I can trust and rely upon. I love you, Noah Hawthorn.'

'I can't say it better than this.' Noah ripped out a piece of scrap paper and recited:

My heart was crumbling, a splattered and squashed mess
 Until along came Ava Montgomery to alleviate my distress
 Happiness then followed me around like a bright burning sun
 Life suddenly became more fun.

Obstacles were in our path, hers more heinous
 Depriving us of any gayness
 My family troubles clouded my vision
 Until our paths were aligned, heading for a collision.

Realising our greatest fears were released
 Meant changing track, goals idealised
 But the only way ahead was together
 Close in each other's arms, forever.

'Gayness!' she laughed.

'I know! I'm still working on it, but you get the gist.' He smothered her giggling with a kiss.

Acknowledgments

Thank you to everyone who helped make this book a reality. To my first reader, Justin, my love and gratitude for feedback, good, bad and crazy! To writer friends who read an early draft – Mary-Lou and Lucy, your feedback was invaluable. To Annie Seaton for her amazing editorial skills and making the manuscript shine. As it says in my dedication, I'd be lost without you! To cover designer and formator extraordinaire, and wonderful writer and performer, Emma Powell. To my neighbour, Liana for her precision in proofreading. To my regular writing group for their wisdom and guidance on character and other discussions over the duration of this manuscript and the inspiration to keep going. To bookstagrammers and reviewers, thank you for accepting a copy to read and review, and to my readers, thank you for once again picking up one of my books. I hope you are loving this Bellethorpe series as much as me. Much love.

About the Author

Leanne Lovegrove is a lawyer, wife and mother and a lover of romance and reading. Her law career created an addiction to coffee but provides countless story ideas. She is the author of romantic fiction novels and novellas. Leanne writes sweeping love stories with happily-ever-afters with strong female heroines and set mainly in the beautiful landscape of Australia. She lives in Brisbane, Australia with her husband and three children.

To find out more about Leanne's books, sign up to her newsletter on her website and receive a free short novella as part of the Bellethorpe series:

Web: www.leannelovegroveauthor.com
Or find her here:

- FaceBook: https://www.facebook.com/leanne.lovegrove.545/
- Instagram: https://www.instagram.com/leannelovegroveauthor/
- Bookbub: https://www.bookbub.com/profile/leanne-lovegrove

Bellethorpe Series

- Christmas, Before (Bellethorpe #0.5)
- Love In Between (Bellethorpe novella #1) **books2read.com/Love-In-Between**
- Caught in Between (Bellethorpe novella #2) **books2read.com/Caught-In-Between**
- Box set of Love In Between and Caught In Between (Bellethorpe #3) **books2read.com/bellethorpeboxset**

Here's what reviewers are saying about the second story set in Bellethorpe, *Caught In Between:*

"My Best Friend's Wedding meets Farmer Wants a Wife meets The Wedding Planner. Caught In Between feels like my favourite rom-com all rolled into one. Blake and Adele's story is passionate, touching and everything a good romance should be. Leanne knows how to make readers fall in love with her characters from the very beginning. Caught In Between is like a full-bodied wine that hits all of the right notes. It is a novella with passion, love and laughter.

If you love romance and wine with some alpacas thrown in, this is the novella for you.

When you pick up Caught In Between expect to keep it in your hands until the end. It is an absolute page-turner."

Melanie Hunter, reviewer

"Leanne's writing is like sunshine on a page with a storyline like a blue sky... refreshing, lovable and liveable. If you are into small town romance with dramas set in Australia this has your name on it."

Pauline Reid, book reviewer

"Caught In Between is a warm and uplifting story that was a complete joy to read. Leanne Lovegrove is the queen of sparkling rural romances. Without fail she always offers inspiring settings, layered personalities and exciting plots. This novella has a strong central love story with an emotionally satisfying and optimistic ending."

Cindy L Spear, book reviewer

"Two things I absolutely loved about this book, one: Blake, what a heartthrob! and 2, those alpacas. They had me in hysterics!"

allbookedout_withmj – Mandie, bookstagrammer

Also by Leanne Lovegrove

Leanne's other novels:

Unexpected Delivery **books2read.com/unexpected-delivery**
Illegal Love **books2read.com/illegallove**
Keeper of the Light **mybook.to/KeeperoftheLight**
A Good Life **books2read.com/a-goodlife**
Her Outback Home **books2read.com/Outbackhome**

Novellas:

Escapades of a Personal Stylist **mybook.to/escapades**
Love on the Sweeping Plains **books2read.com/sweeping**

Anthologies:

Love in a Sunburnt Land Vol 1
Love in a Sunburnt Land Vol 2